T5-AXI-907

PENGUIN BOOKS

KILLING TIME

Wade Hemsworth has worked for *The Hamilton
Spectator* since 1987, where he started as a beat reporter
on justice issues and municipal politics, and is currently
the editor of the newspaper's youth culture section. In
1990, he received a Halton Regional Police award for
his coverage of the Joseph Fritch case.

Killing Time

WADE HEMSWORTH

Penguin Books

PENGUIN BOOKS
Published by the Penguin Group
Penguin Books Canada Ltd, 10 Alcorn Avenue, Toronto, Ontario,
Canada M4V 3B2
Penguin Books Ltd, 27 Wrights Lane, London W8 5TZ, England
Penguin Books USA Inc., 375 Hudson Street, New York,
New York 10014, U.S.A.
Penguin Books Australia Ltd, Ringwood, Victoria, Australia
Penguin Books (NZ) Ltd, 182-190 Wairau Road, New Zealand

Penguin Books Ltd, Registered Offices: Harmondsworth,
Middlesex, England

First published in Viking by Penguin Books Canada Limited, 1994

Published in Penguin Books, 1995

10 9 8 7 6 5 4 3 2 1

Manufactured in Canada

Canadian Cataloguing in Publication Data

Hemsworth, Wade, 1965-
  Killing time

ISBN 0-14-017877-5

1. Olah, Steven. 2. Ruston, James. 3. Fritch, Joseph. d. 1989. 4.
Murder - Ontario - Burlington. 5. Forensic psychiatry - Canada. 6.
Mentally ill - Canada. I. Title.

HV6535.C33B874   1994   364.1'523'0922   C93-094952-8

"Promises" by Roger Curtis Linn and Richard Feldman is reprinted
with permission from Narwhal Music.

"Breathe" and "Time" by Roger Waters are reprinted by permission
from Pink Floyd Music Publishing.

For my parents,
Anne and Gordon Hemsworth

Author's Note

The purpose of this book is not to exploit, but to explore. I offer it as an illustration of disturbing, complex and important problems in the relationship between Canada's criminal and mental-health systems. These problems bothered me and wouldn't go away. I hope those who read it will share this concern, so the problems may be addressed.

Steve Olah and Jamie Ruston gave plenty of warnings. I wish someone had recognized that they were dangerously ill and stopped them when there was still time. Instead, our laws, which guarantee their individual right to liberty, helped to rob an innocent man of his individual right to life.

All of the material in this book that was not the result of my personal observations is based on official transcripts and records and interviews with the persons concerned. In cases of conflict between sources, I have made every effort to reconstruct dialogue and events in the most accurate manner possible.

Contents

Killing
Time

*It's appalling what human nature is capable of,
when at the same time we're capable of such
generosity, empathy, understanding and
consideration.*

Anne Fritch

Prologue

I still don't know if Steve Olah is crazy. Nobody does. After four years, I still don't know what made him smash the life out of a total stranger with the butt end of a fire extinguisher while his best friend held the victim in the kiosk of a late-night gas bar. Maybe it was to see what it felt like. Sometimes that's what Steve says. Maybe it was so he could take the man's car and wallet. Sometimes *that's* what he says. Maybe it was because he felt destined to spend his life in jail and just wanted to get on with it. Sometimes *that's* what he says. Or maybe it was because an irresistible voice in his head was commanding him to do it while drums pounded and torches flickered against a night sky. That's what he *usually* says.

The experts all call Steve a psychopath. Some say he is also a schizophrenic. He is definitely a genius, who once achieved the top intelligence rating for his age group. Steve is cunning, manipulative and egomaniacal. He is also polite, charming, naive and intensely curious.

Joe Fritch was one of 657 homicide victims in Canada in 1989. What made his murder different is that it absolutely defied logic. There was no conflict between him and his killers, as there is in the vast majority of homicides. There was no struggle to speak of. There wasn't even a clear motive. What disturbed everyone most was the sheer randomness of the attack. Everyone who drives a car knows he could just as easily have been in this man's place.

Steve and Jamie Ruston—who is just as sick, but in a simpler way—did something terrible to their hometown of Burlington, Ontario, that October night, writing what to that point had been perhaps the darkest chapter in the city's history.

A community of transplants, Burlington had charmed the families of the killers and their victim. The last in a melting jumble of commuter cities radiating westward from Toronto along the Lake Ontario shoreline, Burlington was made with families like Steve's, Jamie's and Joe Fritch's in mind.

As the Canadian dream city, Burlington is a squeaky-clean, thoughtfully designed community run by an honest council. The Niagara Escarpment juts its rocky spine out of the northern horizon, gently descending through farmers' fields, subdivisions of large homes, a modest downtown, and finally over a thin strip of green parks before dipping into the blue waters of Lake Ontario.

The police who patrol the wide streets there are known across the country as progressive and effective. Burlington had one of Canada's lowest crime rates; not one of the 118,000 people who lived there had been murdered in more than a year before that night.

Burlington, most of it having been built in the previous twenty years, had turned out according to plan. Not only was it one of the most beautiful, sensible communities in Canada, but it was also one of the richest.

Everything was working out for the Fritches, too. Joe had worked hard, earning a reputation among his colleagues as a fair, sensible and quiet man. His diligence had earned him a secure, $91,000-a-year position and a fine home in a place where they could finally settle down and enjoy life.

Their children were bright and growing up fast. Anne Fritch, confident that her four kids were old enough now, had started university in nearby Hamilton, a full-time student working toward a history degree at McMaster. And the Fritches, like so many of their neighbours, knew how lucky they were.

What they didn't know was the other Burlington, the effluent of success, a small pool of the city's youth who had somehow missed the organized sports and activities, whose parents didn't push them to join the famous Teen Tour Band and travel the world, who weren't cramming at home to get into McGill University, Queen's or the University of Toronto.

These were the lost teens, the victims of too much money and too little time from their hard-working parents, bored into rebellion, looking for a new thrill. They cut school, scoffed at curfews, and hung out in the shopping malls, getting drunk from boozy cocktails they mixed in Mac's Milk cups, smoking hash from the ends of their cigarettes, and, for some reason, doing whatever they could to get the hell out of there.

The two worlds collided when Jamie and Steve killed Joe Fritch. They weren't only executing the father of four children and the husband of a loving wife, they were also sticking a knife into the heart of what Burlington thought it was. When the news broke the next day that he had been killed, the community was stunned.

Who, after all, in this sprawling, suburban city, did not gas up at self-serve stations? Who had never found himself in need of fuel late at night? This could have been anyone, and God knows Joe Fritch hadn't been looking for a fight. If one couldn't feel safe conducting such routine business in such a ridiculously quiet city, what kind of security did anyone have?

For more than two years, until the killers were finally brought to trial, the city followed every detail, hoping to get some answers and perhaps some relief. But at the end of two intense weeks in court, there were still no real answers. Sergeant Joe Barker, one of the investigating police officers on the case, worried that with so much attention focused on the pitiable aspects of the killers' lives, the public had become very sympathetic to the murderers and had forgotten the victims.

He knew from the many hours he had spent with the Fritch family that, with the help of respected Hamilton grief counsellor Brenda Symons-Moulton, they had coped exceptionally well with the anger and grief they had been keeping to themselves. Many could try to imagine their horrible suffering, but few beyond Barker knew of their remarkable survival.

The night the trial ended, one of his jobs was to call Anne Fritch and tell her the verdict. He couldn't reach her at first, because she had been writing an exam when the jury announced its decision. When he finally got through to her at about 10:30, Barker also made a suggestion to Anne: that she grant one newspaper interview. He wanted her to speak to me.

Late that Friday night as I sat at my desk in the newsroom of *The Burlington Spectator*, finishing up the front-page story for the morning paper, the phone rang.

"Hello. This is Anne Fritch."

After such a long time wondering what it must have been like for her and her family, but never being able to attach a face or a voice this woman, it was chilling to hear her speak.

She had talked to Barker and would meet me the next day for an interview. But it was not to be at her home, nor were there to be any photographs taken. Then she set one more condition: this would be the one and only interview she would give.

She did not want her face to become known to strangers as *that woman whose husband was killed*. She wanted her family to be as normal as it could.

"I don't want to end up using this as an excuse for anything," she said. "It's hard enough to have this whole affair so public, and if you're a private person, I think it's essential to maintain as much of that privacy as you can."

We met for coffee late the next morning at The Surf, a downtown restaurant popular among police and journalists alike as a no-nonsense diner. The night before, as tired as she was, she had written out a page of her thoughts on her student binder paper.

I will always remember October 18, 1989 as a day of fear, shock and horror, culminating in my having to tell our children of their father's murder. To watch children freeze in their own world of shock and horror, attempting to find a way to express their overwhelming grief, only adds to a parent's feelings of grief and inadequacy. The early months were spent trying to grapple with disbelief, trying to make rational decisions, trying to contain emotions, and trying to get to the next day intact. Having four kids to watch and care for kept me from making any serious mistakes. We have always been a strong family, and now we have become even stronger. I think we all felt that we had to be strong for each other.

A death, especially a death such as Joe's, can destroy you or it can make you realize some of life's values. Joe was interested only in forward movement. He was bent on self-improvement and self-development. He cared very much about people and always had time to listen to them. He had a dry sense of humour and a twinkle in his eye when something amused him. He was quiet-spoken and sincere. He had courage and a deep commitment to his family. Those values are still here—I see them in our kids. He would be very proud of them and the way they have grown through this experience, the quiet strength they have shown time and again.

Something that stands out very clearly is the kind, patient manner of the police officers in Toronto on that Wednesday evening. It continued with Detectives Joe Barker and Jim Chapman, who investigated the case. My many conversations with Joe Barker made me appreciate how considerate and informative he has been throughout. I have been very impressed with the calibre and dedication of [Crown Attorney] Paul Stunt and his team.

Sitting in a private alcove in the restaurant's dining room, Anne Fritch spent the next two hours describing what life had been like for her family after her husband was murdered. She spoke calmly, clearly and precisely. Her round eyes were large enough to portray simultaneously the raw anger she still felt toward the three selfish teens who had treated her husband's life so callously, and the motherly love and strength she had drawn upon to keep her family from crumbling after what they did.

"You can let it destroy you, or you can tell yourself it's not going to do me in, too. One victim is quite enough," she said. "You can let something like this stop you. You can turn to drink. You can lock yourself in your house. You can scream for retribution. But what does that do? For Joe's sake and the type of person he was, and the type of relationship we had, you have to go on. If the shoe was on the other foot, he would."

She remembered clearly what it was like that day when police officers broke the news that Joe had been beaten to death and dropped into the trunk of his car while three teenagers drove it to Toronto and enjoyed themselves on the credit cards they had plucked from his body.

That night, while Jamie and his girlfriend, Cari, were

spending the night on the run, and Steve Olah was lying on a bare steel prison cot, thinking of himself, she was telling her children that their father would never be coming home.

"No adult in my acquaintance has any sort of life experience to deal with this, and I certainly don't, but for a child, there's nothing you can do," she said. "That was the hardest part: seeing your kids in pain."

Sarah, the youngest at ten, was already in bed, and Anne had to wake her up to tell her.

"There's nothing you can say. There's nothing you can do. Parents like to think they can protect their children from the harsher realities of life and, not to overdramatize things, you'd never expect something like this," she said. "You're in a numb state. You're saying the words, and you're just not believing what you're saying. To have to tell the kids, it was just horrible."

Much of the family's strength to deal with Joe's death came from the lessons that he had taught them, mostly by example. He had always been one for self-improvement, and had been his own worst critic. Although he was quick to find fault with himself, he accepted others' faults without judgment.

Of course, he was human. Although Anne's admiration for her husband was clearly vast, she and the children stopped short of deifying him.

Among the children, Jason, the oldest, seemed to have been hit the hardest. He turned twenty two days after the trial. That made him just a few months older than Jamie and a few months younger than Steve.

In the first days after the murder, many people told him he would have to take his father's place at the head of the family. But Anne wouldn't have any of that.

"He's not the man of the family, and he doesn't have to

assume these massive responsibilities. It was just not appropriate to ask a seventeen-year-old to step into a forty-four-year-old's shoes," she said.

At the time, Jason was just two years from finishing high school and had been looking forward to art school. As he crossed the tenuous bridge from boyhood to adulthood, the loss of his father could easily have knocked him off, but instead, he persevered, Anne said.

During the month before his dad was killed, Jason had been having trouble with math. Joe had set aside his own stack of extra work and taken out three math books from the library so he could refresh himself and help his son get through the course. Although he died before he could see how much he had helped, the tutoring had taken hold, and Jason managed to pull through the course with a decent mark. By the time the trial was over, Jason was enjoying the first year of a fine-arts course at the University of Guelph.

"I see so much of Joe in him. This has furthered the maturing. He's an excellent, excellent young man. I'm extremely proud of him."

Erica, then fifteen, Adam, fourteen, and Sarah, twelve, had also shown their potential to carry on without their father, Anne said.

"I think they've come through this, really, with flying colours."

When they took up competitive swimming, Joe had wanted to share in their enjoyment of the water, even though he had a dreadful fear of drowning. He took swimming lessons just to enjoy the pool with them. Only four days before he drowned in his own blood, he had been proud to take his first dive into the deep end.

"He was just glowing with pride to conquer a fear. He didn't need to do that, but it was part of his belief in self-development. You don't let a fear like that stop life's adventures."

Joe Fritch's enjoyment of his children was reaching full bloom at the same time that his relationship with his wife of twenty years was also reaching new heights. In the normal course of any relationship that long, there are peaks and valleys, Anne said. She and Joe were at one of the peaks when he was taken from her. Just ten days before his death, they had combined a business trip to San Antonio, Texas, with a pleasure weekend. It was one of the few extended periods alone together that they had had since Jason was born.

"It was fantastic, that weekend," she said. "It couldn't have been better. It was like a second honeymoon. I'm glad we had that weekend."

That trip was soon after they had attended the opening of *The Phantom of the Opera* in Toronto.

"It was the first time I ever saw him in a tux. God, he was handsome. It was like falling in love with him all over again."

The last time she saw her husband was in the morning, as he was stepping out of the shower. He chattered away happily to her as he buttoned his cuffs.

He was looking forward to an after-work dinner with Aaron Gropper, a close friend. They were planning a private venture in the water-filter business, and Joe was also happy just to be spending time with his pal.

"He was grinning ear to ear. He was so excited about it. Then he said good-bye."

Because their relationship was so strong, Anne said she has been spared some of the self-doubt that others in her position have experienced.

"For a lot of people, when they lose a mate, there's a lot of anger, and a lot of people have deep-seated guilt. I don't have that, and I'm glad, because I could do a heck of a number on myself."

Anne was ambivalent about going to the trial. She was well aware of how her husband had died, and had even identified his body at the morgue, but she didn't have a complete picture of the events until she had read about them in the newspaper, in an effort to prepare herself for the courtroom.

"I didn't understand the extent of the brutality and the horror. When I read that in the paper—I can't even describe my reaction. I realized there was no way I could go and sit in that courtroom with those people and listen to any of this."

Still, she struggled through the hard parts of the trial reports, because she felt it was her duty.

"I had to understand and appreciate what he went through. I had to know."

The family's exposure to Joe's drive and determination had helped the children get through the crisis, Anne said.

"Joe was not only the type of person who allowed you to make your own decisions, but who *wanted* you to make your own decisions. That has helped enormously in dealing with all this. The kids knew intuitively that you are responsible for yourself."

If Steve, Jamie and Cari had known the same thing, none of this would have happened, she said, as her eyes momentarily turned steely again, and the topic put a hard edge on her soft voice.

"If we were all responsible for ourselves, the world would be a hell of a lot better place to live in, and things like this wouldn't happen. Four lives were ruined, and they did it to themselves."

Burlington was a place where Anne and Joe Fritch had

wanted to live. It was tough when the Hudson's Bay Company transferred him from Montreal in 1987, but at least they were happy to be coming somewhere as nice as this.

"I always wanted to live in Burlington. It was such a nice community. It always had such a nice feeling about it," she said. "Burlington, I'm afraid, will never be home, nor could it be."

It can no longer feel like home when almost every day Anne has to drive by the gas station where Joe was killed. She can't avoid the corner of Maple Avenue and Fairview Street, but she still tries to keep her eyes off that Petro-Canada station. When she does look over there, she sees shadowy figures through the translucent glass, and chases them from her mind.

Sometimes, the what-ifs try to take over. What if the traffic lights had been different, and he had taken the usual way home down Brant Street instead of Maple? What if he had left Toronto that night just five minutes later, or five minutes sooner? What if there had been just a bit more gas left in his tank? But just as quickly, she banishes those questions from her mind.

"There's no point dwelling on those things, because that isn't what happened."

Anne Fritch and her family will carry on. They will never forget Joe. But they refuse to let his death end their lives, too. He wouldn't have stood for that.

But the question will always remain. Why?

"To actually remove a life, I don't think I'll ever understand that. It could have been anyone. That's the horror of the thing. It could just as easily have been your dad or your mom. Or me. Or you."

Speaking with this remarkable woman only drove me to

dig deeper for answers. I met several times with Steve's parents, who are equally impressive people: upright, intelligent, bright and caring. Like Anne Fritch, they had learned in a wholesome and realistic way to deal with what Steve had done. They were searching for the same answers, and having just as much trouble finding them. No one could make sense of this.

I wrote to and visited Steve several times at Kingston Penitentiary to figure it out for myself. Each time I felt I was getting close to the answers, something turned me away. He doesn't get many visitors. It's not hard to understand why. The ancient prison by the lake is an imposing fortress of concrete, stone and barbed wire. To get inside, you have to reach between the bars of the front gate, drop the heavy knocker against the door, and wait for someone to open the slit and ask who you are. If you have completed the forms to be accepted as a visitor, the door swings open and you get to go through the metal detector. Guards buzz you through several more doors before you finally get to the visiting room, a large open area where prisoners visit with their friends and families at tiny tables which are bolted to the floor. All that a visitor is permitted to bring in is a sealed package of cigarettes, a book of matches and change for the vending machines. Guards stand watch from behind the glass of a raised platform at the back of the room, while mothers cry at some tables. At others, wives or girlfriends wearing too much make-up and too little clothing offer their men a peek down their blouses. On my first visit, about half of the dozen men in the room were murderers, and I tried not to stare at their bad teeth, long hair and tattoos while I waited for Steve. I tried not to think of how they got there. Finally there was a buzz and a click and Steve walked into the room. He had never really fit into any group in his life, and among the country's worst criminals, he was still a misfit. His eyes were bright, his hair short, and his speech clear and articulate. He was eager to talk about his work on the board of directors for the Lifers' Group in jail. Even though I had brought the package of du Mauriers for him to smoke during the visit, he said please and thank-you for every one. He was happy to talk to me, and to have a chance to tell his side of the story. He explained how the teachers, kids, cops and doctors all teamed up against him, trying to keep him down. He seemed to be making sense, his pleading brown eyes making frequent contact with mine. Soon I was nodding up and down in agreement. Finally, my eye caught his hands and stopped, and I snapped back to reality.

This happens every time. Those hands delivered the forty blows that killed an innocent man. Those hands followed the orders of that twisted mind. I can't see that mind, but I can't stop looking at those hands. I shudder when I think how easy it is to believe and even to like Steve. I understand now exactly why nobody will ever know if Steve Olah is crazy.

Part One

— Chapter 1 —
The Crime

Steve and Jamie had been ready to give up on their plan when, at five minutes to one, the white Buick Regal pulled up to the pumps and Joe Fritch stepped out to gas up.

"This one! This one!" Jamie screamed to his friend, jumping and pointing at the small, neatly dressed businessman who was filling the tank of a family car.

Steve looked out the window and agreed that the thin, middle-aged man in glasses looked like the perfect mark, and he had arrived at the perfect time.

To their left and right, Fairview Street was clear. In front of them, Maple Avenue stretched bare pavement nearly a mile and a half, right down to Lake Ontario. And with it now being an hour past Petro-Canada's official closing time, there would be no more customers. Burlington goes to bed early on a Tuesday night.

The red Canadian flags flying over the station, visible for at least a quarter-mile in all directions, made it the focal point of the open, windswept corner, but there were few around to notice. It had been raining all week, adding an extra chill to the mid-October air, driving even joggers and dog-walkers off the street. The field across Fairview was still undeveloped, and the adjacent shopping mall was empty.

For the teenagers inside the tinted glass kiosk, the wait was about to end. After weeks of planning, and hours of waiting for the right victim to deliver himself, everything was in place.

The buzz from the hash they had smoked through the crude pipe they had made from a Coke can was just wearing off, and adrenalin was taking over. The tools had been set in place long before. The heavy red fire extinguisher, knee-high on big Steve, had been moved from behind the counter to the customers' area. Jamie clutched a black garbage bag.

As the numbers climbed on the pump—fifteen, sixteen, seventeen dollars—Steve stepped behind the booth and crouched low. Jamie, in his Petro-Canada shirt, stayed inside, on the customer side, bending down and pretending to pick up garbage and place it in the empty bag.

Jamie's girlfriend, Cari-Lee Chisamore, perched behind the counter on the corner floor safe, fear rising over what was about to happen.

After clicking the pump up to twenty-eight dollars, Fritch turned and walked toward the doorway, reaching into his blue blazer for his wallet.

Stepping inside, he faced the cashier's window to pay the girl behind the counter. Jamie sprang up and threw the bag over Fritch's head. Steve dashed inside and hoisted the fire extinguisher high over his head, holding it end to end.

As the confused customer tried to break out of the bag, Jamie held him around the waist, and Steve, standing in front of the man, brought down the first blow. The sickening noises of metal on bone, shouts and rustling plastic rebounded off the glass and ceramic tiles. Fritch was still standing.

"Hit him again!" Jamie shouted, panicking. This was not like TV, where victims crumpled neatly to the floor, unconscious from one blow. Instead, this man was still upright, struggling to get out of the black bag. Steve raised the extinguisher and brought it down again and again, ten times in all, but Fritch was still on his feet.

"Hit him again! Hit him again! He's not dead yet!" Jamie screamed, now beginning to lose control as the gruesome reality of killing someone came over him in a terrible wave. But it was too late to stop now. Jamie brought his knee up and drove it into Fritch's groin. Finally, from this insult, he fell, and Steve, breathing hard now, took the fire extinguisher by the handle and began pumping the sharp rim of the bottom into Fritch's head, just above the left ear. By this time, Steve was in his own world, moving machine-like, raising the extinguisher over and over and driving it into the skull of his victim, shearing the booth's aluminum door frame in his mad and careless rush to kill. Finally, Steve heard a crack, and felt the skull begin to soften. After noticing that Fritch's hands were turning grey, he stopped, as many as thirty blows later. Fritch's last tortured breaths drew blood into his lungs, and he drowned.

The job, as his killers had described it, was over. The boys picked over the body and removed the things they wanted: car keys, cash and a wallet full of the best credit cards.

Less than two miles away, Anne Fritch and her four children had gone to sleep, figuring Joe would be home soon. He always came home. Of course, it was usually well before 1 a.m., but tonight was an unusual night because of the special dinner he had scheduled in Toronto with his best friend Aaron Gropper.

The Fritch family slept obliviously, believing they would get back to their comfortable routine in the morning, when the family would scramble to get ready for school and work, and Joe would go back to the office in downtown Toronto.

That's the way it was all over Burlington.

The day after the murder was uncovered, paper boys and girls who worked for *The Burlington Spectator* delivered their neighbours a front page showing this quiet man smiling at the camera, sun warming his forehead in the picture of vacation-time happiness, over the gruesome, ironic caption: "Joseph Fritch: found in trunk."

Even more unbelievable were the three pictures of his suspected killers, pulled from high-school yearbooks and mug shots. These were *children*, for God's sake. Jamie Ruston looked off the page with a half-smile, half-sneer, hair dripping over his dark, wide-set eyes. There wasn't even the mark of a razor on his face. Beside him was his girlfriend's picture. Cari-Lee Chisamore, said to be travelling with her boyfriend, heading for the border, looked even less the part of a killer. She smiled happily. Adulthood had not yet begun to slacken the smooth, taut skin of her young face or burrow the depth of experience into her clear eyes. She was a girl.

And, finally, Steve Olah, on the end of the row, already in custody, looked out from the page in all preppiness in a photo that could as easily have been on the announcements page of the same newspaper, congratulating him on his graduation from the prestigious Appleby College or Hillfield Strathallan College.

Over the following days, the front pages of *The Burlington Spectator*, the *Burlington Post*, *The Hamilton Spectator* and the Toronto papers continued to carry news of the search for the missing teens, who seemed to have vanished. Everywhere in Burlington, and indeed even in tougher Hamilton next door to the west, people expressed fear and outrage. Gas stations reported severe drops in their night-time business.

On the Sunday after the killing, Wellington Square United Church was jammed with mourners for a memorial service. It was two days before Fritch's forty-fifth birthday. From his wife, children, mother, brother and others in the front pews to the mayor and an alderman at the back, more than 250 people represented the shock, grief, vulnerability and terror that had taken over this community. All of them asked the same question: Why?

"I can't give you an answer," Chaplain Dora MacCallum-Paterson told them. Not even this respected chaplain could explain why something so horrible and random could have happened to one of Burlington's adopted sons. Instead, she urged the congregation to seek help from God.

"Why Joe? Why anyone?" she asked. "Tears and sadness and helplessness and rage all flood our being. There are some things we just cannot humanly forgive. Be with this community, joined in solidarity by a true sense of compassion." Before the end of the service, she read out a prepared thank-you from Joe's four children.

"Thank you, Dad, for being, caring, and for teaching, for understanding, for helping us to understand, and especially for just being you. Most of all, Dad, thank you for just being you, because you're special and we love you."

Meanwhile, in their home north of the Queen Elizabeth Way, Burlington's Great Divide, a similar family was at home, dealing with its own crisis. Craig and Diane Chisamore and two of their daughters, Cindy and Shannon, worried about what had happened to Cari, the middle girl, who until now had avoided trouble in any significant sense. Through an interview with the newspaper, they pleaded for her to call home and let them know she was all right.

"We want to know if she's okay, and we want her to know

we're not mad," Diane said. "We want to help her." The last they had seen of her was October 17, when Diane had driven Cari and her scruffy boyfriend to the gas station. The last thing she had said to them was: "Make sure Cari gets on the ten o'clock bus."

Now she was nowhere to be found, travelling with a kid they had never trusted, with a first-degree murder warrant for both of them flashing across the screen of every police computer in the country. The best they could hope for was that she would be arrested.

Craig Chisamore, in many ways similar to Joe Fritch—neat, quiet, distinguished, diligent in his work and his family life—had moved his family all over the country as he rose within the Ford Motor Company of Canada, eventually becoming a senior executive in the parts division at headquarters in Oakville, just east of Burlington.

Like the Fritches, he and Diane had decided Burlington was the perfect place to bring up their family, and they had settled into a large, comfortable home less than two blocks away from Cari's high school, where, until now, everything had been working out very nicely. But between their house and the school was the SuperCentre shopping mall, which provided not only the family groceries but also a place for the disaffected youth of the neighbourhood to hang out and plot to kill a man.

Up north in Kilbride, a village settlement in rural Burlington, Jim Stinchcombe and his wife, Karen, were wondering what the hell had happened to their son Jamie, who went by the last name of Jim's first wife but had been living with them. Jim and Karen had managed to establish a workable, even amiable relationship with Jim's first wife, Cathy. They developed a common policy toward raising their difficult son, trying to make sure he knew he was loved, but also keeping him from playing one off against the other. Jamie knew his limits, and, subject to common-sense rules and discipline, knew he could always come home.

Despite their admirable efforts, life was still a struggle for the Stinchcombes. A hard-working man struggling to raise his family in a modest home where water came from a well, Jim Stinchcombe had recently gone to a special town meeting, a pencil tucked behind one ear, and pleaded for controls against the giant million-dollar homes with swimming pools and underground sprinklers that were making it hard for him to get enough water even to flush the toilet or draw a bath for his children. There had been tears in his eyes as he made his moving speech, and it had helped convince the city fathers to slap a moratorium on building there.

Now, he and Karen had secluded themselves inside that home, one of the original Kilbride houses built before the rich people started coming north. Now absolutely everyone in the village—working class and upper class alike—knew what had happened.

The Stinchcombes withdrew even more as the public pressure mounted. Police and journalists were frequent callers. In their quiet way, though, they were doing the same as Cari's parents. Knowing that his son had dreamed of going west, Jim called his brother in British Columbia and told him to be on the lookout for Jamie and Cari, and to call if he heard or saw anything.

At Frank and Beth Olah's house, not far from the Chisamores', anger mixed with the profound sadness the family was feeling over the death of Mr. Fritch.

Frank, a computer programmer, and Beth, a nursing instructor, had gone through enough trouble over the past several years to know their only son was mentally unstable and capable of the crime they had read about. They had tried their best to make authorities listen to them and take them seriously. But even though she was a working professional within the health-care system, Beth Olah had not been able to make herself heard, and her son had now gone out and killed a man. Even from the time they had heard the first news report about the killing, they had no doubt that he had done it. But whose responsibility was it?

— Chapter 2 —
Steve Olah: Bully to Brilliant Psychopath

Steve Olah had been a worry to his parents even before he was born. Elizabeth, his mother, had serious difficulty during her pregnancy with Steve, her first child, who was born on September 14, 1971.

Two years earlier, Beth, a nurse, had married Frank Olah, a Hungarian immigrant who had come to Canada to work the gold mines in 1957. The trouble with Steve started early in her pregnancy with bleeding and medication to prevent her from losing the baby. During the last month, she developed high blood pressure and toxicity, a condition where retention of fluids threatened her health. In delivery, the placenta detached early from the uterus, and her baby was without oxygen for a short time. Any of these problems could potentially have led to brain damage, but Steve seemed to progress even beyond normal levels, failing to show any of the hallmarks of prenatal damage, such as palsy.

In fact, Steve grew quickly into a large, bright and insatiably curious baby. He learned how to shake his crib over to the bedroom door before he could even walk. At fourteen months, Beth noticed his first steps after she had seen him rooting through the can cupboard. Steve came toddling down the hall toward her, a forty-eight-ounce juice can in each hand.

By this time, he already knew how to talk in phrases, and his vocabulary was remarkable. It seemed he had skipped directly from the babbling stage to conversation. He adjusted well to the birth of his sister, Jennifer, when he was a year old. She was as bright and active as Steve, and grew into an exemplary young woman, a source of pride for her parents. She was active in soccer, volunteered her time to help mentally handicapped youngsters, and in her late teen years—even throughout her brother's murder trial—worked in a clothing store. Outgoing and gregarious even while coping with her brother's frightening behaviour and notoriety, Jennifer helped her friends who looked to her for advice on more normal teenage questions of relationships and parents. The two children, born so close together, had shared equal potential and opportunities, but could hardly have turned out more differently.

As a toddler, Steve's curiosity had led him all over the neighbourhood. He could pick out neighbours' cars driving by and tell his parents who owned them and what make they were. He wanted to know how everything worked. Minutes after unwrapping the watch his grandmother had given him for his fifth birthday, he had it apart on the floor in front of him, trying to see what made it tick. Other parents would remark on how polite he was, and how well he could amuse himself. Before starting kindergarten, the Sesame Street child could already count to 150, identify all the letters of the alphabet, and read and write some words.

"I was told how smart I was from the day I could understand it," he says.

Although he was mischievous, he was a thoughtful child, and his parents adored him, lavishing time and attention on him, encouraging him to explore and expand his fertile and creative mind. At the same time, he was impatient. He couldn't stand anything that wasn't perfect. If he couldn't master something, he would abandon it. But this attitude wouldn't cut it at school, where, in the years before special programs for gifted students were common, group work and structure were necessary to run a classroom.

The problems started in kindergarten at Paul A. Fisher School, in what was then the newest part of Burlington, near their suburban home in Headon Forest.

"Going to school really bothered him, because he had to follow all these rules and regulations. School was just too much for him. He was a Dennis-the-Menace kind of kid, but not in a bad way," his mother remembers.

On one of the first days of school, Steve walked up to the blackboard, picked up a piece of chalk, and wrote a single word: DAMN. The incident upset the teacher. Bad enough that pupils were writing swear words on the blackboard, worse when they came from five-year-olds.

"I knew it was bad, but I thought I'd get more attention if I wrote something like that," he says. "I should have written 'asphyxiation' or 'resuscitate.'"

For Steve, a permanent disillusionment with adults, power and authority started in that kindergarten classroom. He remembers being singled out with one other pupil for early advancement to Grade One. He says he overheard the teachers talking about there being room for only one of them. The other boy was higher up the alphabetical list, and Steve was left behind, crushed.

"No matter how smart you are, things like that tend to affect your self-esteem," he says. Steve says the refusal to skip him ahead in school was too much for a boy who was already coping with the suddenly diffused attention he was getting in a schoolroom. He constantly soiled and wet his pants in class in an effort to draw attention to himself.

"When I look back on it now, I think it's the only way I could get them to say: 'Hey, look. He *is* different.'"

For a time, it worked, and he got what he wanted: individual attention and time alone with adults. But, after the taunting of his classmates, he realized this was not the kind of attention he wanted. He didn't want to be looked on as a baby who needed to be taken away to have himself cleaned up. He wanted control over others, and turned instead to violence and theft.

When the class was to watch a film, he would pull the plug from the movie projector partway out of the outlet. He would convince other students to lay a finger across the prongs, and laugh when they jumped back from the electrical shock.

He didn't dislike them. He just wanted to do something mischievous. He was already starting to get into schoolyard scraps. Bigger than most of the other children, he picked fights with kids a year or two older than he was, and often won.

Steve continued to act up in class, and found himself making regular trips to the principal's office. Finally, Beth stepped in and told them not to send him to the office any more. He *enjoyed* it too much. After all, he got to spend time alone with an adult who seemed to like him, just like at home.

Steve's fractured school record started here and worsened over thirteen years, until it was permanently interrupted by his arrest for murder.

At the end of kindergarten, his parents hoped they had averted the minor crisis, but the next year was no better. Seeking revenge for being passed over, one afternoon he made a naive attempt at arson by lighting matches and dropping them on the outside corner of the school building.

He wanted to burn the place down. The little boy who was with him was scared and told the principal, and Steve was disciplined. It further ingrained his opposition to authority, and started a new hatred that would stay with him: he loathed "rats."

He began taking other kids' unlocked bikes and dumping them down a ravine just off school property. He didn't return for them later. That wasn't the point. "It was more to cause misery than for personal gain," he says.

Already, Steve was checking off boxes in the psychopath's checklist. In order to be considered by psychiatrists to be an adult antisocial personality, or psychopath, one must, by age fifteen, have fulfilled three criteria from a list of twelve. Steve had easily made that mark by Grade Two. If not by age fifteen, then at least by sixteen, he had fulfilled ten of the requirements: excessive truancy, suspension from school for bad behaviour, delinquency, persistent lying, repeated drinking or drug use, stealing, vandalism, grades far below his potential, chronic violation of family rules and starting fights. All he needed for a full score was to become a chronic runaway and have repeated casual sex, and those would come soon enough.

The fights and mischief continued through Grade Two, and, realizing he was quickly getting to the point where teachers could not control him, his parents enrolled him at St. Gabriel's School the next year. They hoped the discipline of a Catholic school would end his disruptive behaviour and instil some respect for authority.

But he was no better there than he had been at public school. One of his favourite tricks was to use plastic sandwich bags to catch bees from the outdoor garbage cans and release them in class, just to make things interesting. To him, the classwork was so far beneath his ability that he didn't see any point in trying. He felt that the system, by failing to recognize his brilliance, was wasting his time.

At the same time he was torturing his schoolmates, he longed for them to accept him. He hid his intelligence from them, because he didn't want to be labelled as a keener or a brown-noser. He hoped they would see him as a cool kid who lived by his own rules and deserved respect for it.

Despite his behaviour throughout school, his teachers liked him. Even though he was a troublemaker, he was still very charming and very bright, and seemed to offer sincere apologies for misbehaving and not handing in assignments. He became very good at getting second chances.

As a result, his report cards were almost without exception paradoxical, carrying some variation on the theme that his teachers were impressed and disappointed at the same time. He cooperated and participated in class, but still ended up with poor, often failing marks. He says there was no reason to bother trying. If he could see clearly from the start of his classwork assignments to the end, there was no point in actually doing the work. His school notebooks record the boredom. While all the assignments start out neatly, accurately and imaginatively, they often trail off. The margins show where his attention went: to elaborately detailed doodles of submarines, dinosaurs and sophisticated maps and mazes.

At home, though, Steve was a much different boy. Although he acted up occasionally, his behaviour bore little resemblance to the stories coming from school. When Steve would act up at home, Frank and Beth preferred to use reason rather than corporal punishment. They would point out why the things he did were wrong, why he shouldn't do them any more, and make sure he understood there were consequences to his actions. He always did understand.

Only twice can his father remember even spanking him: once when he broke a tree in front of the house, at about age seven, and again four or five years later when he refused to go to summer camp. Frank remembers well the first time he scolded his son for lying: "I said, 'Lying can lead to stealing, stealing can lead to robbing, and robbing can lead to murder.'"

He had no idea his son was already well on the way.

One bright spot for Steve and his family was sports. When Steve was seven, he joined a Burlington house league in soccer. He was a successful defenceman, strong and swift, and seemed to enjoy the team. He took great delight in winning, and would be despondent when they lost. Frank coached soccer every year until 1987, splitting his time between Steve's and Jenny's teams, in the interest of fairness. Steve eventually graduated to a city-wide team which represented neighbouring Oakville, travelling to tournaments in other cities.

Despite their doting attention and constant reminders that he was exceptionally bright, Steve's parents knew that somehow he still suffered from an esteem problem. If he couldn't get something perfect, he felt as though he had failed. "Who can achieve perfection?" Frank asked. "No one."

In Grade Four, Steve was heartened when teachers at St. Gabriel's selected a group of bright pupils and were preparing to put them in a special class with Grade Five kids. But the teachers decided to keep the whole grade together, and he was crushed worse than before.

He went home, shut himself in his bedroom closet and set it on fire. Now, Frank and Beth knew their son had a problem so severe that parents and teachers couldn't resolve it alone. They went outside for help, attending counselling with a psychiatrist, but still their son worsened. Steve's hatred for authority was firmly fixed now. He felt the adult world was conspiring to keep him from the place he deserved.

"Then it got *real* bad," he says.

The fights became more frequent, as did Steve's thefts from his classmates. As punishment, he was sequestered behind a cardboard barrier at the back of the classroom for the rest of the year.

"I had taken the wrong path, and it was too late for a U-turn. The die had been cast. It was actually still tumbling until Grade Four, but then it landed," he remembers.

A psychologist who tested him after the closet fire found Steve to be in the 99th percentile of intelligence for his age. In a group of 100 of his peers, he was the smartest. Frank and Beth felt suddenly alone and helpless to deal with their son when the psychologist told them she didn't know what to do with him. She had never encountered a child so bright.

"Your child had to be educated and had special needs. You wanted to get help for him, but you didn't know what to do," Beth said.

They arranged appointments for the family to see a private psychiatrist together and get to the root of the problem. Steve told the doctor, "I'm just like a Coke bottle that you shake up. After a while, the cap just blows off." After several sessions, it was agreed that the best course for Steve would be special schooling, where he could get the attention he needed and wanted.

Frank and Beth borrowed money to enrol Steve at the exclusive Hillfield Strathallan College in nearby Hamilton, a school known for its discipline and high academic standards.

"There was some self-satisfaction," he says. "I was finally *getting* something. I was going somewhere even more special. This is where the first manipulation started. For the first couple of months, I gave the teachers the impression I was a good kid."

And indeed, he was better than before. His marks improved, and so did his self-control. But the schoolwork dropped off when Steve started sensing a new form of alienation. Among the blueblood kids at Hillfield at the time, he felt inferior. He couldn't crack the clique of rich kids that he so desperately wanted to join. "That was the part I hated about Hillfield. They were the good-looking ones. They were good at sports. They were the leaders, the élite."

Meticulous teachers and staff at the school soon began building a paper trail of disciplinary notes and letters about Steve's poor motivation, failure to achieve his potential, and bullying on the school bus. Although most incidents included only minor fighting and disrespect for the driver, one day he stole a nerd's prized leather valise and stomped on it until it was ruined. Steve had to pay for the damage.

As he entered puberty, Steve was chubby and pimpled. His bitterness grew, as did his resolve, not only to make it into the exclusive circle of boys, but to lead it. Not only were his parents not doctors, lawyers, accountants or business executives, he didn't even dress like he was from a rich home. Many of the kids dressed up their grey pants and green school jackets with expensive black loafers and Lacoste and Polo shirts. Steve coveted these clothes, whose alligator and pony crests screamed out to him that the kids who wore them were better off than he was.

"I never got them. I never got the Weejun loafers, either. I would have got them, but my parents didn't have the money."

Despite feeling he was second-class, by the end of four years at Hillfield, he had adjusted enough at least to find a comfortable place somewhere between the outcasts and the élite. The nerds looked up to him and the snobs at least acknowledged him. That was good enough. But when the end of Grade Eight came around, so did Steve's days at the special school. His parents, who in the interest of fairness had also enrolled Jennifer there, could no longer afford the expense. Frank and Beth had not taken a vacation away from home in four years, and faced a mounting debt.

"The one thing I liked about Hillfield was that I had finally found my place," Steve says. "Then it was all taken out from under me again."

The Olahs were forced to send their children back to the public system. Steve enrolled at M.M. Robinson High School, a sprawling low building then at the edge of Burlington's burgeoning northern development, near home.

By the time he started high school, he had also perfected a skill that he would play to the maximum: the ability to manipulate other people.

"He was able to get his way," his mother recalls. "He was able to influence people, to get them to do the things he wanted them to do."

In the summer between Hillfield and M.M., as students call it, Steve learned to smoke drugs, usually hash, or, with his ritzy Hillfield pals, expensive and potent red Lebanese hash oil. From there, he started drinking and the drugs became virtually a daily habit.

At M.M. that autumn, Steve was the new kid all over again. He didn't know many people, and after four years in a uniform, he didn't have the snappy clothes the other kids seemed to value so much.

Still, it seemed to his parents that he was adjusting well.

He participated in student council, and joined Junior Achievement, where young people learn about business by making and marketing their own products. Soon, though, he lost interest in student government and was kicked out of Junior Achievement. He hadn't sold a single one of his products, and it was suspected that he had been stealing money from the group.

Feeling self-conscious and out of place, he turned to the drug-smoking crowd at the school, whom he found more easygoing and accepting. Soon it was drinking and drugs in the mornings and at lunch. Steve says he spent many days in school drunk, even in Grade Nine. At a party at another student's house that year, Steve and a friend broke into the parents' liquor cabinet and passed bottle after bottle of expensive booze out the window while the other kids trashed the house. They stashed the bottles in the nearby Cavendish woods, where the outdoor bar would serve their habit for weeks. If he wasn't drunk during the day, he was often stoned. It was not rare for him to drop three hits of mind-altering acid before class. But drinking and smoking dope were still not enough to get Steve through his school days.

By second semester, he had made friends with several people, including John Ruttan, Andrea Talarico, Cari-Lee Chisamore and Jamie Ruston. Two of them would become his murder accomplices. The rest would become witnesses, or as Steve scornfully calls them today, "rats, every last one of them."

Chapter 3

Jamie Ruston: Contents Under Pressure

Little Jamie stood at the edge of the dock and watched helplessly as his brother, Martin, slipped under the water for the last time. At age three, Jamie couldn't really understand that his older brother had just died, and by the time he was seventeen, he still didn't know how he really felt about the death or about anything, only that he felt bad, and that he didn't know how to feel better.

Martin Stinchcombe's tragic death shaped the equally tragic course of his only brother's life, ultimately motivating him to take the life of another innocent victim: Joe Fritch.

Although he was a bright, mild-tempered boy, James Dylan Stinchcombe's hostility, anger and isolation grew, silent and deadly, within him. Few people in his life had any inkling what was happening to him. On the outside, he appeared gentle and quiet, a friend to stray animals and disabled children. On the inside, he was trying to sort out the feelings of isolation and separation that started with Martin's death and festered as he reached out but failed to find his place in his broken family.

His mother and father, who had separated earlier the same year that Martin drowned, tried their best to be good parents. Jim and Cathy had been married six years. When they split up, Jamie, Martin and Jim moved to Waterdown, while

Cathy stayed in Burlington. Jim had kept the kids because he had a larger home and could more easily schedule his work as a mechanic and glazier to take care of them. But when Martin died, Jim found it too hard to cope, and decided it was better for Cathy to look after Jamie, who moved in with her two weeks after the funeral. Jim moved to western Canada for more than a year before returning to Ontario, when he settled in rural Burlington. Jamie and Cathy added her maiden name of Ruston to his name to make it more convenient.

Jamie saw his father frequently, especially during hockey season. Throughout the moves, no matter where he lived, Jamie's dad always took responsibility for hockey. He would pick him up at 5 a.m. for practice, and was with him through as many as forty games a season. Jamie had been a good skater since taking to the ice at age two. His dad took him to games and practices faithfully, watching his son finesse his way around the ice, preferring to use his skating skill instead of muscle to get the job done. In ten years of hockey, Jamie picked up almost as many gentlemanly player awards as he did penalties. He wasn't aggressive on the ice like his dad and uncles had been. Sometimes, Jim would try to get him to be a little more combative, but it wasn't in Jamie's make-up.

In school, he got along well with his classmates and teachers, and performed well in every subject. From time to time, though, the tip of his unresolved grief would surface. In Grade Two at Tom Thomson School, he wrote a story about being overtaken by a storm while swimming, where he was tossed about, but ultimately rescued. In another story that year, he wrote about falling into quicksand with his father, where only he survives. In Grade Four, he drew a picture of a person saving another person from drowning.

At family gatherings, Jamie was always the favourite among the younger cousins. One of Jim's brothers-in-law ran a group home for the developmentally disabled, and Jamie looked forward to weekends when he would visit the children there. He got on particularly well with the Down's syndrome kids, playing basketball and doing other activities with them, and they asked for him often.

At home, he liked to play with younger kids and was a friend to handicapped youngsters who had no playmates. Nothing in his youth seemed to point to a violent adulthood, especially not a murderous one, but his parents worried that he didn't seem to fit in with the children his own age.

"He always seemed to be a loner as far as I was concerned," Jim said. "I was really concerned that he wasn't hanging around with the kids his own age. It seemed unusual for a child coming into teenage years to be like that."

When Jamie was fourteen, he and his mother and her second husband had moved to a country home in rural Burlington, less than three miles away from Jim and his family, which now included his second wife, Karen, and two young children, Sarah and Sean. The move pleased Jim, because his son would be closer, but having grown up in the city, Jamie couldn't cope with moving to the country, where he had no way to get around and socialize with the friends he did have, mostly kids from hockey. He began losing interest in school. With the restlessness of adolescence stirring him and complicating his angst, the isolation of the country was the last insult to his fragile psyche.

Jamie's parents' first indication that something was wrong with him came with a call from the Hamilton-Wentworth police, who told Jim his son was wanted in connection with a break-in at a home in Carlisle, about five miles west of his home in the north Burlington hamlet of Kilbride. Jim and Karen and Cathy drove to the central police station in Hamilton, where they found Jamie in the youth division. He admitted to them that he had broken into the home, and they told him to come clean to the police. Since it was his first offence, the police recommended family counselling and agreed not to charge Jamie as long as he gave them a statement against his partner, a boy his parents had never met: Steve Olah.

"This was our first brush with Steven Olah," Jim recalled. "When we came out of the police station, both his mother and I strongly indicated to Jamie that Steven Olah was not a good person for him to chum with, for obvious reasons, and Jamie agreed that he shouldn't. He didn't want to go to jail. He liked his freedom and he understood that you just can't go and pull that off and get away with it. You have to pay society for it."

After counselling sessions in the autumn of 1987, Jamie moved in with Jim, Karen and their children the following summer. Jim was working in a factory at the time and got Jamie a position there with him. Since they would get up at five-thirty in the morning for work, it made more sense for Jamie to live there. But Jamie's routine there was very different from what he had been used to at his mother's. Although he loved them and got along with them, he resented the two small children sharing his room and the attention of his father and stepmother. He missed having his own TV and stereo. And he didn't like the extra housework. After the summer, he moved back to his mother's.

But Jamie, always looking for a better deal, eventually came back to his dad's: it was closer to the city, and his father went into town more often than his mother did. As long as Jamie told his dad where he was going to be, he was allowed to stay overnight with friends one night on the weekend, something that his mother hadn't allowed. This time at his dad's, he was "the next best thing to sliced bread," according to Jim, happily sharing and playing with his younger step-siblings, who were now three and a half and one and a half. "It was almost like he wanted to be a child that age again, they played together that well."

But underneath it all, the anger and restlessness of unresolved grief and guilt continued to build, growing with every slight he suffered, every move he made between his parents' homes, every failure. Sometime, somewhere, they were bound to overcome him and explode. Jamie had never learned to understand anger, even though it was running through him like a cancer. Emotionally blunted, he turned against the world that had hurt him, learning to hate rules and authority of every kind. If the world wasn't going to make a place for him, then he wasn't going to bother fitting into it, either. Not even his parents had any idea of the magnitude of Jamie's hostility toward them, himself and everyone else.

Psychological testing after the murder showed what had been happening to Jamie all along. The Minnesota Multi-Phasic Personality Inventory, a series of more than five hundred questions which is viewed in the profession as the most reliable psychiatric screening device in North America, revealed he had deep-seated emotional problems, but also showed he had a reservoir of resources within himself to conceal them. The Weschler Adult Intelligence Scale, which is the most respected intelligence testing device in the field, also indicated his capacity to learn, placing him in the top 2 per cent of the population. The results, combined with those from the familiar Rorschach inkblot and other tests, showed that Jamie was suffering from a chronic emotional disorder, similar in appearance but different from the psychiatric antisocial personality disorder, or psychopathy.

"It is my opinion that Mr. Ruston is an individual who is flooded with intense feelings and just has no psychological ability to articulate them, to acknowledge, and to process them in the way that most healthy people do," court-appointed psychiatrist Dr. Brian Butler said after interviewing Jamie before his murder trial. "I was confronted with that distress within him. The term emotional basket-case is the best way I can try and convey the impression he gave me. He was simply overwhelmed, sobbed uncontrollably, showing enormous distress, and as we worked through the [murder] and afterwards, I was prompting him in trying to get him to describe the feeling behind how he was behaving, trying to identify and distinguish between the fear of the future for himself, regret, empathy for his victim, all of those variety of distressful feelings, and he simply had no ability to try and distinguish those."

Although the problem may appear simple in retrospect, it was difficult for the experts to understand the complexity of Jamie's feelings and actions, let alone to predict what he might do.

"It's hard for me to believe that he acted as he did in this incident—this tragic incident that resulted in somebody's death," Dr. Butler said. "I would have difficulty putting the person he described to me, in that incident, with the person in the interview."

Instead of using his intelligence and self-reliance to heal emotionally, Jamie had used them to build a nearly impenetrable shield. Still, the doctors believed that with proper guidance and long-term counselling, those same qualities could successfully lead him out of the trap, an option which is not open to psychopaths. Psychopaths have no feelings for others. People with emotional disorders have feelings, but can't reach them. The difference between the two was subtle enough not to be discovered in Jamie until it was too late.

Jamie's shell finally cracked on March 11, 1989. It was a Saturday afternoon, and he had been drinking with Steve and another friend at his grandmother's apartment, while she was away. He climbed onto the balcony and threatened to jump. The police arrived in time to wrestle him off the balcony and take him to the emergency room at Joseph Brant Memorial Hospital along the Burlington lakeshore. The officers who took him in said he would have jumped if they hadn't stopped him. In the emergency room, he cried, and said no one wanted him, so he was going to kill himself.

The physician on duty, Dr. Matthew Stempien, filled out a two-page Mental Health Act document called Form 1, allowing the hospital to hold him against his will for up to seventy-two hours for examination. He could have been held until Tuesday afternoon.

Dr. Stempien's report said: "I have reasonable cause to believe that the said person has threatened to kill himself. In addition, I am of the opinion that the said person is apparently suffering from a mental disorder of a nature or quality that likely will result in harm to himself." He noted that Jamie was "depressed, no place to go."

The next day, the case passed from the physician's hands into those of hospital psychiatrist Dr. Sheldon Tobe, who interviewed him for an hour each time on Sunday and Monday. At first, he thought he could reach Jamie and help him.

"When I saw him initially on the Sunday, and he appeared somewhat tearful and upset around the death of his brother,

I thought that perhaps he did have some feelings, perhaps there were some elements there that could be reached in a fashion, that some changes could be facilitated. The next morning, however, when I talked with him about his behaviour, about his concern for other people, he became really quite, quite angry. He seemed to have this deep underlying rage and I really felt at this point that nothing was possible."

By then, the suicide threat had passed, and Jamie had even left the hospital for several hours without permission after the Sunday interview. Upon returning, he was chastised by the staff, and he told them he didn't have to follow their rules if he didn't want to. In a pattern that would repeat itself a handful of times over the next few years, he had come to the brink of crisis and gone back inside himself. Bright and tough at the same time, he had built a deep inner well. Later, he would earn the nickname Summer Storm, for his tendency to flare up, cry briefly and return to his normal, silent self.

"His presentation varied between at times being sullen and angry and resentful at being in the hospital, to other times, depending on the subject matter, tearful and upset," Dr. Tobe reported. Although Jamie had threatened to kill himself, the psychiatrist found no signs of clinical depression in him.

"He did admit that he had thoughts of suicide, and might well have committed suicide on the previous day in the scuffle with the police, and he also admitted that he had had suicidal thinking on and off for many years in his life, but he hadn't acted on them in any fashion," he said. The only meaningful reaction Dr. Tobe had elicited from Jamie was during a discussion of his brother's death, when he became tearful again. But the psychiatrist was frustrated in his quest to understand Jamie's long string of antisocial acts.

Jamie resisted efforts to understand what made him destructive, or to help him change his behaviour. He didn't care whom he had hurt with his petty crimes. He was totally remorseless and determined to live his life the way he felt like living it. He was diagnosed at the hospital as having a delayed grief reaction and a conduct disorder, the psychiatric term used for adolescents who show antisocial, or psychopathic, tendencies. Although Jamie was only seventeen, Dr. Tobe had already found him to be beyond help. Psychopaths are virtually untreatable, since they don't want help, and the doctor's frustration shows clearly in his early report: "At present then, he will remain in hospital. It is hoped that he will respond to some counselling, and may decide to accept some help, move to a group home, et cetera, in order to straighten out his life. On the other hand, he may refuse this totally, and if he does not appear to be a high suicidal risk, will be discharged over the next few days. Overall, the prognosis appears to be poor at present. The patient does not appear to be depressed, has some insight into his behaviour, but at the same time seems to totally lack the common sense or the motivation to make any changes, and in fact, in some way seems to derive some pleasure out of his antisocial behaviour."

The doctor suggested a group home or outpatient counselling, but all Jamie wanted to do was get away from the hospital and do what he wanted. Under the restrictions of the Mental Health Act, there was little the doctor could do. The imminent danger, the prerequisite for confining patients, had passed, and although Dr. Tobe felt Jamie was still a threat to his own and others' safety, he had to let him go without treating him.

"I thought he was one of the angriest people that I had ever come in contact with in my career, and I felt that he did have the potential for some violent act, whether by hurting himself or someone else, somewhere along the line," he said.

Later, the doctor would admit he wasn't surprised to learn Jamie had killed someone.

"Unfortunately, when I heard of it, I wasn't surprised, and as I say, I felt at the time that there was this tremendous amount of anger and I felt that this alleged offence was consistent with the person that I had seen six months previous."

Jamie had clearly been wrong in feeling that no one cared about him. Later, social workers who interviewed his parents found them to be highly caring, motivated and united in their approach to parenting. They had made firm but reasonable rules for him in their homes, and tried their best to get Jamie to comply.

Nonetheless, he had continued to lie, miss curfews, and hang around the people they had told him to stay away from, particularly Steve Olah. Jamie's teachers noted that his once good grades and attitude had started to slide dramatically. Jamie told social workers that he had started taking drugs in the autumn of 1987, and had also started drinking by December. By spring of 1989, he was drinking and taking drugs virtually every day. Jamie described himself as burnt out. He knew what his behaviour was taking out of him in money, health and motivation, but showed no willingness to stop. He said it would take six to eight beers to make him feel intoxicated if he was also smoking hash, and as many as twelve when he wasn't. He was smoking a gram of hash every day he could get it. Although he was manipulative enough to hide his abuse from his family, they could see that their bright, caring boy was changing into a lazy, shiftless slug. His parents and step-parents said it must be the company he was keeping. They knew he was a follower, and that the wrong people could make him do the wrong things. They were correct.

In the youth wing at Barton Street jail during the two years before his murder trial, where outside influences were replaced by rewards to perform, Jamie showed what he was really capable of doing. He reached the maximum credit for good behaviour. He had only two minor blemishes on his discipline record: being found with stolen tea in his cell, and ripping his T-shirt, which cost him three dollars and twenty-one cents. He was considered among the top 10 per cent of the jail's youth population for good behaviour and cooperation. Of course, this paid dividends, such as extra privileges, and Jamie knew well that it could help him later, when it came time for trials and sentencing hearings. Whatever his motivation, he earned a special award for helping slower kids with their work outside school hours, and spent much of the rest of his spare time doing extra work of his own. Ken Ashcroft, the teacher who had started the school program for young offenders at the jail, praised Jamie as one of the best students he had seen. "I can say, based on my experience in classrooms, that Mr. Ruston would be, in any normal high school, in the advanced stream and similarly in the top 10 per cent of that stream."

Jamie's marks were particularly impressive in math and science, ranging into the nineties, compared to the fifties he had been getting outside jail. "He happens to be very strong on logical analysis and computer programs and that sort of thing, whereas he's not quite as able in areas such as poetry. That's only to say that every student has strengths and weaknesses," Ashcroft said. Jamie, in his opinion, could easily have gone on to university. Of all the young prisoners with the same opportunity, only about half the eligible students would even come to class, and only half of those would earn any kind of credits whatsoever. Once again, though, Jamie had waited too long to show what he could do.

His behaviour improved briefly when three weeks after his suicide attempt, he was sent to Dawn Patrol, a detention home in downtown Hamilton, where up to ten boys at a time would serve short sentences for crimes. But there was a strategy to Jamie's improvement. He was still to be sentenced, and any misbehaviour was sure to be reported in court. The day after his sentencing on April 17, he turned surly, sullen and uncooperative, several times being denied passes and privileges after arguing with the staff, damaging property at the house, and failing to live up to promises, such as finding a job and getting drug and alcohol treatment.

Still, in a house full of bad boys, he was far from the worst. A therapist who counselled the family before Jamie was released reported that there was no need for further sessions. She was confident his parents had made their rules and expectations very clear, and that Jamie, with some effort on his own part, could live up to them. What no one knew was that Jamie was completely unwilling to follow the rules of a world that he hated just as much as his friend Steve did.

— *Chapter 4* —
Like Gasoline and a Match

In Grade Nine, Steve and Jamie met, two loose atoms that fused and came apart several times before their final, fatal explosion. Each on his own was bad enough—neither really cared much any more about what happened to him, as long as it was something better than the rut he was in. Their friendship was based entirely on the negative. Their common and only bond was the desire to escape—in their minds through drugs and alcohol, and, more literally, by getting themselves out of Burlington, through a series of ill-conceived, shortsighted schemes. Although each was highly intelligent, Steve and Jamie never planned much beyond the moment.

Before coming together, each was a sick young man in his own right. Their symbiosis formed a third person, fairly separate from their individual personalities. Jamie was a walking, festering ball of anger that had never been released. Without the emotional language to communicate what he was feeling, let alone why, he searched for a partner, a person who would accept him, and perhaps understand him. As a passive person, he wanted someone who would lead him. But as an angry adolescent who had given up on caring about anyone, including himself, he was ready to try anything that might make him feel better.

Steve had always searched for someone he could lead, and

found him in Jamie. He shared Jamie's apathy, self-centredness and isolation. They were at once perfect companions and perfect foils. And shopping malls, drug and booze parties were the perfect places for two twisted souls to find something to break.

Before he met Jamie, Steve had grown tired of his group of friends. The crowd at M.M. Robinson to which he had loosely attached himself started to drift more toward leather jackets and heavy-metal T-shirts to impress the new girls who were coming around. When the owners removed the video games from the Canadian Style Donut shop near Steve's house, there was even less to keep him around that group.

Around the same time, a large shopping centre rose among the new homes: the SuperCentre, a hybrid indoor-outdoor mall. It backed right up to the houses north of Upper Middle Road, and faced another mall across the street. To the east, the Headon Forest neighbourhood opened up. But to the west, across Guelph Line, was its largest source of daytime occupants: M.M. Robinson High School. Anchored by an expanded grocery department store at the west end, the SuperCentre also included a combination Harvey's hamburger and Swiss Chalet chicken restaurant. In the western indoor portion of the mall, there were several small specialty shops: the usual mall fare. The corridor of the mall opened onto a circular food court, with large plants and about twenty small tables. These served the customers of a pizza counter and a doughnut-and-coffee shop. At the back of the circle a long, narrow hallway led to the washrooms and pay phones. At the front was a row of doors leading to the outdoor strip that made up the east end of the mall, including a McDonald's restaurant, a Mac's Milk convenience store, and a beer store.

The food court soon proved a popular place for high-school students to congregate before, after and often during class time. Steve, living nearby, found himself spending more and more time here.

He started socializing with a new group of friends, including Jamie Ruston, Cari-Lee Chisamore, Andrea Talarico, John Ruttan and Geoff Berendse, derisively nicknamed Goof, mostly because of the less common, British spelling of his name.

Steve found it easier to blend in with the kids in this group, because they didn't neatly fit either of the high-school polarities. "It was tough for the first couple years after Hillfield," he recalls. "But there was a small group of kids who were middle-class, but not preppies or rockers, either."

But even among this group, Steve formed only one meaningful bond. Geoff, a round-faced, streetwise youth, was a lost sheep because he was a newcomer to Burlington. Andrea, dark-haired and pretty, was part of the package that came with Cari. Where Cari was easygoing and forgiving, Steve felt Andrea was aloof and snotty, but not intolerable. Nick Santini, Andrea's boyfriend, had always had troubles with Steve, dating from schoolyard fights in Grade Three. Steve never trusted him. John Ruttan, lanky and clean-cut, could never really be close, either. He stayed at the edge of the group, since he was as interested in athletics as he was in friends. That left Steve with one true ally: Jamie.

"All Jamie did was smoke dope, and that was fine with me. He didn't care what I did," Steve remembers. Likewise, Steve didn't care what Jamie did. It was a perfectly unproductive friendship. Drugs and drinking were the foundation and nearly the entire structure of their relationship. "I enjoyed getting high with him, and he enjoyed getting high with me and that's just the way it went," Steve says.

They cemented their friendship at rowdy teenage gatherings before splintering off more and more on their own. At weekend bush parties, where fifteen or twenty kids would congregate in the Cavendish woods west of the high school, Steve and Jamie would often find themselves alone together, sharing a joint or doing bottle tokes, smoking from the top of a pop bottle with a hole smashed in the bottom. They would light a cigarette, place a small chunk of hash or smear some hash oil on the ember and catch the smoke inside the bottle while holding the top closed. When the hash had burned off, they would open the top and drink off the cool smoke.

Jamie and Steve also developed a taste for the longer-lasting, hallucinogenic high of LSD. They began dropping acid often. One of their favourite games to play when they were high was watching people and sizing them up, trying to figure out what they were thinking. Steve and Jamie found they were always coming up with the same answers, and Steve figured he must have found a kindred spirit. They spent their days and nights looking for drugs, using them, and killing time being high, either by walking around, or shooting pool and playing video games at the Golden Nugget Arcade, where banks of machines blinked hypnotically in the downtown darkness, reflecting in their reddened eyes.

Often, they'd go to Jamie's grandmother's when she was away, or even boldly smoke drugs right in Steve's bedroom while his parents watched television just feet away, not distinguishing the sweet odour of marijuana from the cigarette smoke wafting out from behind his door. "They knew I was smoking. They didn't know I was smoking drugs. My parents are really naive about that stuff," Steve says. Their naiveté was fostered by Steve, who, although he was drinking and smoking up constantly, managed to manipulate and deceive them so well that they hardly suspected the extent of his abuse. Once they caught up to him, though, a large and frightening picture made itself clear, one in which drugs and alcohol were only a small part. By that time, the secret Steve had taken over the boy they had raised.

The first time Steve's parents became aware of his criminal activity was Easter weekend of 1987, when a police officer showed up at the door and told them their son had been caught shoplifting cigarettes at the SuperCentre. (He was later ordered to write a three-hundred-word essay as an alternative to being processed as a criminal.) Late that same night, Steve, without a driver's licence, took his mother's Hyundai Pony from the driveway and drove it alone to Niagara, about a half-hour drive south. Along the way, he picked up a hitchhiker and charged him five dollars for gas. But on the return trip, he drove the car into the ditch along a sharp curve on a service road, attracting the atttention of the police. He was not charged. Shortly after that, Steve and Jamie broke into the home in Carlisle. From there, it was a two-year blur of red lights flashing in the driveway, police stations, hospitals and courtrooms that didn't end until Steve and Jamie had been arrested for murder. During this time, Frank and Beth were still trying to deal with their son, but felt they were losing control over him and over the direction of the care their exceptionally gifted and increasingly wicked son desperately needed.

Between age sixteen and eighteen, Steve went through a string of jobs, being fired from every last one. He worked in a Wendy's fast-food outlet, in the kitchen of another restaurant, at a gas station, in a warehouse, at a grocery store, at an art-framing shop, as a handyman at a seniors' home, as a telephone solicitor and as a construction worker. Sometimes, he would be fired before he had worked a single shift. It was never long before Steve was fired for not showing up at work. Frank and Beth became used to the phone calls from employers asking why he hadn't shown up. Somewhere along the route between home and work, he had detoured. They didn't know where he was going, but learned that he had gone many of those times to idle, smoke drugs and drink with Jamie and the others. Once, they bought him an expensive bicycle so he could get to and from work directly. Not long afterward, Frank caught Steve trying to sell it to a friend.

Still, Steve always promised to reform, and, with his glibness, never had trouble talking his way into a new job. All the while, his parents suspected that he might be using drugs, but could never get any hard evidence to prove it. Small amounts of grocery money, loose change and other cash were disappearing, but they could never put their fingers on exactly how much or when it was taken. Liquor bottles always seemed to have less in them than the last time they had checked. Whenever the subject of his behaviour or stealing came up, Steve deflected attention away from it. Frank and Beth felt there was little they could do. Steve consistently broke curfews, and they finally gave up trying to confine him after discovering he had just been taking out his bedroom window and leaving after they went to bed anyway.

They knew he was being secretive, devious and dishonest, but couldn't catch him at it until Steve slipped up and left a pipe and an oxygen mask in his room. When Beth found them, she furiously threw Steve out of the house. He went away for a few weeks, living, she and Frank believe, with Cari and Jamie in a sublet student house near McMaster University in Hamilton.

They let him move back home when he promised to attend a drug and alcohol rehab centre in Burlington. But, as with his schoolwork, promises always led to requests for extensions. Excuses waned into refusal and Steve never went.

Steve and Jamie hit the depths of the first phase of their friendship in November 1988. Finding themselves at loose ends, without drugs, booze, money or anything to do, they waited in the parking lot of a small strip mall at Brant Street and Upper Middle Road near Steve's house, outside a Mac's Milk store, hoping to steal a car and leave Burlington altogether. Steve wanted to go to California. Jamie wanted to go to British Columbia. They could sort that out later. At least they could agree that west was the way they wanted to go. It was more of a dream than a plan. They didn't even have a map, much less a destination, or even a clean set of clothes with them. The pathetic scheme was doomed well before it got underway.

They watched customers pull up and run inside for milk or cigarettes. They waited and waited for one of them to leave the keys in a car so they could take it, but no one did. Finally, a Hostess potato-chip truck pulled in to make a delivery. The driver left the keys in the truck while he went inside to do his business. With the driver's door out of the delivery man's line of sight, Steve and Jamie climbed in the truck. Steve, who knew at least the basics of driving, took the wheel. He started the truck and revved the engine, but went nowhere. The parking brake was on. Finally, he got the truck moving, and prepared to make a getaway, heading north for Highway 401, thinking they could take it all the way across Canada, not realizing it would end at the Windsor border with Michigan. Not even Steve and Jamie were foolish enough to think that a pair of teenagers who could barely control a stolen chip truck were going to get past customs.

But their caper hit its fatal snag well before Windsor. The slow truck, which Steve couldn't get past ninety kilometres an hour, was running low on propane after two hours on the road. They found a Superior Propane pamphlet in the truck and figured they would pull off the highway and find an outlet. Steve was confident he could bluff his way into getting a free tank of fuel on the company account. Aylmer, Ontario, a rural community and home of the province's police training academy, was the next exit off the highway. Steve and Jamie drove nervously around the streets of the small town. They figured they would be okay as long as they didn't get close to a police car or another Hostess truck, but at one of the first traffic lights, another Hostess driver spotted them.

"Who are you?" he yelled to them.

"Replacements," Steve answered.

"Oh yeah? Where are you going?"

"Back."

"Back where?"

"Headquarters."

"I think you had better give me the keys," the other driver said.

Steve gunned the engine and tore away from the lights. He and Jamie dumped the truck behind a apartment building and ran. Nearby, they found a red pickup truck, engine running, with no one inside: just what they needed. Steve drove again, and headed south from Aylmer as fast as he could go. Soon a car caught up with them, the driver shaking his fist; it was the owner of the pickup truck, who had seen them pull out. Steve drove even faster now, passing cars on the right and spraying gravel by running two wheels along the soft shoulder. Like the chip truck, their new pickup was also nearly out of fuel, and Steve pulled in behind a church so they could bail out again. He and Jamie ran through muddy cornfields and ravines, until they were surrounded in one field by provincial police, and they finally gave up.

After that, Steve was assessed by another psychiatrist, whose report predicted he would likely commit a serious crime soon. By the time of Steve's murder trial, though, the report had been lost.

Steve's next brush with the law came two months later, just a few days before he was to appear in court on the theft charges stemming from the Hostess truck caper. Rather than face the judge, he decided to run away. He waited up until 1 a.m., when he could be sure his parents were sleeping. He sneaked into the kitchen and slid a piece of cardboard under his dad's key ring, lifting it gently so the keys wouldn't jangle. Clutching them tightly, he went out the window, carrying a sleeping bag filled with canned food and extra clothes. Although he had stolen his mother's compact Hyundai before, he wanted his dad's more comfortable family car for the long drive to Montreal, where he would dump the car and walk across the unguarded border to the United States. He had told a friend about his plan to take off, and now dropped by the boy's house to pick up twenty dollars gas money he had left for Steve in the mailbox. Steve drove all night, passing Montreal, hitting the Eastern Townships by about 8 a.m. He cruised the roads parallel to the border, looking for a place he could dump the car and hike across to the States. But there was always another driver too close, or the terrain wasn't good for hiking, so he continued to drive until late in the morning. Finally the coast was clear, and Steve pulled off and parked the car near some woods. He put on all his layers of clothes, but had locked the keys in the trunk before he realized that the winter hat he had brought was also locked inside. Rather than damage the car by breaking in, he left the hat behind, and started hiking into the woods, figuring by the map he had brought that it would be about a ten-mile trek across the border. Steve pushed through thick underbrush until he found a snowmobile trail. Although it made easier walking, it led him in an arc instead of straight across the invisible border. The ten-mile walk soon became an ordeal, and the −30° Celsius temperature chilled him deeply. He walked until after dark, and was dead tired now, after two days and a night without sleep. Exhausted, he sat down and thought about rolling out the sleeping bag and going to sleep for the night. But he knew he would freeze to death if he stopped, so he pushed onward. Finally, when the No Trespassing signs were in English, he figured he must be in New York State. He walked until he found a group of buildings, and knocked at the first house with a light on to ask if he could sleep in the barn.

An older woman came to the door. Steve told her he was a traveller on his way to New York City and asked about the barn. Looking at him suspiciously, the woman told him the barn belonged to the family in the next house and sent him to ask them for permission. Steve knocked there, and a pretty young woman said Steve would have to ask her husband, who was in the barn milking the cows for the evening.

The farmer told Steve he looked tired and could spend the night in his home with his family. Inside, they dried his clothes for him and fed him. Steve was feeling better as he played with the children and later reclined on the sofa, watching television with the family. He was keeping his eye on the reflection of the front door in the mirrored wall in front of him, in case the police should come. Steve felt something warm dripping on his neck and looked in the mirror a little closer. His ears were thick and red from frostbite, and the blisters were oozing pus onto his shoulder. The children began to notice too and looked at him peculiarly. An uneasy feeling was creeping over him, when there was a knock at the door. Two border patrol officers, alerted by the older woman at the first house, took Steve back to the RCMP on the Canadian side. The Canadian police had received the bulletin from Halton that Steve was wanted for stealing his parents' car. They called Steve's parents and took Steve to the hospital, where he was treated for frostbite. The next day, Frank and Beth came to take him back home. Figuring he was in enough trouble with the law already, they did not have him charged for stealing the car. Steve made his court date after all, and was sentenced to eighteen months' probation. In April, Jamie was sentenced to three months in a youth detention home.

But before that, while Steve was on probation and Jamie was waiting to be sentenced, they took another run at the law. In March, finding themselves again without money, cigarettes or drugs, they planned a midnight break-in at a variety store at the Mount Royal Plaza, a strip mall off Guelph Line in an older section of the city. Like the criminals they had seen on television, they dressed in black for the job, and waited outside the store for the right moment. Ray, a friend who had joined them, smashed the front door of the shop with a shovel. Jamie stood watch outside, while Steve and Ray filled two large garbage bags with cartons of cigarettes. Jamie screamed out when he saw a police cruiser approaching, and they all ran out the back door, setting off an audible burglar alarm. They ran through the snow, hopping backyard fences, but not dropping their loot. Ray holed up inside a tool shed, making it easy for the police to follow his footprints and nab him with one of the bags of cigarettes. Steve and Jamie, running through culverts and fields, managed to get away with the other bag, which they sold for two hundred dollars and a free hour of pool at an arcade. Later, they blew the money on drinks at a downtown restaurant. Two days after the break-in, confronted by their parents who had been contacted by police, both boys turned themselves in. Steve got thirty days' custody at the Syl Apps youth detention centre in Oakville. Jamie spent the month at the Barton Street jail in Hamilton, after his father refused to post bail for him.

Steve saw less of Jamie during what he describes as the most stable period of his adolescence. Although he was still drinking and using drugs, he was doing so much less, and wanted to spend time with his first girlfriend. Steve describes their relationship as "weird."

"She didn't like to use vulgar terms like banging. It was always 'making love,' or some bullshit like that." Still, Steve needed the closeness of the relationship, and in his own way, felt that he was in love with her. He was crushed when she called him in Florida, where he was vacationing with his parents, to tell him it was over. He returned, more frustrated than ever, and cut his hair short to mark the change in his life and attitude.

When he came back, Steve met Jamie at a teenage party at an abandoned quarry in north Burlington at Kerns Road, where an old couch served as a perfect bench with a sweeping view of the city. Steve and Jamie separated themselves from the group and started talking again about getting out of Burlington. This time, though, the conversation had a more serious tone, and both of them knew they meant it, and would not stop until they had reached their strange goal. Both of them knew they would do anything to get out, and would keep trying until they succeeded or were caught. Still, they never applied their considerable intelligence to making a plan that would work. Steve especially was looking forward to getting on with the life he felt destined to spend in jail.

— Chapter 5 —
Steve's Last Cry for Help

Frank and Beth Olah's hopes that their son would grow out of his criminal and bizarre behaviour ended violently on a summer evening, August 3, 1989. After a normal family dinner at home, Steve excused himself and said he was going out to meet some friends, as he often did. Although they knew he drank and used soft drugs, they had no idea of Steve's extensive abuse of both. For five years, he had been drinking alcohol almost daily, and keeping it from them by coming home late after they were asleep, and by lying and manipulating in the way that comes easily to psychopaths.

This night, Steve met some friends at about dusk in the schoolyard at Paul A. Fisher School, a few blocks from home. Among them was a recently estranged girlfriend, from whom he claimed to be happily separated but for whom he still harboured a great deal of feeling. He and Rocky, his friend for the past ten years, split a mickey.

"I was buzzed, but I wasn't really drunk," Steve remembers. "I can drink a twenty-sixer without getting really drunk."

The mickey was like nothing to Steve, but before it was finished, he felt a jealousy welling up inside him, and had convinced himself that Rocky was coming on to his old girl-friend. In his unwarranted paranoia, he commented rudely about them, taunting his friend into throwing the first punch.

Right then, something snapped inside Steve's brain, perhaps the final, tenuous connection that had restrained what remained of conventional, moral thinking from breaking away into untethered psychopathy. In a blind rage over what his clouded mind was telling him, he lashed out, fists flying, as if on automatic pilot.

"As soon as he punched me, that's when I lost control," Steve said. He delivered a smashing blow that caught Rocky in the eye and bridge of the nose, and then, at the sight of his injured friend, momentarily restrained himself and took off. Rocky's nose was broken. Later, Steve himself would define these terrifying, confusing seconds as the dying moments of his conscience. Terrified as the bad side took over, he used the last of his compassion just to hold himself back from further violence.

"I thought, 'My God, what have I done? I've got to get somewhere safe.' At that point, I knew it wasn't just Rocky I was going to hurt. It was going to be other people. That thought scared me. I knew something bad was going to happen, and I wanted to get somewhere safe."

Filled with remorse and confusion, he ran home, out of control and in need of help. "Even in my most deluded moments, I still grasped the logic for some reason," he said. As usual, he hopped the back fence and entered his split-level home through the back patio door on the lower level, where his father was watching television. It was just before nine-thirty.

Steve walked by without saying hello—again. That was nothing out of the ordinary for a seventeen-year-old boy. But Frank noticed a wild expression on his son's face. As Frank settled back to his television program, a strange grinding noise, in long strokes, caught his attention. It was coming straight through from the kitchen above. Curious, he went upstairs to see what was going on. As he stood in the doorway to the neat kitchen, he saw his son pulling a long carving knife through a sharpener that was resting on the counter.

"Steven, what are you doing?"

"Get the fucking Southern Comfort from the bedroom!" Steve hissed, suddenly looking up, pointing the knife and motioning toward the back of the house. The wild expression had grown wilder still. Frank did not recognize his son behind the brown eyes, which were now flaring impossibly wide. Steve's hair was pulled out in all directions, and he was sweating and flushed.

Before this, Steve's parents had rarely even heard him swear. Now Beth, who had been in the upstairs living room, had heard enough to bring her running.

"Let him have the booze!" she screamed at her husband. She was scared. She couldn't smell the playground mickey on her son, but his glazed and dilated eyes told her he was in serious trouble. He was definitely more than drunk, she knew. She tried to bring reason to the situation by bargaining with her son.

"Okay, Steven. We'll give you the bottle, if you give us the knife."

Steve forced his father down the hallway as a hostage, watching him pull the bottle of bourbon from the small, rarely used liquor cabinet. He snatched the bottle, but refused to relinquish the weapon. His frightened father was helpless in the face of this fury.

Despite her shock and terror, Beth Olah maintained, at least outwardly, her professional calm and reason. She grabbed the receiver from the wall phone in the kitchen, and started dialling the three-digit emergency number to get help. She had pressed the first two digits, 9-1, when a hand reached around the corner as if in some cheap horror movie and slashed the telephone cord before she could punch in the last 1.

"You're not going to call the fucking cops!" he screamed at them both.

Steve quickly ran to the two other phones in the house and cut their cords, making it impossible for his parents to get help to subdue the son who, until now, had never shown any type of aggression toward them or his sister, who was away on a camping trip that night.

"We're all going to go down to the hospital now," Steve announced, reaching for a tumbler from the cupboard. "I belong in the nuthouse."

He poured himself at least eight ounces from the nearly full forty-ounce bottle, and guzzled it down without stopping or even wincing.

Using the knife and bottle to threaten his frightened parents, Steve forced them to the driveway and made his father climb into the driver's seat of Beth's Hyundai. He made his mother sit in the back seat, while he rode up front beside his father. Steve yelled as Frank fumbled with the unfamiliar controls.

He forced his father to drive fast, through the red lights between home and Joseph Brant Memorial Hospital, nearly four miles away. There was hardly a word in the car. His parents were silenced by the fear that a wrong word from them might drive Steve to hurt or even kill them.

Steve continued to slug booze straight from the bottle. As terrified as she was, Beth Olah thought to herself: "At least we'll get some help now." Frank's thoughts were similar: "Surely, they'll put him in a straitjacket now. He wants it himself."

At the hospital, Frank pulled up directly in front of the

emergency-room entrance. Steve held the knife to his father's belly. With the other arm crooked around his mother's neck, he held the bottle over her head and kicked open the doors, instantly commanding the attention of everyone inside.

"Pay attention to me!" he screamed at the horrified staff, hammering at the window to the nurses' station. By now, Steve's blood-alcohol level had rocketed to more than three times the legal limit for driving.

"Get me a straitjacket!" he screamed again, still bashing on the window as more nurses and orderlies began to arrive on the scene.

"Give us the knife," said a nurse, calmly but firmly. "Give us the knife, and we'll give you the straitjacket."

"Please, Steven, give it up. Everything will be fine," Frank urged desperately.

Finally, Steve threw the weapon into the half-open window, and it skittered across the floor.

"Here's the fucking knife! Now get me a straitjacket. I need help!"

He released his father, but now placed his mother in a headlock, holding the bottle over her head, threatening to kill her or anyone else who interfered with him.

Frank was ushered away from the scene, while Beth tried to speak quietly to her son. By now, the police had arrived. Three constables from the Halton police force pried him away from his mother and tackled him. They handcuffed him and shackled his legs. Just after 11 p.m., they loaded Steve into a cruiser for the drive to St. Joseph's Hospital in Hamilton, where there are emergency psychiatric facilities designed to handle such cases.

Once he had been physically restrained, he grew wilder still, completing the transformation from a voluntary patient to a hostile one. Whatever recognition Steve had had earlier of needing help was now gone, and he threatened to hurt or kill everyone who tried to restrain or help him. But at least he was in the hands of professionals who would know what to do for him, Frank and Beth thought.

At St. Joseph's, a fifteen-minute drive away, Steve the prisoner was reclassified a patient again when hospital staff replaced the police handcuffs and shackles with leather restraints to bind his arms and legs. Within minutes, he was out of the restraints, and had to be subdued and restrained again. He had been working out and was in peak physical condition, which, combined with his rage and drunkenness, made him virtually impossible for anyone to handle. After he had been bound again and left in an isolation room furnished only with two foam mattresses, the Halton officers were permitted to leave. But by 2 a.m., Steve had once again slipped out of the bindings, and was screaming more loudly and obscenely than ever. He was ramming his head into the wall, had ripped the covers off both mattresses, and had smashed the light fixture in the room. He stalked around the cell-sized room, using the zipper he had ripped from a mattress cover as a whip, successfully holding hospital staff at bay. He finally smashed the Plexiglas bubble on the door. At two-thirty, a nurse called for more police help. This time, it took six officers from the Hamilton-Wentworth police to get Steve back into handcuffs and leg irons.

A nurse at the hospital wrote in her emergency nursing record that the police had agreed to leave their restraints behind, since the hospital's were not adequate, but that the Inspector who had supervised the call spoke with emergency room physician Ken Dwyer about the "politics" of police and the Mental Health Act, before leaving at 3:15.

At 4 a.m., Steve was still screaming as loudly as ever, under strict supervision in the inescapable police leg irons and cuffs. All the while, his parents, who had had to drive to the hospital in their own car, sat in the waiting room in shock and confusion, listening to their son's raging screams echo down the hallways.

Dr. Dwyer, after observing Steve and taking a brief history from his distraught parents, pulled out a very powerful and rarely used tool from the doctor's arsenal: a Form 1, the same document which had been used to hold the suicidal Jamie Ruston five months earlier. After several hours of Steve raving and beating his head and hands on every wall, ceiling and door within reach, and threatening virtually every nurse, doctor, police officer or parent who came near him, Dr. Dwyer concluded that Steve was "suffering from a mental disorder." He felt that releasing Steve, even to jail, would be dangerous for himself and those around him.

He wrote: "requires medically safe and secure environment in hospital," and recommended that a more thorough assessment be carried out once the seventeen-year-old had had a chance to dry out.

Dr. Dwyer told Frank and Beth that later in the morning, the staff's chief emergency psychiatrist, Dr. John Deadman, who was highly regarded in his field, would come in and interview Steve.

By then, Steve had calmed considerably, although he would not cooperate with psychiatric assistant Russ Whitworth or the doctor when they tried to interview him over a period of ninety minutes.

"I remember a guy came in and said, "Have you been drinking?' And I said, 'Yes,' and that was it. I didn't have any assessment. I don't remember any assessment," Steve said later.

The psychiatrist, a veteran of thirty years, concluded that Steve's problem had to do with drinking, not insanity, and rescinded the Mental Health Act order, sending Steve instead to the Barton Street jail.

In the space at the bottom of the hospital's Emergency Psychiatric Service Consultation form, Dr. Deadman listed "substance abuse" as the primary diagnosis, and "conduct disorder" as the secondary. This lesser conclusion serves as a catch-all for a number of personality disorders in young people, among them antisocial personality disorder, more commonly known as psychopathy.

Since Dr. Deadman didn't perceive that Steve represented an "imminent" danger, he said he was forced by the Act to release him. His report recommended "patient should be dealt with through the legal system."

Steve was taken to jail and processed as a prisoner, not a patient. What little optimism his parents still held now began to fade, and they started to lose trust in the mental health and criminal justice systems.

Ten weeks later, in the back of a police cruiser, under arrest for murder, Steve would tell the officers who had arrested him: "If they would have committed me when I wanted, none of this would have happened."

Later, psychiatrists for the defence, who examined Steve and his history in a slightly more relaxed and cooperative setting before the trial, found that this incident was definitely an indication of a budding psychopath and paranoid schizophrenic, a rare combination, but one of the most dangerous known to the field.

Once he was moved to the Barton Street jail, Steve came under the care of Dr. Guyon Mersereau, staff psychiatrist there. Dr. Mersereau prescribed heavy dosages of anti-psychotic medication to even out Steve's mood swings and regulate his sleeping patterns. Steve was initially in the habit of staying up until 4 a.m. and sleeping until 11 a.m.

Dr. Mersereau later described Steve as one of the most dangerous patients he had ever seen, even considering his long-standing experience at one of the toughest inner-city jails in the country. Staff members who supervised him daily also recall Steve as one of the most frightening prisoners they had held, because of his volatile combination of intelligence, hostility, strength and instability.

Feeling they had been failed by the public system, Steve's parents proceeded to press charges against their son, not as punishment or retribution for the terror he had put them through, but as a way to show they were serious about having something done for him. Some control was better than none at all.

For Beth, who had given her career to the health field, the failure to treat her son as a mentally ill person was especially disillusioning. If even she, a health-care professional, could not press the right buttons to cure an impossible and dangerous situation, who could?

The family sought the advice of their lawyer, Paul LaFleur, a young barrister who had moved to Burlington from Windsor. Like Frank Olah, he came from a blue-collar background, and could sympathize with the family's plight.

The towering, prematurely grey lawyer told them that if they wanted help for Steve's psychiatric problems, they had three choices: they could leave him in Barton and let the system continue treating him as a simple criminal, they could send him to Toronto's Clarke Institute of Psychiatry, or they could seek bail for him and get private help outside the system.

The Olahs, still believing that their son was sick, rather than evil, refused the jail option outright. They wanted help, not punishment. LaFleur told the family that the Clarke had unreasonably high patient-to-doctor ratios, and Steve could end up there for a very long time just waiting for a proper assessment, let alone treatment.

"If I had to go through it again, I still wouldn't recommend that a patient go to the Clarke," LaFleur said later.

Instead, he advised that they could seek bail for their son, if they were willing to take him back into their home, with a judge's order that he seek and maintain psychiatric care. Dr. Mersereau at the jail also advised Beth Olah that private treatment was the best option for helping her son. The Olahs chose this route, since it not only meant that they would have direct control over the situation, but also that their son would be close to home, instead of in downtown Toronto, at least a half-hour's drive away.

When his parents and lawyer visited him at Barton Street, Steve kept telling them "*him* made me do it." His eyes were still as wild as they had been that night with the knife and the bottle. LaFleur said that, even as a layman, he could tell Steve was far outside himself.

"When I went to see him in Barton, it was clear he was in psychological trouble," he said. "He was trying to look at someone over his shoulder [when no one was there]. I said, 'This guy is out of it. This guy is nuts.'"

But without a judge's order for treatment in the criminal wing at Hamilton Psychiatric Hospital, getting him into the facility was out of the question. There are just six beds there for such assessments at the hospital, which serves a population stretching from Niagara through Burlington to Hamilton-Wentworth and Brantford, about one million people. Such an order was impossible to get unless it had a psychiatrist's endorsement. At the bail hearing on the charges of assault with a weapon, Steve was released on a

$3,000 bond, under the strictest set of conditions ever encountered by LaFleur: that he attend school, be under the care of his family physician and whomever she designated, take his anti-psychotic medication, obey his parents, live at their house under an 8-p.m.-to-6-a.m. curfew, not associate with James Ruston, take no alcohol or non-prescription drugs, keep the peace and not possess any weapons. It was September 21. They could have won bail earlier, but Frank and Beth had spent six weeks trying to arrange an appointment with a psychiatrist. There was no way they were going to try to handle this alone. They were surprised at how hard it was to find a psychiatrist in Burlington who would treat their son. The public health nurse at school couldn't help them. The Counselling and Human Resources Institute in Burlington had a waiting list that would have left them without help for several weeks. Child psychiatrists wouldn't see him because he was nearly an adult. Adult psychiatrists said he was too young for them to treat. Finally, Frank and Beth agreed to seek bail when one adult psychiatrist's office in Burlington agreed to take Steve as a patient. Six weeks after he had threatened to kill them, Steve's parents were driving him home again. All three of them were scared, but some optimism had returned. They were following the best advice they could get for dealing with an impossible situation.

"While we were driving home, Steve said, 'Something's finally happening so I can get cured,'" Beth recalled.

"He sounded very happy," Frank agreed.

But between the time they had left for the jail and the time they returned with their son, the psychiatrist's office had left a message on their answering machine: the doctor would not take Steve as a patient. There was no explanation. Terrified again, they scrambled for a replacement. Beth's doctor arranged to have the psychiatrist who came to her office once a week see Steve, even though she was only scheduled to do assessments, not treatment. The psychiatrist set up weekly appointments and prescribed the anti-psychotic drug Largactil, renewing the prescription each visit.

In a bid to restore order and structure to Steve's life, his parents bought him a journal so he could keep better track of his appointments and commitments. They enrolled him in yet another school, hoping he could get a new start.

Now he was to attend Central High School, in the heart of downtown Burlington. Frank and Beth Olah were reluctant to tell school officials about their son's history. Since they were under no obligation to do so, they opted to let him have the fresh start they felt he deserved, and let him enter classes directly on September 25.

They felt they had done everything possible for their boy: they had forgiven him, sought the best advice they could, risked having him back in their home, sought psychiatric help, and tried to establish more productive routines for him.

And for Steve's part, it all seemed to be good. He enjoyed his new start, although he was showing the early signs of being uncomfortable outside jail, where he said he couldn't cope with all the space, freedom, choices and ultimately, responsibilities. The first entries from his journal show these mixed emotions:

Saturday, September 23, 1989.

It's 9:07 p.m.
This isn't a diary because I won't write in it every day, I know I won't. I just got it to keep track of thoughts and feelings.

I get poetic sometimes, and I wanted to have a place to write down some of my poems. This will not, however, be strictly a book of poems.

It's for writing down anything. Just in case I die or go to jail, I'll be able to see what was going through my head at the time. Maybe I'll let my psychiatrist read a few selections. I don't know.

Sunday, September 24, 1989.

It's 12:04 a.m. Hope springs eternal. I heard that somewhere. I hope it's true. I hope I can handle all the things (school, being out of jail).

My parents are showing so much understanding! They don't seem to see any barrier too strong to prevent them from helping me. It feels good for once to have my parents care. They've so far blended the perfect proportions of strictness and freedom. Something has changed between us. I feel like an equal.

They're going to let me smoke in my room, which is unbelievable in itself, but they're only imposing one condition: an Air Ecologizer. It's almost too good.

It's 9:55 p.m. A lot happened today. We enjoyed an excellent breakfast in Niagara-on-the-Lake on a boat tour, and went shopping in the downtown area.

When we got home, I beat Dad in a game of Computer Scrabble, then I went out for a walk. I found myself at a loss when deciding a route to take. It was weird. I'd been confined in my travels to such a small area I was taken aback by all the space. Jail does that to you.

I felt it this evening. Jenny was bugging me to help her on her art project, and then yelling at me for any advice I could give her. It tried to take over. Over such a small thing. I could feel the anger and frustration and resentment giving it power, but I couldn't stop it.

Something really weird happened. After Jenny finally figured out that I'm the wrong person to ask for help, Mom gave me a hug and calmed me down. It was the way she did it that freaked me out. It was like she read my mind. She knew the struggle I was having with it, and she made it go away.

I'm sort of worried about starting school tomorrow. I mean, it'll be okay, I know I can handle it. I've been to a new school before. That's within my realm of experience. It's the unknowns that frighten me. It feeds on fear. It senses my weakness and tries to seize control. It's evil.

The "him" that Steve had talked about inside Barton had now become an "it," but continued to haunt his thoughts, only to grow more imposing as the diary, begun in average penmanship and near-literary writing, slowly disintegrated into the unreadable, meaningless ramblings of a madman. Psychiatrists later testifying on Steve's behalf said that at this point Steve's delusions, once founded in general paranoia about people trying to dominate him, were crystallizing into something more powerful, concrete and destructive.

Tuesday, September 26, 1989.

It's 10:18 p.m.

I'm seeing ——— before class tomorrow. What a dilemma! I'd like to get together with so many nice girls, but I don't really have the time.

Miss ———, my extra help teacher, is dressing provocatively, and her intentions are not entirely wasted. She looks really good. I'd probably get shit for screwing a teacher, but I'd still like to try. She'd be great in bed.

A real cute chick called ——— in my science class keeps flirting with me. Whoa. I'd really like to get her cherry. She's only 15, though.

Then there's ——— in English. She's a petite brunette with a dynamite smile and great tits.

Choices! It's getting me confused more than anything else. I'd like to have them all. It could probably be done, but I just don't know if I could do it. That's four girls in one school. Heavy.

Miss ——— would be the easiest. She's older and more susceptible to physical advances. ——— would be a delicious challenge. I'd make her want to so badly, then I'd let her down. Then pounce in a truly

*passionate escapade of truly momentous proportions. Chicks, man, they
drive you nuts!*

Myriad facets,
Points of light, stars in the sky.
Constellations, zodiac,
Roll the dice.
Crapshoot.
Poker.
Crimson twilight off blonde highlights
Pitter-patter
Cardiac-ejaculatory arrest.

Wednesday, September 27, 1989.

It's 7:06 a.m.

   *We bought an air purifier yesterday, and this is the first day I'm
allowed to smoke in my room. My parents suggested it. I didn't even
need to ask. Pretty good.*

It's 7:36 p.m.

Promises

I don't mind if you never come home,
I don't mind if you just
Keep on rolling away on distant sea,
Cause I don't love you and you don't love me.

Cause a commotion when you come to town,
You get on your smile and they melt,
Your lovers and friends, it's all very fine
But I don't like yours and you don't like mine.

Reprise

Da la, la, la, la, la, lah,
Da la, la, la, la, la, lah

I don't care what you do at night,
Oh, I don't care how you get your delights,
I'm gonna leave you alone, I'll just let it be,
I don't love you and you don't love me.

Chorus

I got a problem
Can you relate?
I got a woman
Calling love hate.
We made a vow: We'd always be friends,
How could we know that promises end.

Reprise

I tried to love you for years upon years,
You refused to take me for real.
It's time you saw what I want you to see,
And I still love you and you just let it be.

Chorus.

Reprise

Repeat reprise and fade

— performed by Eric Clapton

Thursday, September 28, 1989

It's 10:05 p.m.

    This is a copy of a poem I wrote in late July 1989. I reread it tonight, and it holds a new relevance for me. In reading it, I surprised myself with the scope of my visions, and the eloquent way in which I expressed it.

Hello, my name is love. For you I can sail on the wind
and soar like a dove

For you I can break all convention,
leave tradition in the past
Or hurt you.

If I kiss you tonight, sweetly,
I will kill you tomorrow, surely.
Hot, humid, passionate love, but not.

I feed on feelings and excrete pain.
I have no feelings and feel no pain.
My morals are nonexistent, and I don't discriminate.
Hello, my name is love.

Friday, September 29, 1989

It's 4:39 p.m.

    I met a really nice girl in English class today. I couldn't believe how blue her eyes are. She is blonde, and laughs a lot. She also sits right across from me, so I get lots of eye contact.

    I'm going to be really bored tonight. It's Friday, and I have nothing to do, except either vegetate or do homework. It is really depressing.

    I found out today that Jamie was looking for me at Central the other day. Obviously, he doesn't comprehend the consequences of his actions.

I'd get thrown right in the can for even talking to him. I never did see him, though.

Sunday, October 1, 1989

It's 9:35 p.m.
Was just thinking.

Late that other night
I might have said some things
Done some things
That maybe caused a fight

Climbing high and soaring fast,
Diving deep,
Then flying on the heights

Wednesday, October 4, 1989
It's 5:51 p.m.

Thursday, October 5, 1989

It's 12:53.
I'm still up from the last entry! I'll be dead tired in school tomorrow. It doesn't seem to matter how tired I am, I still can't seem to get "up" for school.
Pink Floyd plays across the room.

"Race towards an early grave ..."

Perhaps it's some kind of omen. I don't know if I believe in omens and all that superstitious poppycock. It's like god. A bunch of spooky coincidences, and everyone starts believing it.

I had a weird omen the other day. It came to me in the form of a dream. I dreamt that I would meet (that is would meet, the future tense of the verb. I knew somehow that it was something that had already taken place. Somehow, I knew) a beautiful redheaded girl with bounteous bosoms and a tight little ass.

More than that, though. She was a truly beautiful person. Kind and sweet and generous, I know I was deeply in love with this person. And I knew it would happen. The dream will become reality. Pink Floyd still plays across the room.

*"Hanging, haunting,
quiet desperation is the English way . . ."*

*"Quiet desperation!" I wish! Maybe it was quiet once, but the desperation is loud and clear now.
I'm going to sleep.
Goodnight.
Shut up!*

Thursday, October 5, 1989

It's 9:54 p.m.

[Steve cited the full lyrics to the song "It Can Happen" by the group Yes, but wrote nothing more.]

Monday, October 9, 1989

It's 1:03 a.m.

I was lying in bed when a thought crossed my mind: what a big mess I've gotten myself into.

I mean, not that it's just hit me now. I know the legal ramifications. It hit me in a totally different way . . . dark, jail-like places jittered through my mind, then acceptance, familiarity, almost like I belonged. Like I was supposed to be there. I had a strange longing to be back in Barton.

All of a sudden, being in jail was important to me. Did I really want to be outside?

My acquaintances (I don't call them friends and relatives because I don't feel close to anybody. My parents, especially. I feel a tie to my mother, physically. A strong one. But not closeness, caring, to anyone. People are just people to me, everybody. Just people, with no differentiation between loved ones, friends, even strangers seem alike to me. Just people.) and I don't seem to be on the same wavelength anymore. (I used to have an excellent relationship with Jamie. We were closer than brothers. Identical in goals and itinerary. We had achieved, as nearly as possible, a mind-meld. Our protocol, ideas and personalities were perfectly in line. I felt understood, really understood, by another human being.)

I don't really like being with anyone. Even Rocky, whom I admire greatly, does not strike me as a person that I like. I don't really like anybody. (Interestingly enough, as I write, thoughts go through my head. Subversive thoughts, malicious and evil thoughts of domination, manipulation; of power. I know it is as smart and sneaky as I am, and is making me think these thoughts.)

Enough.

In the final entries of the journal, which was eventually found among Steve's belongings in the back of Fritch's car, the delusional "it" becomes more and more powerful, Steve engages the unseen force in actual written arguments. By the last entry, *it* had won.

Thursday, October 12, 1989

It's 11:42 p.m.
I'm going to do a big job. Not just a big job, but a BIG job!

A hijacking, or something, maybe a bus, then hijack a plane for the getaway. Or a bus!? Hijack a bus. Go across the Mexican border in a bus! Tons of hostages; tons of weapon-stopping armour.

— Chapter 6 —
The Big Job

As Steve's control over the force he called "it" grew weaker, his desire to do his one "Big Job" grew stronger. He wanted out of all the places he felt had held him back for so long: his school, his home, and the quiet, peaceful place he had somehow distorted into his own hell—Burlington. Even the idea of jail seemed better, somehow, than staying there.

Feeling less control over his life than ever, Jamie wanted a major change, as long as he didn't have to work for it. He didn't want to wait, especially since he was coming up to his eighteenth birthday, when suddenly his crimes would be judged by adult standards, and the maximum three-year sentence for juveniles would no longer apply.

They were ready to do anything. At school and at the SuperCentre, their friends had begun to notice the change in Steve's and Jamie's attitudes, too. On a Thursday afternoon two weeks before the murder, they stood outside in the smoking area at M.M. Robinson with their friend Geoff Berendse.

"We've got to do one major big crime. Soon," Steve said, dragging dramatically on a du Maurier. "We shouldn't have got caught for that chip truck, but the fucking driver saw us. And we wouldn't have got picked up for the smoke shop, either. We planned that perfectly, except for that fucking little rat who squealed. This time, we're just going to steal a car and fucking drive. Maybe we'll go over the border to the States, maybe to Florida, or maybe out to B.C. Where do you go when you're in trouble, Geoff?"

"I go to the Eaton Centre in Toronto."

They finished their cigarettes, and Steve left. Geoff, the only one in their group with his own car, drove Jamie over to the gas station for work.

The next week, Andrea Talarico and her boyfriend Nick Santini were idling in the food area at the SuperCentre with Steve and Cari. Andrea Talarico and Cari-Lee Chisamore had become best friends after meeting in a class at M.M., six months after Andrea's family had moved to Burlington from Thunder Bay. Andrea was one of the few people at school who knew Cari and Jamie had been dating for the past three weeks.

Andrea was only slightly acquainted with Steve. She had met him just after he got out of the Barton Street jail, but Nick had known him for about ten years, from Steve's first try at the public school system. They had been good friends once, but when Steve started to go overboard with drugs and drinking, Nick deliberately distanced himself.

Steve was picking at the edge of the table as the teenagers chatted about nothing much. Bored, he kept mentioning jail, saying how he liked it there and how he knew he was going back soon. Finally, he broke off a piece of plastic from the edge of the table, and threw it down for everyone to look at.

"What's that for?" Nick asked.

"I could kill someone with this, you know," Steve pronounced. "All I'd have to do is poke out their eye, and that would be it. I wonder what it would be like to kill someone."

"You're sick," Nick said, disgusted. He knew Steve had really changed.

"One thing I want to do before I die is kill someone," Steve persisted, looking around the table for shock, approval or whatever reaction he could get.

No one answered. It was a weird thing to say, for sure, but Steve was like that. He was always boasting and trying to get a rise out of people. Everyone put it out of mind.

"Let's leave," Nick said, taking Andrea's hand.

On Monday, October 16, less than forty-eight hours before the killing, Beth Olah got a call from Steve's shop teacher at Central. Her son hadn't been in class that morning, and had missed other classes. The teacher wanted to know if something was wrong. Beth phoned the school office, and learned Steve had been skipping classes regularly for two weeks. She was shocked. It was the first indication that Steve had gone back to his old ways. Although he had stopped taking his medication several days earlier, and had resumed his old drinking and hash-smoking habits, missing school was the first breach of the bail conditions his parents had been aware of. Steve had so many faces that he could keep up several charades at the same time, and had clearly fooled his parents. Because he had shown them such a willingness to get better, and because they wanted to boost his self-esteem by showing they trusted him, they did not supervise him taking the pills.

Cari was supposed to meet Jamie after school at the SuperCentre that afternoon. After her last class, she crossed Guelph Line to the mall to meet him. She waited, but he didn't come, so she went home for dinner. She returned to the mall at 6 p.m., hoping to find him there. Moments after she arrived, Steve and Jamie stumbled in. They were carrying a Mac's Milk pop cup, filled with booze. They reeked. Cari and Jamie argued about Jamie standing her up earlier, and the boys left. Cari went home, mad: mad that Jamie had missed their date, mad that he didn't care, mad that he was drunk, and mad that he was with Steve, again.

Ed Boutillier was at the SuperCentre with a couple of pals, Mike Courtney and Jason LaPorte, when Steve and Jamie returned. Ed, a lanky, low-key teenager, had moved away from home while he was still in high school. He had a part-time job at the Sunoco station on Fairview Street at Maple, right across from the station where his friend Jamie worked. When he saw them, he could tell they were stoned and drunk. Steve moved slowly, and his eyes were red. Jamie, by contrast, looked crazed. The whites of his eyes were showing below the circles of his eyeballs, as if he were on the edge of convulsion, fighting to concentrate through the haze of hashish and booze. They asked Mike if he had any drugs to sell.

"I don't have any," Mike answered. "I don't do drugs any more."

Steve and Jamie looked at him as if he were some kind of traitor.

"Where have you guys been lately?" Mike asked.

"We've both been in jail," Steve said, a slight smile curling his lips. "I've got to go back to jail."

"When?"

"Maybe tonight. Have you got ten bucks, Mike? It's for something very important."

"For what?"

"We need some gas money."

"But you don't have a car."

"By the end of tonight, we might. We'll kill someone if we have to. What do you think would be the best way?"

"Oh, so *that's* why you might go back to jail."

"Yeah. I want to get my time over with now."

Jamie just laughed, trying to give the other guys a mean look like he had seen in the movies. Nobody believed they really meant it. Steve was always bragging, and Jamie pretended to be tougher than he really was. No one gave them any money, and finally, Steve and Jamie got up from the table to leave.

"Where are you going?" Ed called after them.

"To jail," Steve said without slowing down.

He and Jamie stepped out into the pouring rain and ran south on Guelph Line, in the direction of downtown Burlington. The other guys sat there, quiet. Mike thought to himself: "Those guys are crazy. They're losing it."

At home, Cari's anger had subsided, fermenting into worry over what trouble Jamie and Steve might get into. She went back over to the mall, where she found Ed and his friends still sitting in the food court.

"Have you seen Jamie and Steve? I was supposed to meet them here."

"They left about ten minutes ago," Ed said. "They said they were going to steal a car. Maybe they'll get a little farther than they did with that stupid chip truck, eh?"

The boys were all laughing, but Cari was not amused. She looked at her watch urgently. She said she had to find them. It was just after eight: Steve's curfew time.

"He's crazy, you know," she said. "Jamie's going to get in a lot of trouble if he stays with him."

Cari got up and walked over to the pay phone to call Steve's house, where his mother told her Steve wasn't home yet. She walked back to the table and said she was worried because they were still out.

"They asked us for ten bucks gas money for the car they were going to steal," Ed told her.

"I hope they don't get caught," Cari said.

"You know that if they get caught, they're going away for a long time," Mike said.

"Where *are* they?" Cari asked no one in particular, rubbing her face. "I wish I could find them."

"What are you doing hanging around with those guys, anyway?" Mike asked. "They're trouble."

"Because we've known each other for a while and we're really close friends, okay?"

Ed and Mike teased Cari, toying with her to get her more worried.

"You know, Steve doesn't mind jail," Ed said. "There's no hassle, no work, free room and board."

"Yeah," Mike said sarcastically. "Life is so full of hassles. I wish I could just go live in a forest in a cabin with nobody around."

They all pushed their chairs out from the table and stood up to leave. The boys headed out by the shops at the far end of the SuperCentre. Cari went out the exit off the food court, and headed for the Mac's Milk a few doors down in the outdoor strip of the mall. She told the clerk she was looking for Steve and Jamie, but he told her he hadn't seen them recently. He called the police station for her to see if Steve was there. He wasn't. She looked for two more hours before giving up and going home to bed.

Frank Olah got home late from work that night, at nine-thirty. His wife returned a half-hour later. Steve wasn't home and they didn't know where he was. It was now well past his curfew, and they were worried, especially after the phone call Beth had received from the school that morning. They were afraid. Beth called the police, asking them to arrest him for breaking his bail conditions. She expected the police to go looking for him, but through a misunderstanding, no cruiser was dispatched. She was told she would have to speak to Steve's probation officer in the morning.

While Beth worried, Steve and Jamie were on the other side of town, in a car dealership on King Road in west Burlington.

Steve and Jamie had heard it would be easy to get a car from Bannon's Automotive, because all the keys were kept in the office and it was easy to break into. That was true enough. They went in through the air-conditioning vent and found the keys. But matching the right keys to the right car in the dark while half-drunk and stoned proved too difficult. They gave up and walked the several blocks to the Mr. Submarine shop on Plains Road, around the corner from King Road. Now, they were angrier and more anxious than ever.

It was past 11 p.m. when dispatch at Burlington Taxi radioed veteran cabbie Fred Springer to pick up a fare at Mr. Submarine on Plains Road in west Burlington and take him to Joseph Brant Memorial Hospital.

When Springer's taxi pulled up to the shop, Jamie Ruston got in and told him to take him to Kilbride instead, offering no reason for the change in destination. By the time the cab had climbed the long hill to the north end of Cedar Springs Road, the meter read $18.60.

"I don't have the money. I must have left it with my friend," Jamie said, holding out his empty wallet. "I can pay you tomorrow night at work. I work at the Petro-Canada Station at Maple and Fairview. I'll give it to you then."

"Okay, give me your wallet for security."

Jamie handed over the wallet, and Springer checked through it to make sure it was really Jamie's. He knew it was when he saw Jamie's M.M. Robinson photo I.D. card, his birth certificate and his probation card. He held on to the wallet as security and said he would be by the station the next night to trade it for the fare.

Steve's parents were frantic by the time Steve called them to pick him up at the sub shop. Frank jumped into his car and raced across town.

Steve's eyes were wild, his hair was pulled out in all directions, and his clothes were filthy. His parents hadn't seen that look since the night he took them hostage at knife-point.

They told him they had called the police, and that he would have to answer to his probation officer for breaking his curfew.

At 5 a.m., Steve was wide awake. The hole in his stomach lining was burning red hot, and he vomited. When his parents woke up later, he told them he couldn't go to school that day. Beth left for work in Hamilton as usual, while Frank packed for a business trip he was taking to his company's headquarters in Akron, Ohio.

Later that morning, Andrea went with John Ruttan, who had recently dated Cari and remained her close friend, to the SuperCentre for lunch. They met Cari and Jamie there. John had been friends with Jamie for about three years, but noticed he had changed since Steve got out of jail. John didn't see Jamie as often. He was always with Steve now.

Andrea went over to the doughnut shop and got coffee

and a bagel. As she sat down with her friends at the table, she could tell Cari was anxious. Andrea knew about the fight the night before, and knew Cari was still giving Jamie the silent treatment.

The girls started their own conversation, while Jamie told John he was planning to take off. Last night, he said, he and Steve had broken into a car dealership and taken several sets of keys, but they couldn't match any of them to any of the cars on the lot, and had left empty-handed. Now, they were more determined than ever to get a car. Jamie said he would kill someone if he had to. He'd do it by hitting him on the head.

"But you'll go to jail if you get caught," John said.

"I like open custody," Jamie said. "But I don't want to go to a real jail."

Cari and Andrea turned for a moment to the boys' conversation. Out of concern for Cari, Andrea jumped in with a blunt question.

"Why do you want to go away, Jamie?"

"I just want to have a good time. I don't want to work for it, either," he answered.

Jamie turned away again to speak to John, and Cari and Andrea went back to their own conversation, but they kept one ear on what the boys were saying. They couldn't help but overhear Jamie ask John: "How would you kill someone? How hard would you have to hit somebody before they die?"

Cari heard it too, and sat dumbfounded by her boyfriend's question. "Shut up, Jamie. That's gross."

But John laughed it off, and picked up the conversation again. Cari sat stupefied, and now Andrea could understand why she looked so worried.

"Washroom," Cari mouthed to her friend, shifting her eyes toward the women's room down the corridor from the food court. She looked more upset, and was much quieter than usual.

Andrea finished the bagel, and got up with Cari. On their way down the hall, once they were out of earshot of the boys, Cari finally opened up to her friend.

"Jamie and Steve *are* planning on taking off," she said.

"Where?"

"I don't know. They're just going."

"Don't worry. They're not really going to go anywhere."

"I *am* worried. I think they *are* going, and I'm worried about how they're going to go, and what they'll do to get there."

"Like, what did they say they would do?"

"I'm not sure, but Jamie's been talking about stealing a car at the gas station. What do you think they would do with the guy from the car, Andrea?"

"I don't know."

"Do you think they'd kill them?"

"I don't know, Cari."

"They've got the guts to do it. I know. Jamie says they'd just drop the guy off at the border, but I don't believe him. You heard him talking about how to kill someone. I just don't know."

But Andrea refused to take it seriously. She figured Jamie's threats to leave were just a way of getting the upper hand in the quarrel that was still going on from the night before.

"Don't worry about it. He's not serious," Andrea said.

"I'm telling you, I *am* worried. I don't want him to go."

By the time they returned to the food area, other students were coming and going from the table. Jamie asked Cari to call Steve's house for him. His bail prevented him from contacting Steve, so he knew that he wouldn't get through if someone else answered the phone. Cari refused because she didn't want Jamie to hang around with Steve, but one of the recent arrivals from M.M. made the call. Jamie went over and took the phone. He wanted to tell Steve about his new idea: to use his job at the gas station to steal a customer's car.

"We decided at that point that we would have to abduct a person," Steve said later. "We would wait for suitable people to drive up. We figured we could pick and choose because not very much traffic comes through the gas station that time of night, if someone drove up that was suitable. We'd look for that type of car first, like either a luxury or a sports car. And then when the person got out of the car, how they were dressed, whether they would have credit cards or cash, or what the story would be."

Back at the table, Andrea used the opportunity to get more information from Cari.

"What's wrong? What's the matter?" she asked.

"I'm never going to see Jamie again."

"Come on, don't worry. Look, I'm going to English now. Are you coming?"

"No. I'm going to stay with Jamie," Cari answered, as the worried look on her face intensified.

Jamie returned to the table after a few minutes, but didn't say what he had talked to Steve about. The crowd was breaking up. Andrea got up to leave.

"Hey John! Wait up. I'll walk back to school with you."

John walked back to the table where they had been sitting and picked up his jacket, and Andrea used the opportunity to lean over and whisper to Jamie.

"You'd better not hurt her. She cares about you, you know."

But Jamie just sat, smiling wryly.

"Remember what I said," she told him.

She called out to Cari, "I'm not working tonight, so you can call me if you want to talk about anything."

"Don't worry, I will."

When they were alone, Jamie told Cari about the botched car-lot theft. She was still angry with him for standing her up, but she was so worried about him leaving that she listened.

"If we're going to get a car, we're going to have to take one with someone in it," he said. "We'll have to make the guy drive."

"Please don't do it, Jamie. I don't want you to go. I don't want you to get in trouble."

"Don't worry, we'll be okay," he reassured her.

"You're leaving because of me, aren't you? You're upset with me."

"No, no, no. It's just that me and Steve, we can't stay in Burlington. We've got to get out. We're in trouble all the time, and I've just got to make a new start somewhere else."

They continued like this until 3 p.m., when they went over to Cari's house two blocks away. Jamie was carrying his gym bag, with his Petro-Canada shirt inside. Cari didn't know he was also carrying a long kitchen knife.

Jamie asked Cari to come with him to work that night, and to be with him until late. She agreed. She wanted to talk him out of the robbery and running away, and if not, at least to squeeze in every last minute she could get with him before he left.

"Maybe you should come with us," he said.

"No way," she answered flatly.

He still wasn't saying when he and Steve were going to take off, but Cari figured it would be that night or the next day. She knew that Steve would be coming to the station later that night.

What she didn't know was that Steve and Jamie had been discussing an even larger crime, one that would simultaneously serve their desire to escape from Burlington with money and a car, and possibly satisfy their curiosity about the one aspect of crime they wanted to experience before they died: killing a man. They had talked around the idea for days now, even calling it the Big Job, just as Steve had written in his diary. During their hours together—spent illegally, considering the probation order—they walked around, talking and dreaming of this Big Job. When Steve cut classes, he spent his time with Jamie, walking around the blocks of the pleasant neighbourhood, the original settlement area of Burlington. In particular, they liked to talk under the spreading shade tree in front of Steve's school. While they were in the schoolyard plotting the murder that would take his father's life, Jason Fritch was inside, blissfully unaware of the impending collision between his life and theirs.

When Craig and Diane Chisamore came home later in the afternoon, they resigned themselves to the fact that they'd have a guest at their dinner table: Jamie Ruston.

They didn't care much for Cari's new boyfriend, but they were working hard to be fair with her. They loved their daughter deeply, and tried not to let their concern get in the way of her life. Craig, tall and distinguished-looking, called her his "social butterfly." She was the middle child: four years younger than Cindy and five years older than Shannon. Craig and Diane had been married twenty-two years, most of it spent moving around Canada with his job at Ford. The family moved for the first time to Burlington in 1976, while he worked at the Canadian headquarters in Oakville. After eight years, he was transferred to Edmonton, and then the family returned to live in Burlington in 1986.

In the three years since they had moved back, Cari had proven she was an independent spirit. She had left home the year before over a curfew battle, only to return three weeks later, having learned how much she needed her family, and promising to keep better hours. Since then, the whole family had come closer together. Although Cari's behaviour had improved considerably, she was still cutting classes occasionally, and her parents wondered about the company she was keeping. They weren't pleased about Jamie's scruffy appearance or his criminal record, and in the few times they had met him before that dinner, he hadn't said much to make them feel better. Still, Cari seemed to believe in him, and they were trying to show her they trusted her to make her own judgments.

"She talked to her mother a lot about him," Craig said. "She cared a lot about him, but it wasn't a love relationship. We were aware that he had had some scrapes with the law before. She, on a number of occasions, said that just because somebody did something wrong once didn't mean they were a bad person. She wanted to guide him down the right road."

Steve, on the other hand, had been barred from their house after Cari had heard him making rude sexual comments to Shannon.

At 6 p.m., Diane called Jamie and her daughter up from the basement for dinner. By the end of the meal, it was getting close to Jamie's 8 p.m. start time at the gas station, and he was still miles from work. He had planned to take the bus, but because of the late hour and the heavy rain that was pouring down for the second night in a row, Diane offered to give him a ride. Cari still didn't know if her parents would permit her to go with Jamie to the station.

They had let her go many times before, even though they didn't like the idea of her hanging around for hours in a gas bar with a boy they didn't entirely trust. Since tonight was a school night, Cari worried they might make her stay in, but her mother said it would be all right, as long as she took the 10 p.m. bus back home.

"You make sure she gets that bus, Jamie," Diane said as they got out of the car into the rain.

"Okay," he said.

"We'll see you later, Mom," Cari said, trying to look casual, but she was worried. Jamie had told her before dinner that they would be leaving that night.

Jamie headed for the kiosk, where Sharon Patrick was finishing up the paperwork from her shift. Jamie told Cari to wait until she left before coming in. It was against company rules to have friends in the kiosk, either in the customers' or employees' area, and Jamie had already been warned by the manager, Gary Hackman, not to let Cari into the kiosk. But Jamie wasn't too concerned about the rules any more. He was on the last shift of his two-month tenure at Petro-Canada.

At first, like many cashiers, he had come up short on his deposits. After a talk with Hackman, the shortages began to shrink, and then, in the last few weeks, had begun to creep up again. Hackman docked Jamie's pay for the money that he was obviously pocketing, to the point where he was working just to cover the money he owed. Jamie agreed to quit rather than being fired, and the next day he was supposed to come and pick up what little was left of his last paycheque.

Jamie exchanged greetings with Sharon Patrick as she did her paperwork, while Cari walked over to the telephone booth on the other side of the lot and called Andrea.

"I'm at the station. My mom just dropped us off here," Cari said.

"Why are you calling me from the pay phone?"

"Why do you think?"

"Well, what's going on with Jamie? How did it go between you guys this afternoon?"

"They're going," Cari pronounced. "Steve's coming by here about midnight. Jamie asked me to go with them."

"Why?"

"If they leave, I'll never see them again."

"Don't go, Cari. You know they're only going to get into trouble. Where are they thinking of going?"

"Anywhere but here."

"Hey, maybe they'll go to Thunder Bay," Andrea joked, trying to ease the tension.

"Hey, yeah. All four of us should go together," Cari said, returning the joke. "But I do want to get out of Burlington."

Andrea could tell she was serious. She tried to keep the mood light, yet still get her message across not to go. By the end of the conversation, Andrea felt she had talked Cari out of going along with Jamie and Steve, and confirmed that she would meet her friend at the mall at eight the next morning, as usual. But then Cari said: "If I'm not there, don't worry about me, okay?"

"What do you mean? You *will* be there, won't you?"

"Yes. If I have any doubts or anything, I'll call you."

"You phone me any time you want, Cari."

But that was the last time she talked to her friend.

Bob Yates, who worked at the Petro-Canada car wash on the same lot, often socialized with Jamie after closing the car wash, when he would return the keys to the gas bar. Because of the rain that night, Yates hadn't had any customers, and he joined Cari and Jamie at eight-thirty, after closing up. Yates, a quiet young man, wasn't saying much, but Jamie was excited. He told him he was going to run away to the United States, sell seashells on the beach, and lie around. Before that, though, he said he and Steve and Cari were going to get a hotel room and party before sending Cari back home in a limousine. Cari said she didn't want anything to do with it.

Every time a car came in, Jamie gave it the once-over, saying he'd like to take it and throw the driver in the trunk. Yates figured he must be joking. Jamie took the phone in the kiosk after Cari had called Steve's house and got him on the line. Yates could only gather from Jamie's end that Steve was on his way down to carry out some plan, and that he was supposed to bring drugs with him.

Jamie called Player's Pizza on Brant Street, and ordered two subs and two bottles of pop to be delivered. In the meantime, Springer, the cab driver, returned to collect his fare from the night before, and Jamie paid him with four five-dollar bills from the till. Springer handed over the wallet and left.

While Jamie was checking out cars at the gas station, Steve and his mother were sitting down to a late supper on Cartier Crescent. Steve was feeling better, and with his father away and his mother at work all day, had used part of his afternoon to cook her a special dinner. He was angry with her for getting home late. But as they ate, Steve told her he had had a quarrel with his sister. "I'm just finding it hard being back in school, Mom," he said. "It's that, it's everything."

"Steven, you know you have our support. Whenever you're worried about anything, you know you can talk to us," she said. "You're taking your pills like you're supposed to, aren't you?"

"Yes, of course." Steve was lying. He hadn't taken them for several days.

But Beth didn't know that. She had wanted Steve to think she and Frank trusted him to take care of himself. He had seemed eager to get better, and she knew that he wouldn't forget to take the medication that was supposed to help him get there.

After dinner, Steve watched television with his mother, not telling her who it was when Jamie called from the station. He acted normally, but inside he was anxious for her to go to bed so he could sneak away and meet up with him. He was already behind schedule.

Finally, Beth got up to go to sleep in her room upstairs.

"I think you should get to bed soon, Steven. You need to get some sleep."

"Don't worry, mom. This program is over at eleven and I'll go to bed then."

As soon as she had settled in bed, Steve went to his room on the first floor and pulled the covers off his bed. He arranged a pile of clothes on the mattress and a soccer ball on the pillow, throwing the covers over them to make it look as though he were sleeping underneath. He climbed out his bedroom window, as he had many times before, and headed for the Mac's Milk store at Brant Street and Upper Middle Road to call a cab.

Just before 11 p.m., the taxi pulled up to the station. Steve climbed out, carrying a black knapsack, and once again, Jamie dipped into the Petro-Canada till to pay the driver.

Steve broke out a small chunk of hash a friend had dropped off at his house that afternoon. Now, he and Jamie took a Coke can and poked a hole in the bottom near the rim, lit a cigarette, dropped a small piece of the hash onto the heater, and shoved the smoking ember into the bottom hole. Putting a thumb over the drinking hole in the top, they took turns trapping the hash smoke inside and then taking it all in with one big toke.

Steve and Jamie passed the crude pipe back and forth, although Cari and Bob refused to join them. Bob left the kiosk to run home in the rain.

Although Steve and Jamie were both catching a buzz, they were nowhere near stoned. Compared to their usual drinking and smoking habits, this was just a snack. As they enjoyed the lightheadedness of their modest high, they started talking again about the job ahead of them. At ten minutes past midnight, Geoff Berendse's Mazda RX7 sports car pulled up to the pumps. Marino Peric was in the other seat. Cari and Steve were with Jamie inside, all behind the counter together. Geoff and Marino went in by the employees' door.

Jamie was counting up the evening's receipts at the counter.

"Hi guys. How are you?" Geoff asked. "What are you doing still open?"

Jamie looked up at the clock.

"I hope they pay me overtime," he said mockingly. Cari, uncharacteristically, was silent. Geoff thought this was weird. Then he noticed the tip of a black plastic garbage bag sticking out of the top of Steve's pants. Steve was pointing to it, and jumping up and down, obviously excited. This was risky behaviour, considering he and Jamie were planning to use the bag in a murder, but Steve couldn't resist the opportunity to draw attention to himself.

"What's that for?" Geoff asked.

"It's a condom for a black man," Steve joked.

"But aren't you supposed to be in for your curfew?"

"Don't worry about it. I'll be back in the morning."

After a few more minutes of idle conversation, Jamie asked if Geoff was there for gas. Geoff said yes.

"Just put in five bucks and leave," Jamie said. He seemed impatient.

Geoff pumped five dollars' worth of gas into the car, and handed the money to Jamie. He bummed two cigarettes each from Steve and Jamie, and stood idle in the booth until Jamie turned to him and spoke in a grave tone.

"You have to leave. We're going to do something big," he said mysteriously. Berendse figured they were going to smoke drugs. He had no idea what Jamie really had in mind.

"Well, does anybody want a ride home?" he asked.

"Yes, I'd like…" Cari started, but then Jamie cut her off from what was her perfect opportunity to leave the scene of an impending murder.

"No. We'll take a cab home," he said for her.

Inside the kiosk, Jamie and Steve were glad to be rid of their friends, obviously excited to get on with it. Cari sat anxiously, virtually helplessly, as they shaped their vague idea into a concrete plan.

The possibility of killing their victim grew into a probability, and finally, a certainty.

"We decided that we would have to, or else how were we going to keep the witness quiet?" Steve said later. "And we figured if we kidnapped somebody, we've got to feed him, we've got to transport them, we've got to take care of them, we got to tie them up, we got to do all this shit. I said if we kill him, we can just stick him in the trunk and leave him—and bury him some time."

They took the heavy red fire extinguisher from its bracket under the counter and carried it to the other side of the kiosk, where the customers would stand to pay. Jamie picked up the extinguisher and held it over his head. But he didn't have full command of the heavy cylinder, so Steve took it from him, along with the responsibility for inflicting the blows on their intended victim. Steve gave Jamie the garbage bag. Cari sat scared and quiet, losing hope that they were bluffing.

Finally, just before 1 a.m., a car pulled up to the pumps, a white Buick Regal, last year's model. The driver was alone.

"We saw him get out of the car and we saw that he was wearing a suit and a trench coat and he looked kind of skinny and he was wearing glasses at the time. And, you know, he didn't look like anybody that would do us any harm, and he looked like we could take him pretty quickly," Steve recalled.

The businessman got out of the car, and reached for the nozzle.

"This one! This one!" Jamie said, reaching for the light panel, turning off the outdoor canopy lights that had lured Mr. Fritch from the roadway and into their crude trap.

Fritch was startled by the lights going off, and pivoted momentarily toward the booth before returning to the mindless task of pumping his gas. Outside, Steve had ducked out the employees' entrance and was crouching low behind the booth so Fritch couldn't see him.

Jamie had moved to the customers' area where he was acting out a cruel pantomime, bending low to the floor, placing imaginary trash into the real garbage bag, while Cari sat behind the counter. Whether she was aware of it or not, she was an important prop in this drama. When Fritch walked in, he presumed that she was the cashier and stepped up to the window, reaching into his blazer for his wallet. But before he or she could say anything, he was plunged into blackness, his nostrils sucking stale, vinyl air and his ears filling with plastic rustling.

Shouts. A girl screaming. The door hissing open. Fritch, confused and reflex-driven, struggled to raise his hands over his head for air and light. But crashing through the plastic came the side of the metallic cylinder, ringing heavy and hollow on the hard bone of his own skull. No air, no light, no room, no idea what was happening to himself, only struggling to wrestle free and make it stop. More blows and shouts. Less air. Ten hard, ringing smashes across the top of the head, and still, he stood. An angry young voice screamed he wasn't dead yet, and commanded his execution.

Suddenly there was a blow from below as a knee plunged into his groin. Reflex drove him to the ground, where the blows now continued, harder than before, and he began to drift into unconsciousness. Again and again the boy stood over the man's helpless, hooded body, pumping his bizarre weapon into the black plastic, until he heard a crack and the final sucking gasps of the customer, whose lungs were filling with his own blood.

At last the blows stopped, and he was dead on the cold floor.

The Criminals

M.M. Robinson High School yearbook photo of Steve Olah released to the media after the murder.

Police released this photo of Cari-Lee Chisamore as they combed the country for her and Jamie Ruston.

The Halton police mugshot of Jamie Ruston, taken seven months before the murder, was released to help the public identify the fugitive killer.

Paul Stunt's last murder trial as a Crown Attorney was one of the most difficult he ever faced. Stunt called Steve and Jamie callous murderers out for a thrill kill.
Spectator photo

Halton assistant Crown Attorney Susan Lawson, who prosecuted the case with Crown Attorney Paul Stunt.
Spectator photo

Hamilton lawyer Jeffrey Manishen represented Cari-Lee Chisamore with Martha Zivolak.
Spectator photo

Toronto criminal lawyer
Bill Trudell who, with
Janet Leiper, represented
Jamie Ruston.
Spectator photo

Paul LaFleur, the Olahs'
family lawyer from
Burlington, recommended
the family seek bail for Steve
even after he attacked his
parents. LaFleur said Steve's
chances for proper mental
treatment were much better
outside criminal or mental
institutions.
Spectator photo

Steve Olah's senior trial lawyer Alan
Cooper.
Spectator photo

Halton police principal investigator
Sergeant Joe Barker.
Spectator photo

Halton police principal investigator
Sergeant Jim Chapman.
Spectator photo

Toronto homicide detective
John Line.
Spectator photo

The Places

The tree in front of Central High School in Burlington, one of the places where Steve Olah and Jamie Ruston planned their "Big Job."
Spectator photo

The Petro-Canada station where the murder took place.
Spectator photo

The Carlton Inn in downtown Toronto where Steve Olah, Cari-Lee Chisamore and Jamie Ruston watched movies, slept and ate breakfast after the murder, using Joseph Fritch's credit cards to pay for it all.
Spectator photo

View from behind counter at Petro-Canada station, photographed the night after the murder, when police closed the station to comb it for evidence.
Halton police photo

Discolouration in grouting of the kiosk floor near the customer entrance led police to pry up the tiles.
Halton police photo

Underneath the tiles, police found bloodstains still vivid from the night before. The blood matched the victim's type.
Halton police photo

Underside of murder weapon (gas station fire extinguisher), marked and dented from hitting the floor, with dark bloodstains on the inside rim.
Halton police photo

Joseph Fritch's body was found in the trunk of his Buick Regal in a downtown Toronto parking garage.
Halton police photo

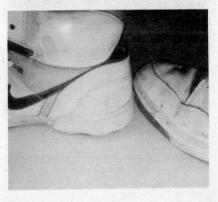

Jamie Ruston left these bloodstained runners behind at the Toronto Eaton Centre Florsheim shoe store after trading them in for fancy Italian loafers paid for with the victim's American Express Card.
Halton police photo

Prisoner-escort
officers lead
Steve Olah
from prisoner van
to Burlington court
in one of his first
appearances after
the murder.
Spectator photo

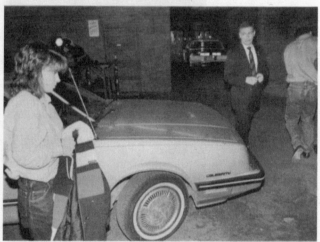

Police lead Jamie Ruston (back to the camera because his identity
was protected by the Young Offenders Act) and Cari-Lee Chisamore
through the basement of Halton police headquarters in Oakville after
returning with them from B.C. Sergeant Jim Chapman is at centre.
Spectator photo

Jamie Ruston and Steve Olah on their way to court during their trial.
Spectator photo

Sergeant Jim Chapman leads Cari-Lee Chisamore, who was originally charged with first-degree murder, from Burlington court in one of her first appearances.
Spectator photo

Cari-Lee Chisamore returned to court from prison to testify against Steve Olah and Jamie Ruston, who was once her boyfriend.
Spectator photo

Sergeant Joe Barker, left, and Sergeant Jim Chapman lead Jamie Ruston and Steve Olah through the freezing rain to the prisoner van following their convictions for first-degree murder.
Spectator photo

Chapter 7

"We Just Did It To Have a Good Time"

"Go out and get in the car, Cari," Steve said, still breathing hard from the effort.

"I can't move," she protested, crying.

"She's got to get in, man, if we're going to get away from here," Steve said, and walked out. Wanting just to get out of the booth, she followed him. The car was parked right outside the door. She walked around to the passenger side, where Steve had already opened the door for her.

She sat silently, eyes closed, waiting for the next step.

Inside, Steve and Jamie picked up the body. Steve, being far stronger, grabbed the corpse under the arms, and Jamie held the feet, while blood continued to dribble out of the garbage bag and onto the ceramic tiles.

But each time they were ready to take the body out to the car, a police cruiser drove by, first one from the west, then one from the east and a third from the south. None stopped; no one could have imagined this was happening. Finally, the last cruiser was out of sight. The crime was now fifteen minutes old, and the way was totally clear.

Cari heard Steve and Jamie laughing with each other before she felt the weight of the body being dumped inside, and heard the trunk slammed shut again. She felt more scared and sick than ever.

"There's blood on there," Jamie said, looking at a smear on the white paint. "We'd better clean that off if we're going to be driving around."

Steve grabbed a Kleenex from Fritch's car and wiped off the blood, while Jamie headed back inside the kiosk to start the clean-up.

While Jamie mopped up the blood and hosed down the murder weapon, Steve climbed into the driver's seat beside Cari. He started the car and gunned the engine, making a hard left, taking the car behind the automotive plaza and out of sight. Opening her eyes for the first time as Steve accelerated, she noticed a man asleep in the driver's seat of a parked tow truck.

"There's a man in there!" she screamed.

Steve veered, but caught the right rear fender on a parked van, causing a loud bang. But the man did not stir, and Steve finally came to a stop between the van and the tow truck.

"Keep your eyes closed," he said calmly. "I've got to wipe off my hands."

As he continued to wipe the blood on his jeans, Steve turned to her and said, paternally, "You might need some help after this. For me, it's just a rush, but you'll need help later."

"You scare me, Steve," she said, repulsed.

"Don't worry, I'm not going to hurt you," he said in an absurdly calm tone.

"But you've just murdered someone! Don't you know that's a sin? It's the worst sin you could possibly do, Steve!"

"Don't worry about it," he said. "I'm not religious."

Finally, after another fifteen minutes, Jamie had finished cleaning the kiosk, wiping it so clean that five hours later, Elke Sears, the morning attendant, would have no idea of the horror that had happened there the night before. Jamie even scrubbed the grout between the tiles. He wanted to make the kiosk look as normal as possible. He even left Peric's five dollars in the cash register, along with the night's receipts. Taking that money would have been *stealing*.

Although he had started the next day's business at 11:51 p.m., he didn't finish his paperwork from the night before, but that was nothing new. He used the sink in the employees' washroom to wash the blood and fingerprints from the fire extinguisher, but neglected to return it to its bracket under the counter. It was dented and chipped along the sharp rim that surrounded the convex bottom, but in its upright position didn't show the marks of its bizarre use. Jamie brought in the oil displays and wheeled them into the employees' section. Satisfied that everything was too clean for a murder to be traced to the scene, Jamie prepared to leave. But there was one problem: the mop. It was soaked and stained in blood, and since no amount of rinsing seemed to get it out, he took it with him. He turned on the alarm, but forgot to lock the customers' door, not knowing that the open door would be a giveaway. He also missed the drop of blood about the size of a dime outside the employees' door.

Figuring he had given Jamie enough time, Steve brought the car around to the front of the booth again, opened his door and moved the seat forward. Jamie tossed the unclean-able mop into the back seat and climbed inside. He was holding the Coke-can pipe. Steve pulled off the lot, turning right onto Fairview Street, looking for an exit onto the highway.

"Where are you going?" Cari asked.

"Toronto," Steve answered.

"I want to get out right now. I just want to go home," she told them.

"That wouldn't be a good idea right now," Steve said. "But don't worry. We'll get you home later."

He pulled onto the Queen Elizabeth Way and drove the only direction he could: south toward Niagara. But they wanted to go east to Toronto, where they figured they could ditch all the clothes they were wearing and buy new ones. Toronto was large enough for them to blend in without risking a border crossing in a stolen car, carrying a body in the trunk. Steve took the first exit, at North Shore Boulevard, only a mile from where the killing had taken place, just beyond Fritch's own backyard.

He pulled a U-turn on North Shore and got back onto the highway, this time heading north and eventually east along Highway 403 for Toronto. Jamie reached up from the back seat and put his hand on his girlfriend's shoulder.

"I can't believe we did it," he said to Steve.

Cari pulled away from his touch.

"What's your problem?" he asked her.

"Just leave her alone right now," Steve advised. "It's going to take her a little while to get used to this. Why don't you fire up some more tokes?"

As they drove, Jamie began going through the contents of the wallet. There was an American Express card, a Royal Bank Visa card and a Triathlon car-leasing card. These, along with the cash and driver's licence, were what they had been looking for. Jamie put them in one pile on the back seat. In another, he placed the useless items: receipts, business cards and the family pictures that Fritch had carried with him. Jamie looked at one and felt a brief pang of remorse, but continued nevertheless. He put everything back in the wallet, now sorted and ready to serve their needs.

On the way down the highway, they smoked the rest of the hashish.

Steve had wanted to find a grand hotel to stay in to celebrate their accomplishment. He was planning on the Royal York at York and Front, but didn't know how to get there. He drove well beyond the intended exit, and had to turn back.

"All the frigging one-way streets fucked me up," Steve complained later.

Eventually, he ended up driving north on Yonge Street, and finding the Carlton Inn, beside Maple Leaf Gardens.

Steve parked the car on the ground-level parking lot across from the front of the hotel, between a Red GMC van and a red Toyota Tercel. He took the wallet and checked it over again, in preparation for the first fraud he would commit with Fritch's credit cards. The three of them went first to the second floor of the hotel, looking for a public washroom where they could make themselves presentable enough to check in.

Steve and Jamie went into the men's room and cleaned the rest of the visible blood off their hands. Jamie stayed in the washroom while Cari and Steve, presenting themselves as a couple, went to the lobby to register. Neither was carrying any baggage. It was now 2:12 a.m.

"Uh, we'd like to have a room for the night," Steve said.

"Well, let's see ... we're pretty crowded tonight, but we've got some space in the middle floors and then some higher up. There's a room I can give you on the twenty-second floor, second from the top," said the clerk, Nathan Lapkin. "Will you be paying cash, sir?"

"No, I'm not going to pay cash," Steve said.

"Then I'll need to see your driver's licence or some other identification," Lapkin replied.

"Well, we've got American Express, or I've got my Visa."

"Oh. Credit cards. Fine. Sure, no problem," said the clerk,

who then took an impression of Fritch's Visa card, and ran it through the authorization machine. It was valid.

Steve signed the bill: *John Bill* Fritch, getting both first names wrong. In the space for his address, he began writing an actual address in Burlington, on Headon Road, but then, as an afterthought, added *Vermont* in the space for province. The cost of the room was eighty-nine dollars, and they were assigned room number 2226, a double. Steve handled the whole transaction, while Cari stood quietly by.

They took the lobby elevator up to the second floor and picked up Jamie before getting back in and riding up to their room. They had a clear view of the parking lot and the car from their window.

"Perfect," Steve said. "This way, we can see if he tries to break out or anything."

Even though they had all heard Fritch's last breaths, they felt there was still a chance that he could be alive. All three teens were thirsty, so Steve took the elevator back down to the lobby to get change for the pop machine. He bought three cans of pop from the machine on his floor and returned to the room, where the three of them started watching pay-per-view movies. First, though, Steve called the front desk and requested a 7-a.m. wake-up call. They caught the ending of *Ghostbusters II*, and then the entire showing of *Roadhouse*, starring Patrick Swayze.

"In one particular scene in the movie, the hero gets in a fight with this guy and the guy pulls a gun," Steve said later. "And Swayze with his hand rips the guy's larynx out and Jamie says, 'He just killed that guy,' and I said, 'Yeah, but he pulled a gun on him.' Then he looked at me and said, 'Geez, we just did it to have a good time.' And that was the only mention he ever made of it."

At 4:30, the movie was over, and everyone was hungry.

"None of us could get to sleep, 'cause we were all pretty shaken up and pumped on adrenalin, and so I went to the store," Steve said. He left the hotel and walked to the Hasty Market across Carlton Street, where he spent $68.55 on a carton of du Maurier cigarettes, deodorant, chips, aspirin, toothbrushes, toothpaste, shampoo, shaving cream and razors. Now there was less than $30 of Fritch's cash left, but Steve had bought the supplies he figured were essential for his and Jamie's trip out west.

Cari and Jamie, in one bed, fell asleep shortly afterward, while Steve stayed up until about 6 a.m. watching mindless late-night television, flipping the channels between drag-racing and other junk.

Although he was the last to get to sleep, he was the first to rise. He awoke on his own at 7:30. There was no wake-up call. He went out to move the car because he didn't want to leave it in any one place for too long. He paid eight dollars and drove to a parking garage behind the hotel, on Wood Street, driving up the ramp to the second floor, without stopping to take a ticket. There were workers preparing to do renovations on the floor where he stopped. Anxious and inexperienced behind the wheel of a car, he drove the Buick into the wall, scraping the front grille, and got out, trying to look nonchalant.

"We're working here today, so maybe you could park a little bit further down," one of the workers said to Steve. He drove to another empty spot on the other side of the building, but not before scraping the white paint off the side mirror.

He went back up to the room, where he woke Cari. They let Jamie sleep. He always slept late. At 8 a.m. Steve and Cari went down to the hotel restaurant, Windows, for breakfast. Cari ordered pancakes, but didn't touch them. Steve, on the other hand, easily consumed two eggs, sausage, three coffees and a milk. He paid with Fritch's American Express, leaving a $1 tip on the $13.18 bill, this time signing J.G. Fritch.

They got back to the room just before nine, and woke Jamie.

"Let's go shopping. The stores open in five minutes," Steve said exuberantly.

Jamie took a quick shower, and they all left the room carrying the supplies Steve had bought at the convenience store. They went down to the lobby, where Steve used Fritch's Visa card to pay the bill for the room and movies.

Beth Olah went to wake her son for school at 7:30 and discovered his trick with the bedclothes. She was frantic with worry. She phoned the police as soon as the probation office was open and told them that Steve was missing, again, and that she wanted him to be arrested. She called their lawyer, Paul LaFleur, and told him the story. "I didn't feel there was much more I could do," she said later.

Anne Fritch woke up alone, and wondered why she hadn't felt her husband getting into bed with her last night. She searched the house, and then started making calls to try and find him. She didn't want to panic the children, but this just didn't happen. She was worried, but certainly had no clue what had become of her husband.

Steve, Jamie and Cari got to the garage, where they put their belongings in the back seat of the car, while Fritch's body still lay curled in the fetal position in the trunk.

On the way out of the garage, Steve walked up to the booth and asked the attendant if he should have picked up a ticket earlier.

The attendant said, "Oh, you must be the guy who didn't take a ticket," showing him a piece of paper with Fritch's licence plate number, 354 FEC, on it. "Just give me six bucks."

The trio walked south on Yonge Street. It was now about 9:30. First stop was Sam the Record Man, where they bought a dozen rock tapes for the trip. On the way, they went through the wallet, and Steve and Jamie dropped all the "useless" contents, including Fritch's family pictures, in garbage cans along the way.

Next stop was the Eaton Centre, further south along Yonge.

They went to Club Pelle, a leather specialty shop in the mall, where Jamie picked out a $499.99 full-length black overcoat and Steve selected a bomber jacket, $399.99. They paid by American Express, with no problem. Jamie wore his new coat out of the store, placing his black suede bomber into the shopping bag, with the knife he had brought from home still in the pocket, along with a book of matches from the Carlton Inn.

Next, they hit Eaton's, where once again Steve produced the American Express card to pay for several pieces of clothing, mostly shirts and socks, almost all from the expensive Ralph Lauren section. Total bill: $808.38. Steve signed J.B. Fritch at the bottom of the receipt and they left.

Next, they wanted shoes, and headed for one of the most expensive shoe stores in the mall, Florsheim, where the sister-and-brother team of Fernando and Leonore Martins was working. It was about 11 a.m.

Leonore helped Steve, who was still wearing runners and jeans stained with blood. He chose a pair of brown-and-green Italian brogues, $125. Jamie selected a pair of size 9½ black Italian loafers, $140, and took off his blood-smeared white leather Nike high-tops to try them on. "I think I'll walk around with them on for a bit," he told Fernando, and stood up to admire his new shoes.

Meanwhile, Leonore had brought out the brogues, which Steve decided to buy. "Hey, Jamie, what do you think of these?" he asked proudly.

"Pretty good, man," said Jamie, still smiling at his own shoes and showing them to his girlfriend, who was lingering in the doorway.

"You guys take American Express?" Steve asked.

"Oh, yes," Leonore replied. "But would you mind if we wrote up two separate bills? We work on commission."

"Okay, fine," Steve answered. The Martinses stood at the counter writing up their respective bills. Jamie was still wearing his new shoes, while Steve had left his in the box. Leonore ran the card through the instant authorization machine in the front of the store. An electronic message came across the screen, telling her to call the authorization centre.

Steve and Jamie were just over two hours away from their planned departure for British Columbia. They were going to put Cari on a bus for home, and then go live the easy life on the road.

Fritch had been dead less than twelve hours, and already they had racked up $2,000 in goodies for themselves, almost all of it on AMEX. And although Fritch always paid his bills on time and his card had not been reported missing, this unusual spending pattern was enough to tip the officials at American Express, who noted the number of times the card had been used for major purchases in the past few hours. Using their electronic authorization machine, they asked the store clerk to call personally.

"Just a minute please, sir," Leonore said to Steve, "I've just got to call this in."

She disappeared with the card to the back of the store to call in. A person on the other end asked her the expiry date of the card and the number. Leonore was then transferred to a second person, to whom she gave all the same information.

"We're quite sure this card is being used fraudulently," said the woman at the other end. "Is the customer still in the store?"

"Yes."

At the sales counter, the atmosphere began to grow uncomfortable.

"We never have any problem with the card," Steve said to Fernando, while Jamie began to fidget nervously.

"Don't worry, it usually takes a little while with the AMEX," Fernando said, although he was beginning to believe that there must be a problem.

"You know, you two guys look a lot alike," Steve said, forcing conversation. "You could pass for brother and sister."

"We are," Fernando said, laughing.

"Oh sure. You're just saying that," Steve said.

"Hang on a sec. I'll go and check what's happening back there," Fernando said, also disappearing into the back.

"What's going on?" Fernando asked his sister, who was still holding the phone to her ear.

"It's a stolen card," she said.

Immediately, Fernando returned to the front of the store to make sure the pair didn't leave.

"Boy, it's sure taking a long time," he told the young men. "But don't worry. Sometimes, it takes even longer than this."

By now, he was just stalling for time, waiting for the police and further instructions from AMEX, which were being given to his sister.

"Hold on to the card. Do not give it back to the person.

Now, we're going to ask you a few questions. I only want you to answer yes or no."

The credit authorization person went through a standard set of questions designed to build a description of the suspect without arousing suspicion. "Now go out and tell the customer that you're still trying to get through."

Leonore obeyed.

"It should just be a couple of more minutes," she called over to Steve.

At this point, Cari actually walked into the store.

"Great shoes, guys," she said, focusing on Jamie's.

"Those really look good on you, Jamie."

By now there were other customers in the store, and Fernando was dividing his attention between the one he was serving and the boys, not wanting them to leave, but at the same time not wanting to appear too anxious.

Jamie and Cari drifted toward the door slowly, and eventually stepped into the mall again, carrying all but three of the shopping bags.

Fernando reluctantly left their sight to go to the back room again to get a pair of shoes for his new customer.

"Sir, can you come back here for a moment, please?" Leonore asked Steve.

"Sure," he said, walking toward the back.

"The people from the credit-card company want to talk to you," she said, passing him the receiver.

At that moment, two Metro Toronto police officers assigned to the mall walked into the store. Cari and Jamie sauntered away casually and took the escalator to the lower level, where they could keep the front of the store in view.

The credit authorization centre kept Steve tied up on the phone, testing him with questions about balance, payments and family status. Steve sensed what they were up to, but stayed on the phone.

"Hey, this isn't some kind of trick, is it? You're not trying to keep me here so the police can show up, are you?"

"Oh no, sir. We're just working to transfer a line of credit from your Royal Bank account." Someone signalled the person that police had arrived in the store, and he lied to Steve. "Okay, put the lady back on and I'll give her the authorization code."

Steve emerged from the back, only to find Constables Simon Knott and Dave Roberts waiting. It was just before quarter to twelve.

"Which one is he?" Constable Roberts asked Leonore discreetly.

"That one," she said, pointing to Steve who, remarkably, was still standing casually at the front counter, asking questions about whether his shoes were ready. He wondered to himself if the officers had seen the look of shock light up his face for the split second when he first noticed them.

"Is anything wrong with my card?" he asked.

"What is your name?" Constable Knott asked back.

"John."

"John what?"

"John Fritch."

"Do you have any other identification on you?"

"Just these other cards."

In fact, Steve had Fritch's driver's licence with him, but he didn't dare produce that, since he looked nothing like the middle-aged victim's photo card. So, rather than have the police go through Fritch's wallet, he took it out himself, from the right rear pocket of the blood-stained jeans. He handed Constable Roberts three cards: the American Express, the Royal Bank Visa and the Triathlon leasing card.

"The name on this card is *Joe* Fritch," Constable Roberts said, before his partner cut back in.

"What is your real name?"

Steve answered truthfully, but was still nowhere near ready to admit the whole thing. He tried a different tack.

"Steven Olah."

"Where did you get the cards?"

"I found them on the street in Burlington."

"All right, Steve, we're arresting you for the fraudulent use of a stolen credit card," Knott told him, and read him the standard rights from his notebook.

"Do you understand?"

"Yes," Steve answered. He was experienced at this part.

Roberts quickly frisked Steve, finding three receipts, Fritch's brown leather wallet, Fritch's driver's licence and a small amount of cash.

He handcuffed Steve behind his back, and Leonore told them about Jamie, describing him as tall and thin, with blond, spiked hair, wearing the new shoes and a full-length black leather overcoat. She gave a slightly less complete description of Chisamore, before the police turned back to their collar.

"Did you use these cards anywhere else?" Roberts asked.

"Yes."

"Where?"

"At Eaton's three or four times."

"Anywhere else?"

"Yes. We used the Visa at the hotel where we stayed last night."

"Where is the stuff from Eaton's?"

"In my car."

"Where is your car?"

"A couple of blocks from here, on Yonge Street."

Roberts asked to use the telephone, and called 52 Division at Dundas and University for a cruiser so they could bring in their prisoner. Now, Steve changed his strategy again. He knew he wasn't going to be getting out now, but wanted to buy some time for his friend to get away. He figured Jamie would send Cari home, and run alone. Meanwhile, both of them were watching from the lower level, with only a partial view of the front window of the Florsheim store.

"Watch the bags," Jamie told Cari. "If you see them move, then we'll know Steve's busted for sure."

After the police took Steve away, Fernando took the remaining shopping bags and put them into the back room. There was the bag with Jamie's old jacket, another containing Steve's new one, and a third from the record store, carrying all the tapes they had bought at the start of their short spree. After several minutes, Cari and Jamie decided it was time for them to strike out on their own.

"How much money have you got?" Jamie asked Cari. He himself didn't have a dime, since Steve had been carrying the stolen wallet with all the credit cards and what was left of the cash.

"Ten dollars."

"Okay, we've got to get out of here," he said, taking her hand and heading south toward Union Station.

Meanwhile, Steve was placed in the back seat of a cruiser, and the officers ordered him to take them to the car. Steve purposely took them to the wrong garage. Now, he was momentarily back in control again, and enjoying it.

Later, when Fernando had to move one of the bags, Jamie's knife dropped onto the floor with a thud. Fernando could tell it wasn't something they had just bought. It was slightly worn. It was a weapon. Fernando was scared; he knew it had been more than a pair of con-men he and his sister had served. He fished around in the pockets of the jacket and found a coffee mug and the old Coke-can pipe.

Steve told the police officers that the other things he had bought were in his car, on Yonge Street. He forced them to drive around for fifteen minutes, until it became absolutely clear that he was lying to them.

"It was just a little wild goose chase to give Jamie some time," Steve said later.

The officers drove him back to 52 Division, where they turned the prisoner, the cards and the receipts over to fraud squad veteran Sergeant George Reynolds, a fatherly but streetwise officer with twenty-five years' experience. Meanwhile, Roberts called Fritch's office, where secretary Sandra McGuire told him that Fritch had not come to work that morning and couldn't be found. Next, the officer called Fritch's home, where there was no answer.

Reynolds had entered interview room 204F, where he was alone with Steve. At this point, he figured he was just dealing with another in the long string of misguided young hoods he had seen over the years. He introduced himself, and asked the young man the usual factual questions about his address, date of birth and school status. Steve answered truthfully on all counts.

"It is my understanding that you were arrested earlier by two police officers in the Eaton Centre for using a stolen credit card. Is that correct?"

"Yes."

"Did the officers explain to you that you had the right to retain and instruct counsel without delay?"

"Yes, he did."

"Do you understand that right?"

"Yes."

"Where did you get the three credit cards?" he asked, holding them out to the prisoner.

"I guess I found the guy's wallet, so I picked it up from the sidewalk from Fairview and Guelph Line. It was eleven or eleven-fifteen last night," Steve said, lying and naming the busiest intersection in Burlington, across from the Burlington Mall.

"Who was with you?"

"I don't want to say now."

"Have you used the credit cards?"

"Yes."

"Would you tell me where?"

"Carlton Hotel, Sam the Record Man, some Italian place. We got leather jackets there. Eaton's twice. Florsheim shoes, where I got busted."

Reynolds, feeling sorry for Steve at this point, broke into a more personal conversation.

"Look, Steven, you're only eighteen. You've got a criminal record, you're on probation, and you're coming up in court again soon on weapons charges. Now, you're facing these stolen-credit-card charges. Do you plan on continuing like this and ruining your life?"

"I can't cope out here," came the frank reply. "I know I need some help."

"Maybe the best thing for you would be for you to get into a trade, like bricklaying. There's a shortage, you know. Think about it."

Reynolds excused himself after five minutes. He spoke with his colleague, Sergeant Stan Brar, who offered to try and track down Fritch and ask him about his credit cards. He tried calling the Hudson's Bay Company, where a secretary said she was very concerned about Fritch, since he had not come to work that morning, and had missed an appointment with some business people from Montreal. A phone call to Fritch's house showed that his family was equally worried after he had failed to come home the previous night.

Reynolds, after being briefed by the constables, recruited Constable Gary Logan, a plainclothes fraud officer, to join him in the interview. He told Logan that Fritch appeared to be missing. Then Reynolds and Logan entered the room, where Steve was still sitting calmly on a wooden bench.

"It appears that the American Express card in the name of Mr. Fritch was used to check in at the Carlton hotel last night. Did you use the card at the hotel?" Reynolds asked.

"Yes."

"How did you come to Toronto from Burlington in time to be here for the seventeenth of October?"

"We took the GO train in."

"The hotel check-in receipt has a check-in date of October 17, 1989. How were you able to get to Toronto and check in at the hotel less than an hour after you found the credit card?"

"That hotel slip, the date is wrong. The clerk made a mistake. We didn't get in 'til after 2 a.m."

Steve was right about the time, but at the Carlton, the next day's official business does not start until a few hours after midnight.

"Who was with you when you checked in to the hotel?"

"I ain't telling you. If I fink out on a guy, it's like signing my death warrant in jail."

After twelve minutes, the officers stood up and excused themselves to go and track down more information before continuing to question Steve. Reynolds felt there was a lot more to this than the simple use of stolen credit cards.

When they went back in, they picked up where they had left off, with Reynolds still handling the questioning. By now, Steve was looking on it as a game.

"He came in, and we had the funniest conversation I've ever had in my life," Steve recalled later. "He knew that I had murdered Mr. Fritch. And I knew that he knew, but he never said that I murdered Mr. Fritch, and I never said I murdered Mr. Fritch. And we're kinda both skirting the issue. It was hilarious, actually."

"I would like to talk to you about the small brown wallet and the three credit cards you told me you found. Are you certain that you didn't take them from a car?" Reynolds asked.

"No. I just picked it up from the sidewalk, like I told you before."

"I feel there is something else here besides just using stolen credit cards. How were you able to get to Toronto?"

"We drove in, in my Chevelle."

Momentarily ignoring the obvious lie, Logan cut in and took over the questioning: "Where were you prior to finding the brown wallet and the credit cards?"

"We were drinking in a field."

"Which field?"

"A hydro field."

"Which hydro field?"

"Behind the post office."

"What were you drinking?"

"C.C."

"Where is the bottle?"

"I don't know. In the field."

"Wasn't it muddy in the field?"

"I was on the gravel pathway and it was dry."

Logan looked at Steve's black lace-up runners. He asked

him to take one off. Steve pulled off his left shoe and passed it to the officer. Logan looked closely at the seam between the sole and the upper.

"For being in a field last night, which would have been wet and muddy, these shoes appear to be as clean as new."

"Well, what do you expect? They got clean from walking on the fat rugs in the hotel."

Steve was thinking fast now. His mind was racing. This was fun.

Reynolds had been studying Steve's hands. There were cuts on the first two knuckles of his right hand, three smaller scratches behind the ball of his right thumb and a burst blister on the palm of his right hand, about an inch and a half long. These were not the marks of fraud. They were the marks of violence. Reynolds now resumed questioning.

"I notice there are some fresh small cuts on your hands. Where did you get these cuts?"

"They're from my cat." Then Steve made the most bizarre statement of the afternoon, one which later was to become one of the most controversial of his murder trial: "I know you're thinking about little old ladies that push shopping carts."

"Why would you say that about old ladies? No one has mentioned little old ladies to you," Reynolds replied, as perplexed as he was annoyed.

"You tell *me*. They're *your* brains. I pick it up in your vibes."

Now Steve was much more animated. He was anxious, excited and actually smiling.

"I have changed my mind. I have decided to tell you who was with me."

"Who was it?"

"Jamie Ruston, R-U-S-T-O-N."

"How old is he?"

"Seventeen."

"Where does he live?"

"In Burlington. Just a little ways from my house."

"Where is he now?"

"He's probably going west on the 400 right now."

"How can you go west on the 400?"

"Well, you know what I mean. North on the 400 and west on the TransCanada. He's never been there. He's always wanted to go out west."

"Why would he go out west to avoid our investigation of these credit-card charges when we don't even know that he used the cards?"

"Well, you've got probable cause to charge him."

Steve knew all the jargon.

"What makes you say we've got probable cause to arrest Ruston when you're the one that used the cards?"

Steve looked off into space. When he didn't answer, Reynolds sensed the opening, and tried to widen it.

"I would also like to know why you think Ruston is headed out west when you have the car keys."

"Oh."

Steve hadn't planned on this part. He sat up straight in his chair, and looked at the floor before answering. "Okay, okay. You show me that you've got Jamie in custody and I'll tell you the whole truth. I don't have to talk to him or anything. Just let me see that you've got him."

"If we have the car keys here, where is the car?" Reynolds asked, ignoring Steve's offer.

"It's in the parking lot behind the hotel where we stayed, but it's not in the hotel parking lot. It's in the above-ground parking on the first level in the far right corner."

The officers excused themselves again, leaving Steve in

the interrogation room. If, as they had suspected, there had been an assault, kidnapping or murder, then it was likely that the car would provide some clues.

Reynolds passed the keys to Logan. Logan told another officer, Constable Craig Morton, that they were going to the parking lot on Wood Street to find the car driven by this fraud suspect and that they were looking for a 1988 white Buick Regal, licence plate 354 FEC.

At the same time, the officers from Eaton Centre, Knott and Roberts, were sent to seal off the room at the Carlton. A few minutes later, Reynolds got a call from dispatch, telling him that Logan and Morton couldn't find the car in the place Steve had described. Reynolds went back inside the interview room, annoyed.

"Do you want to tell us how you really got the car keys?"

"Well, we killed the guy. We took his keys. We put him in the trunk," said Steve, calmly.

Immediately, Reynolds left the room again to tell his supervisor about the murder admission. What had started as an everyday fraud investigation of a common teenage delinquent had suddenly escalated into a potential murder case.

Reynolds called the homicide squad, and was in the middle of asking an officer there if he should take Steve out to find the car when another call came in. Logan and Morton were still having trouble finding the car, but were staying at the scene waiting for further instructions. Reynolds told them that they were now also looking for a body. They called back a couple of minutes later. They had found the car, with a body in the trunk, and were ordered to stay there until the murder investigators arrived.

Reynolds phoned the homicide squad again, where he spoke to Staff Sergeant Mike Hamel, a big, easygoing man. He told him what he knew so far.

It was more than an hour and a half later when Hamel and Sergeant John Line, a dapper man in an expensive suit with his white hair combed back, were able to come to the fraud office.

Reynolds filled them in before handing the case over to them. At 3:37, Hamel and Line left the station to check into the scene where the body had been found. Line had the keys to the Buick, and he and Hamel went to the Wood Street garage, where there was another officer monitoring incoming and outgoing traffic. The uniformed officers, Logan and Morton, were still watching the car.

At the same time, coroner Dr. Murray Naiberg arrived at the scene. Hamel took the keys and opened the trunk. There was Fritch's body, lying end-to-end, in a fetal position with the legs curled up. He was fully dressed, and the black garbage bag still covered his head. At 4 p.m., Dr. Naiberg officially pronounced him dead. Hamel noticed, as the identification officers came to begin their photography work, that there was fresh damage to the car, along the right fender and right door. There was also blood on the left rear corner of the car.

The homicide officers returned to 52 Division. Now it was their turn to talk to Steve. He was still in room 204F, still sitting on the same bench.

"Hello, Steven," Hamel opened. "This is Sergeant John Line and I'm Staff Sergeant Mike Hamel. We're from the homicide bureau. Do you know what that means?"

"Oh. That's murder."

"That's right. Now we're going to ask you some questions. Please answer slowly—I'm taking exact notes of everything that's said."

"We killed the guy and put him in the trunk," Steve said plainly.

"Stop right there," Hamel said, raising his hand from his notepad.

"I have to read this to you," Line said.

He read Steve the standard Charter of Rights primary and secondary cautions, advising him that he had the right to contact a lawyer before answering any more questions, and that he was under no obligation to answer any questions. He also told him that he was not to allow other officers to influence him by making promises or threats. Any answers that he volunteered, though, could be used later as evidence. Steve said nothing.

"Do you understand?" Line asked.

"Lawyer? Christ no," Steve said. "I want to plead and go to jail. I don't mind twenty-five years."

Line started off the interview.

"Where did this happen, Steven?"

"In Burlington. That's where we live. Do you know Burlington?"

"A bit."

"Fairview and Maple, west Burlington. It's in a Petro-Canada station. Jamie worked there."

"What happened?"

"We wanted to kill somebody. Anybody that drove in. He drove in for gas. Jamie put the bag over his head. I had this extinguisher, a fire extinguisher. I smashed it over his head. He went down. I kept hitting him. I think thirty, forty times."

"What happened after that?"

"Jamie cleaned up the place. We put him in the trunk of the car."

"Who else was involved?"

"For the record, Cari, the girl involved, didn't do anything. She was telling us to stop. She will be a good Crown witness. She's not involved."

After a few minutes more of routine questions, Line and Hamel excused themselves. They discussed the case, and phoned Halton police to let them know what had happened.

At 6:17, Line and Hamel went back into 204F.

"We're going to make a tape recording of this conversation. Is that okay with you, Steven?"

"Yeah, sure," Steve said. He was still looking relaxed, smoking cigarettes, wearing the same clothes he had worn during the murder.

He was getting ready to make a full confession to the crime, including virtually every detail of what had happened, as if he were reading it from the police blotter himself. He was still enjoying this.

After several minutes of recapping for Steve what had happened so far that day and reaffirming that he had been read his rights, Line got to the heart of the question.

"You realize you're going to be charged with murder?"

"That's correct."

"You understand that?"

"Yes."

"This murder, can you describe it in your own words?"

"Uh, I would say, um, that murder is when someone is killed, not accidentally, by someone else. Either premeditated or otherwise."

"Okay. What is your definition of premeditated?"

"Uh, premeditated would be when the people that are planning on murdering someone plan on murdering that person, like they planned it beforehand that they're gonna murder someone."

"In this particular case, what did you tell us before?"

"I had told you that, uh, that we did in fact plan out the entire routine that we followed, but we did not plan on killing the particular victim of the crime."

"Okay. And, of course, that interview that we held with you before, we told you about a lawyer and you said you did not wish to have a lawyer present. Is that correct?"

"Yeah, that's correct. At the time, I stated that I wished to plead guilty and just go to jail."

After more clarification of rights and cautions, the police continued their questioning.

"Now, you told us previously that you and your friend James had a plan."

"That's correct."

"Go ahead and just describe to us that plan."

"Okay. The plan was, well, Jamie had this idea that we could go out west, like out to B.C., and we figured that the only way we could get out there would be either to get a car or a large amount of money or a credit card or something like that. And Jamie working at the gas station turned out to be a bonus, because we decided that when he was working night shift, like until twelve, I would come over sometime in the evening and wait for a possible person to come along that we could, uh, abduct, and possibly kill, and take their automobile, their money and their credit cards. And use them to our benefit."

"You say that you planned to rob someone, abduct someone, take their car, their credit card and drive out west?"

"Yes. As things fell into place, like as events went along, it did become clear to us—both of us, I might add—that there was a certain way we should do that, and that involved using his job at the gas station and the fact that people did pull in there and we could pretty much have our choice of what kind of car and credit and all the stuff that we wanted to take."

"Okay. So the prime motivation was, then, money? Was a robbery and money?"

"The prime motivation in this case..." Steve hesitated. "You have to understand. I've been going for psychiatric treatment. I've been assessed several times and James has been assessed several times and I know for a fact that neither of us has got it all on the ball. I wouldn't say we were out for money, 'cause neither of us really cares about money that much. We'll spend it as easily as we get it. I would say probably that our motivation was just to get away. Neither of us has a real easy time dealing with everyday pressures. We both smoke drugs, we both drink heavily, and sometimes you just want to get away. We tried it before. We tried several times before, just to get away, and every time, we ended up getting caught, and this was just another time to get away."

Line asked Steve about his psychiatric background, and Steve told him vaguely about the August incident with his parents.

"Okay, Steve. Now when we spoke to you before, my partner and I, you mentioned a female."

"Yes."

"Can you provide us with her identity and where she may live?"

"I can provide you her identity. I would like to make it clear for the record that she was not involved in any way with the crime and she did not wish to be involved in any way with the crime. She, however, does have information that would be beneficial to the Crown."

"Okay. So you're telling us that she was not part of this scheme. She was never brought into this scheme. She was never there when the crime was discussed. Is that what you're telling us?"

"That's correct. She had no foreknowledge about what we were doing."

"Okay, what's her name?"

"Her name is Cari, C-A-R-I, Chisamore C-H-I-S-A-M-O-R-E."

"How old is Cari?"

"I believe she's eighteen."

"Do you know where she lives?"

"She lives in Burlington, but I'm not sure of the street address. She does live near the SuperCentre, though," he offered.

Steve then, in the same even tone of voice, told the officer every detail of the day of the killing, from the time he got up in the morning to the actual beating, robbery and flight from the gas station. As he was describing the breakfast he ate the morning after the killing, Anne Fritch was in another office at the station, where Reynolds was telling her that three teenagers had killed her husband, taken his credit cards and car, and two of the kids were still missing.

Back in 204F, Steve continued freely spinning his tale. Line had barely to ask anything beyond clarification questions. Steve told the officers that he had wanted to wait until after his probation, with its 8 p.m. curfew, was over before committing the Big Job. But, he said, Jamie talked him into doing it sooner, while Jamie was still seventeen, and liable to only a three-year jail sentence.

"Jamie is not eighteen and not a legal adult. And that was, I believe, his prime motivation for wanting to commit the crime now, as opposed to later," Steve said. "He had a sense of urgency in wanting to commit the crime."

"Did he discuss the fact that, 'Listen, let's do it now because I'm still a youthful offender?' Is that what you're saying?"

"Yes."

After almost an hour of hearing chilling details come from

this boy's mouth, the officers wanted to know how all this had affected him.

"Steve, what do you feel right now?"

"Uh, you mean, like, how do I feel about having killed someone?"

"Yes."

"I don't know. Usually what happens with me is that when I do something wrong, like every time I've been arrested, the cops say, 'Oh, he behaves well, he's polite and everything, he's cooperative.' Then, like a couple of weeks later, a couple of days, maybe a couple of hours, I don't feel terrible, like I don't feel guilty or anything. But I know that there is something wrong. There's this inner turmoil in me all the time and, uh, it's just insane."

"Do you know what I mean when I say remorse?"

"Yes."

"Do you feel remorse right now for taking this man's life?"

"Well, I've thought about his wife, eh? And, uh, I don't know. If it was my husband, like if I was the guy's wife, I'd probably want to hang me out to dry. Like, I've thought about it that way, and I've thought how she would feel. And I don't know. If I could take it back I would. But, you know, it's kind of pointless to say."

After precisely sixty minutes, the officers turned off the tape recorder.

As Steve moved through the police process, Jamie and Cari were still intent on getting as far away from Toronto as they could.

"How do you get to Union Station from here?" Jamie asked Cari.

"This way," she said, taking his hand and dragging him south toward the train station at Bay and Front streets.

At Union Station they studied a map to figure out how far they could get for ten dollars. "But if I go with you, then I won't be able to get home after that," Cari said, naively.

"You can't go home right now anyway," Jamie said. "You're going to get blamed for all of this just like me."

She looked upset now.

"Oh, we'll see," Jamie recounted briefly. "Maybe you can go home tomorrow."

At the station, Jamie, who was carrying all the clothes they had bought at the Eaton Centre, handed a heavy shirt to Cari, and kept one for himself. Their first day as murder fugitives was much colder than their last day as high-school students.

They took a train to Richmond Hill, twenty miles to the northeast. Now they were broke. They had not eaten since the early morning, and had barely slept in two days. They sneaked into a high-rise apartment building and slept in a stairwell, using their shopping bags for pillows and Jamie's new leather overcoat as a blanket.

As Jamie and Cari were preparing to bunk down in the stairwell, two Halton police officers, veteran detectives, were getting their assignments.

Already, a squadron of identification officers had begun combing the gas bar for more clues. Although the station had been re-opened and busy all day, there was still plenty for them to find. There was a set of ten fingerprints on the door near the floor. One was smeared with blood. The door frame was sheared where the fire extinguisher had grazed it. In the grouting between several slightly loose floor tiles near the door was a dark brown stain. Underneath the tiles was blood, still vivid. Jamie had cleaned up quite well, but not well enough to hide a murder from the experts.

Detective Sergeant Graham Barnes, head of the Major Crime Squad, called Jim Chapman, a compact, tanned sergeant with a big, toothy smile, who was at home eating dinner.

"Toronto's got a body in the trunk of a car. It came from a Petro-Canada station in Burlington. Get down here as soon as you can."

Chapman showered and dressed. He didn't know when he would be home again.

At thirty-eight, he had put in sixteen years hustling up Halton's punks. This would be his eighteenth murder investigation. He had covered the range of homicides, from domestics to bikers and mobsters.

He would work this time with Joe Barker, two years younger and two inches taller, at six feet. Sergeant Barker was a more loosely constructed man with a dark moustache, sleepy eyes and glasses. Both men had grown up in Hamilton's tough east end, and although this was Barker's first time as a principal investigator in a murder case, he was every bit as gritty and determined as his partner.

Barnes told Chapman and Barker that there had been a murder at a gas bar not far from the police station, and two young suspects were still on the run, somewhere.

One, Steve Olah, had been caught in Toronto and was being held downtown. He had already made a statement, and provided the names and descriptions of a James Ruston and a Cari-Lee Chisamore. Barker prepared a two-paragraph press release, giving a bare-bones account of what had happened and asking for the public's help in finding Jamie and Cari.

Meanwhile, Chapman drove to Toronto with Detective Colin Parcher, to be briefed by the Toronto officers and collect the first of the suspects. At 9:43, he met with Line,

Hamel and another officer, who gave him a copy of the taped confession from Steve, information from the staff at the Carlton Inn and the keys to Fritch's car, which was being held for examination at the Centre of Forensic Sciences garage in downtown Toronto.

At 10:56, after the information and evidence had been exchanged, the Toronto police turned Steve over to Chapman, who would take him to the Halton regional police headquarters, then located in Burlington's neighbouring town of Oakville.

Chapman explained to Steve that he was arresting him for first-degree murder and gave him his rights again.

"Yeah. They explained all this. I can get a lawyer and all that," Steve said. "I told them everything already."

"Okay. Let's go to Oakville," Chapman said, after finishing his obligatory reading of rights. Steve was tired and dishevelled. He had not bathed in two days. Chapman drove the unmarked cruiser, while Parcher sat in the back seat with Steve, whose hands were cuffed. Parcher took notes, in full view of the prisoner, of what little conversation took place in the car. As they pulled out of the 52 Division parking lot, Steve started the conversation.

"Jamie's got a knife."

"Where would he carry the knife, Steve?" Chapman asked.

"In his clothes."

Steve then sat silently for a moment, raising his hands up to his nose and then pulling them away again, disgusted.

"I didn't know blood smelled so bad," he said. "I've still got it under my fingernails."

He explained to the officers how the crime had been committed, and how they drove to Toronto, got the room and watched movies. Then he switched back to the kiosk, describing how they cleaned up all the blood so no one would know what had happened.

"Why the bag on the head?" Chapman asked.

"We didn't want him to see us. We were planning on abducting him, but what better way to keep a person quiet than not having him around?" Steve said matter-of-factly. "And to catch the blood. Can you imagine if there hadn't been any bag?"

"When he came to get gas, did Cari know what was going to happen?" Chapman asked.

"Yeah. We talked about it in front of her."

"When, though?"

"About twenty minutes before the guy arrived."

Then Steve started asking questions of his own.

"What's life now? Twenty years?"

"To be honest, it depends on the court, but first-degree is twenty-five, but that varies with parole. Are you tired?"

"Yeah. I only nodded off for an hour at the hotel."

"Why not sleep longer?"

"We wanted to get going. I wanted to be on the road by 2 p.m. to B.C."

"Well, what were you going to do with the body?"

"We were going to bury it in a shallow grave by the Lake of the Woods."

Then there was another pause before Chapman returned to more practical matters.

"Have you eaten?"

"Yeah. They gave me a burger and a coffee and I have an ulcer," Steve said. His stomach was hurting him now.

"You okay now?"

"Yeah, but when I lay down ..."

"Are you on medication?"

"I'm supposed to be on ..." Steve tried to answer, but had

lost the name of his ulcer medicine. "I'm not sure of the exact medication, but it was pronounced Zantac. It's at home."

"We'll get it for you tomorrow. Is that okay, Steve?"

"Yeah, I guess so."

"Did you have a car?"

"No."

"Any ideas where he would sleep tonight, Steve?"

"I don't know. I was thinking about that, but he's so unpredictable."

"Other than Zantac, are you on any other medication?" Chapman asked, pulling off the highway onto Trafalgar Road in Oakville, and heading north toward headquarters.

"I was supposed to be on tranquilizers. They're supposed to calm me down. If they would have committed me when I wanted, none of this would have happened."

"Would he steal a car?" Chapman asked, thinking ahead to the search for Jamie.

"Yes, he'd wait at a store for one, or take a hostage," Steve said.

"Would he kill someone?"

"Being a police officer, I'd be careful," Steve warned. "He doesn't like police."

Chapman asked one last question before pulling into the station at the end of the twenty-five-minute drive.

"Is there any chance that he'll turn himself in?"

"Very little chance," Steve said. "He'll run."

After lodging Steve for the night, Chapman drove to the Burlington detachment to compare notes with Barker. Since there was no tape player in the station house that night, they went to the back parking lot to play the confession tape in Chapman's car. They listened to it three times through, until nearly 4 a.m. They agreed to meet at Oakville the next morning at eight. During the four hours in between, neither man slept, going over and over in their minds what had happened, and how they were going to catch and convict the young people who were responsible.

"You don't sleep," Barker said. "You just stare at the ceiling."

"I've got to steal a car," Jamie pronounced a few minutes after 6 a.m., as he and Cari walked out of the apartment toward the shopping mall across the street.

It was as though the link between Steve and Jamie had not been severed. Steve had predicted exactly what his friend would do.

It was even colder than the day before. Jamie and Cari had awoken sore, tired, hungry and shivering. Cari hoped Jamie would use whatever car he stole to drive her home. She didn't have any idea that by now the whole Halton police department was mobilizing in an intensive search for her and her boyfriend, that their parents had been notified, and that their descriptions had been sent to every police force and border crossing in the country.

"I've got to get away from here. I've got to find some connections who can help me get even further away from here," Jamie said, looking serious and still sounding like a movie character. They were at the mall now.

At that time of day, the only place with any traffic was a doughnut shop. They walked up to a *Toronto Sun* newspaper box outside the store The whole front page of that day's tabloid stared back at them out the window.

The haunting image was a full-size, smiling picture of Joe Fritch, whose benign face, featuring a moustache and a fringe of reddish-brown hair, was not unlike Cari's own father's.

Inset into the corner were their own pictures, under the headline: "Teens Sought in Murder."

The paper told them there were national warrants for their arrest on murder charges. This was Cari's first realization that she, too, was being linked directly to this killing. At first, she had thought the police must have figured she had been abducted by Jamie and Steve, or, at the very most, that they wanted her as a witness. Wrong.

They were calling her a murderer just the same as the other two. She was more scared now, and knew that going home was out of the question.

What the paper told Jamie was that they had to get as far away as they could, as quickly as possible, before they were recognized.

Beside the newspaper box was an inconspicuous grey K-Car with the motor running. The driver was inside, getting his morning coffee.

"We've got to take this," Jamie said, urgently. "Get in."

"But we'll get in trouble," she said. Her naiveté was tragi-comic.

"Look. We're not going to be able to get in any more trouble than we're already in. Get in," Jamie said. "And you're in just as much trouble as I am."

He was right. And although by now in a way he revolted her, part of her was still attracted to him. She was being pulled in two different directions. On one side were her parents, who would always help when she was in trouble. But there was no trouble bigger than this. Could even they help her now? On the other side was her boyfriend, who seemed to be offering an escape from the impossible situation that they now shared. And if she needed anything to tip the balance in Jamie's favour, there was always the butcher knife she believed he was still carrying in his pocket. He had never threatened her, but still, she had been there when he helped kill another person, and she knew he was even more desperate now than he had been then. Anything could happen, she thought.

She got into her second stolen car that week.

He backed out of the spot and started driving fast, heading north.

"Hey, there's a briefcase in the back seat," Cari said.

"Get it up here," Jamie said, quickly looking over his shoulder, hoping that his face wasn't already too familiar to be recognized as he drove. He just wanted to get far away. Fast.

Cari hauled the briefcase into the front seat and turned it toward Jamie so he could open it.

When he lifted the lid, he saw a manila pay envelope, and found just over $500 cash inside, mostly in large bills.

"Holy shit," Jamie said, feeling providence was at last taking a hand in helping him get away. "I'll hold on to this."

For Jamie and Cari, the find was not a minute too soon. It changed them from desperate, penniless teenagers with no options into bona fide fugitives with plenty of choices. Jamie's plan to escape from Burlington had been bruised, but not broken.

"I've got to phone my parents," Cari said, as her inner pendulum began to swing toward home again.

"No way," Jamie said. "The cops will have the phones wired."

They drove for an hour in silence, as Jamie planned and Cari worried.

"I've got to see my uncle John in B.C. He'll know what to do," Jamie said, mentioning his father's younger brother for the first time since the killing.

He and Cari continued, stopping in Barrie, about fifty miles northeast of Toronto. Yesterday's shopping spree for fine designer clothes, leather jackets and Italian shoes suddenly shrunk into a mission for the essentials: toiletries and clean underwear, just as their fine Buick Regal had been replaced by a utilitarian K-Car. They now pulled onto the lot of a Bargain Harold's discount store. There they bought four pairs of women's panties, a tube of Close-Up toothpaste, a package of girls' sports socks and three pairs of men's dress socks. For some reason, Jamie bought a six-dollar tie. He paid the $26.11 bill with a hundred-dollar bill and eleven pennies. They went to a laundromat to wash all the clothes they weren't wearing. Included in the load were Jamie's clothes from the murder, which still carried the bloodstains of nearly thirty-six hours earlier.

While Cari and Jamie were washing the last traces of blood from his clothes, Steve was still in his stained jeans and denim shirt, seated in another interview room, this time at Halton police headquarters. It was just after 10 a.m., and he was now rested. While his friends had slept in a stairwell, he had slept on a bare, iron prison cot in the basement of the Oakville station. Since he hadn't yet been interviewed here, the police had segregated him from other prisoners by holding him in the separate women's cell, which had been empty.

Like the Toronto police interview room, this one was sparsely furnished, with a table, two chairs and a washable white board for writing with magic markers.

The important difference between them was that the Halton interview room was equipped with a video camera, which recorded the sights and sounds of the interview. Barker stood behind the camera in the next room while his partner asked Steve the questions.

Steve sat slouched in one chair in the corner, under the clock and calendar, while Chapman sat across the floor from him with a notebook in hand.

After making sure Steve was aware of the videotaping and

understood his rights, Chapman said he would give him a few minutes more to think about what he wanted to do. Chapman left the room, and the videotape recorded Steve sitting listless in the chair, arms crossed, staring at the floor. Chapman returned and started the interview. As in the Toronto police interview, Steve's monotone rarely fluctuated as he described the horrible and minute details of the murder that he and his best friend had just committed.

"Starting when you left your house, just in your own words, Steven, just go over what happened. What was going through your mind that night, any conversation you can recall with Jamie and Cari with respect to this incident. And, if you don't mind, as you're going through your story, I may stop you every so often just to clarify a point, if that's okay."

"Okay."

"Can you just tell me where you start off, when you and Jamie were with each other a couple of days prior to this incident? Was there any discussion at that time that led up to the occurrence at the Petro-Can gas station?"

"Yes, there was."

"Okay, can you tell me what that was? And exactly what the conversation was, as best as you can recall?"

"Uh, we'd been planning what we'd called the Big Job for about a week before we actually did it. Maybe a bit longer."

"What is the Big Job? What planning did you do?"

"The Big Job is the incident that we're going to relate here. And the planning that we did was just discussing how we would do it."

"Okay. What, when you and Jamie spoke about it, did you have? What was your plan that day, as opposed to what actually happened?"

"Our plans that day were to abduct a person by forcing him into the trunk of their car with a knife and taking their car, their credit cards and their cash."

"Where did you and Jamie have this discussion?"

"We discussed it several places. There's a doughnut shop in the SuperCentre and we talked about it, um, walking around. We walk all kinds of places. And we just talked about it down at Central High School under the willow tree. We talked about it everywhere."

Just as he had for Line, Steve spelled out every last detail of the killing to Chapman, as flatly as before, except for the part when he described the actual hitting.

"Okay, the guy finished pumping his gas, came up to the door, opened it, went inside. And then I went in right behind him. He was up at the counter at that point. And I picked up the fire extinguisher. It was placed so I could pick it up. I picked it up so that it was lengthwise like this," he said, showing Chapman what he meant. "And Jamie shot up, put the garbage bag over the guy's head so that he couldn't see us, and I bonked him over the head a couple of times. And he didn't fall down, and Jamie says, 'Again, again, hit him again.' So I bonked him, I don't know, thirty or forty times, and he wasn't moving any more, and he was, uh, I don't know. His hands were turning grey anyways. We figured at that point that he wasn't dead because we could still hear, uh, breathing, or, uh, clogging or something. Breathing. So maybe some air was in his lungs."

"How much would that fire extinguisher weigh, would you guess, Steve?"

"I guess maybe fifteen, twenty pounds."

"Do you have any idea how many times you hit him?"

"I'd say approximately thirty to forty times. All in the head."

"Were you able to tell from his position which side of the head you were hitting, or what?"

"Okay, when I first started hitting him, he was pretty much facing me. Jamie was off to this side with the garbage bag, holding him down. And I hit him with the broad side of the fire extinguisher. And that didn't do much, except, you know, make noise, and then Jamie kneed him in the nuts and when he went down, I started using the end of the fire extinguisher."

"Which end?"

"The end without the handle."

"The bottom."

"Yeah. It's rounded on the inside, but it's got a steel rim that goes all the way around. And it's really hard and heavy, eh? And I started dropping it down on his head like that, when he was down on the ground. And I'm pretty sure I fractured his skull."

"You're indicating you're holding onto the handle."

"I was just like this, just like that," Steve said, now rising from his chair and miming his actions. "I'm holding the handle and dropping it on his skull," he said, motioning like a person pumping water from a well.

"Okay. Why do you think you broke his skull?"

"Because I heard a crunching noise and the extinguisher sunk in a bit," he said, slumping back into his chair.

Chapman, inwardly horrified but outwardly calm, asked how Jamie and Steve had split the duties.

"He's supposed to put the bag over the guy's head so that he can't see either of us."

"Okay. Your job is the fire extinguisher?"

"My job at that point was just to knock the guy out, okay?"

"Uh huh."

"But, uh, we got so carried away, we figured that all of a sudden it became far more important to keep hitting this guy. Because, like, we never knocked anybody out before. It took maybe ten shots before the guy went out. And then when he went out he was still wiggling and he was still breathing. And we're like, 'Oh no. What are we going to do with this guy?' So we figured he's better off dead anyways, in the condition he's in."

Steve then told Chapman exactly what happened afterward, down to the amount of money Fritch had in his wallet and pockets: "ninety-seven bucks in bills and about a buck thirty-five in change."

Later in the interview, he recalled the entire breakfast menu he and Cari had enjoyed, and even the waiter's name: "Our waiter's name was David. He's a blond guy. I think he was homosexual," Steve said.

As the bizarre interview—which had gone almost too easily for Chapman—wound down, the detective asked Steve about his clothes.

"While we're at this point, I notice on the legs of your pants there's some staining."

"Yes."

"What do you believe that to be?"

"I believe that to be the remains of Mr. Fritch. It's blood from him. There's some down there on my leg, there's a little bit up here, some over here. Mostly splatters, I guess, from his head. There's some over here, on the cuff of my shirt," he said, pointing out all the marks for the camera.

Operating the camera in the next room, Barker was chilled. Steve seemed to *like* what was happening to him.

"This was his starring role. He thought, 'If I talk to a lawyer, he's going to tell me to shut up.' He was king, in his mind, and he knew: 'I'm the most important thing they've got going.' Up until that point, he was a nobody," Barker said later.

At the end of the interview, officers from the Identification Unit took away Steve's clothes to be analyzed, as well as samples of his hair, fingernails, blood, urine and saliva. His photograph and fingerprints were registered.

Chapman and Barker could hardly believe what had happened in the last hour, neither as police officers, nor as men.

"The way he described it, the hair on the back of the neck stood up, and I got goosebumps at several points," Chapman said. "You thought, 'My God. What have we stumbled into? This is the scariest thing I ever heard of.' This could have happened to anyone. Everyone gets gas, and it wasn't even that late. With every other one, there's some kind of reason. I thought, 'I wear a suit. I drive a nice Mustang convertible.' That sent shivers up and down my spine and to this day it still does."

"I said, 'Jesus Christ,'" Barker said, "'We drive by that gas station every day.' It could have been any one of us. For a pocketful of credit cards, some cash and a fancy car. That's what it boiled down to."

After the laundry was done, Jamie and Cari pulled up to a motel near the shore of Lake Simcoe.

"You'd better go sign in," Jamie said.

"What am I supposed to do?" she asked. "My name's in the paper, too."

"Tell them your name is Melanie Brooks," Jamie said, drawing the name out of nowhere. Like Steve, he was also enjoying his role as a big-time criminal. Cari presented herself at the desk as instructed. She had grown bolder, and was willing to pass herself off as someone else now in order to protect her boyfriend. And herself.

At the motel, they watched the news, which included a report about themselves, and they knew that they had to move quickly. Still, Jamie, practically hearing a soundtrack in the background of his adventure, liked watching himself on TV. He liked being one step ahead of the police, and was determined to keep it that way.

Frank Olah's trip to Akron had gone well. His friends dropped him off at home early in the evening. He was happy, and carrying a gift for his son: a T-shirt bearing the legend "Real men wear black." He walked into the house. It seemed too quiet. "Hello! I'm home, everybody!" he called out cheerfully.

His wife and his daughter silently took him to the kitchen. "Sit down," Beth said. "Steven's been arrested for murder."

The next morning, after he and Cari checked out of the motel, Jamie parked the K-Car in a lot close to the lake. It was getting just a little too hot to keep using it, he figured. He and Cari walked along the railway tracks, out of sight, back toward town, where they bought two one-way bus tickets to British Columbia, at $139 each. They had with them two black garbage bags of clothes. Jamie bought some muffins and juice to have along the way. Once again, they were almost out of money.

After the last pit stop of their four-day trip, Jamie and Cari were riding in blessed anonymity somewhere between Calgary and Vancouver when the family and friends of Joseph Fritch were packing a downtown church for his memorial service. The crime had so horrified the community that the mayor, Roly Bird, and a local alderman, Yvonne Roach, who had not known the victim, attended on behalf of the city. News cameras, behind trees and bushes near the road, waited for the grieving family to exit.

On Monday, Cari and Jamie, now as tired and broke as they had been in the Richmond Hill apartment building, arrived in Vancouver. Jamie called his uncle John's apartment in nearby Burnaby. Jamie's dad had already called ahead and warned him to be on the lookout for his fugitive son, but when Jamie called, his uncle was out. Robert McBain, a Hamilton native who had been sharing the rent on the apartment with Stinchcombe for five months, answered the phone.

McBain had returned home from work at about 5:30, and was not expecting his roommate for another ninety minutes at least. When the phone rang and it was Jamie, McBain was not altogether surprised. He had known Jamie was on the run from a murder in Burlington, and he didn't want much to do with him.

"Hello, is John there?"

"No, he's still at work."

"This is his nephew Jamie calling. I need to talk to him. I'm at the Greyhound station downtown."

"Well, he'll be home in a while. Why don't you take the bus out here?"

McBain gave Jamie directions to take the city bus to Lougheed Mall, across the road from the high-rise, one of a knot of dozens in the neighbourhood.

"Give us a call when you get there, and John should be home by then," McBain said, and hung up.

Stinchcombe got home around 7:15 p.m., and fifteen minutes later, Jamie called again. Stinchcombe went across to the plaza and picked up Jamie and Cari. They looked road-weary and scared. Back at the apartment, all four ate dinner together, in almost total silence. Afterward, Jamie excused himself from the living room and took a shower, while the others watched television.

"You know, I didn't think any of this would really happen," Cari said to the two men. "I was really just going along with them to Toronto to say good-bye."

They all continued watching TV. When Jamie was finished his shower, Cari took her turn.

At eleven, McBain went to bed, but had trouble sleeping. He knew there were murderers in his house, and he couldn't help thinking about Fritch. After all, McBain had two young daughters of his own back home. He sympathized much more with the victim than he did with his roommate's kin.

When he got up at seven the next morning, he called John to his room.

"We've got to get hold of your brother," McBain said.

"Don't worry. We've got [Jamie] talked into turning himself in," Stinchcombe reassured him. "He's going to do it later today."

John called his sister Cindy in Guelph, where it was now 10 a.m., to have her relay the information to Jamie's dad in Burlington.

As he left the apartment, McBain walked past the two couches where Jamie and Cari were sleeping. He saw their clothes slung over a dining-room chair. And he saw the newspaper clipping about themselves they had been carrying.

Stinchcombe, after a brief appearance at work, returned home to wake up the sleeping fugitives. "What are you going to do, Jamie?" he asked.

"I think I'm going to try and cross the border," Jamie answered. He obviously had changed his mind about turning himself in.

"You'll get caught the first time you try. Guaranteed," Stinchcombe said. "Look. You can't live here. I'm not going to get you a job. You can't keep running, Jamie."

He spent another two hours talking to the two of them, with Cari helping talk to Jamie, and finally, they agreed to turn themselves in that day.

At work, Robert McBain was having a tough time concentrating. Although he was satisfied with Stinchcombe's explanation, the idea of those wanted killers sleeping in his apartment continued to gnaw at his conscience.

Finally, he called the Vancouver police.

It was 9:15 when the phone rang at the desk of detective Don Bellamy, in the homicide section of the Major Crime Squad.

"Hello?"

"Yes, sir. I want to pass along some information about a murder at a gas station in Burlington."

"What is your name, sir?"

"Rob."

"Okay, fine. What murder are you talking about?"

"You know, those kids who killed the guy at the gas station, in Burlington, in Ontario."

"Okay. What information did you want to pass along?"

"Well, the two killers they're still looking for are at my apartment right now."

"Where's that, Rob?"

"It's in Burnaby," he said, giving the detective the specific street and suite number on Carrigan Court.

"Okay. What number are you at right now, Rob? I'll get back to you in just a few minutes."

McBain gave his work number and hung up.

Bellamy called Peel police in Ontario to ask about this killing, and to check if it had really happened as McBain had described. Yes, that was all correct, said the Peel officer, reading from a Canadian Police Information Centre bulletin that had been sent across the country.

The Peel inspector offered to have Halton police call Bellamy directly.

Bellamy's phone rang at 9:30. It was Joe Barker. Bellamy set up a conference call with three other Vancouver detectives. Barker described the crime and the suspects to them, and offered to send the information via CPIC, to help them get a search warrant for the apartment.

At ten, Bellamy called Rob again at work, and arranged to meet him at a Coquitlam club called The Two Parrots. At 11:30, they all met. Bellamy was with detectives Bruce Ballantyne, Brian Ball and Grant MacDonald. The police, in planning to arrest the fugitives, asked McBain more questions, which he answered readily, as he drew a floor plan of the apartment and gave them the key to get in.

At 12:22, Bellamy put the key in the lock and entered with three other detectives to back him up in case of trouble.

But there was no trouble.

"Vancouver police. Don't anybody move," Ballantyne said to the three motionless figures who were seated casually in the living room.

Cari was on the floor, Jamie sat on a loveseat, and his uncle John was sitting on a couch.

Bellamy and Ballantyne approached Jamie.

"What's your name?" Bellamy asked.

"Ruston."

Bellamy put one hand on Jamie's shoulder and used the other to pull out his badge.

"My name is Detective Don Bellamy of the Vancouver Police Force. It is my duty to inform you that I am placing you under arrest for murder, as the result of a Canada-wide warrant for your arrest."

Jamie stared blankly, saying nothing.

Bellamy read him his rights.

Ballantyne took over, and walked Jamie to a bedroom to isolate him from Cari.

At the same time, the other two detectives were putting Cari through the same routine. Ball introduced himself to her, announced she was being arrested for murder, and read her rights to her. MacDonald noted in his statement for court that Cari was very calm, "unusually so," he wrote.

In the bedroom, Ballantyne searched and handcuffed Jamie. He found only fourteen pennies in his back pocket. The handful of pennies and a garbage bag of clothes were the net proceeds from killing an innocent man, stealing two cars, and riding non-stop across the country.

"You don't seem very surprised at our arrival," Ballantyne said to the youth.

"No. We were just sitting around talking about turning ourselves in."

After Jamie showed the officers which clothes were his, they took him out of the apartment. After six days of searching and Canada-wide warrants, the arrest took only twenty minutes. In the lobby, the officers sat Jamie in a chair and read him his rights again.

"Do you understand?" Bellamy asked.

"Yes. That means I can call a lawyer."

"You can call a lawyer from headquarters. I have the name and number of one for you." Stinchcombe, at the apartment, had given the officers the name and number of a Toronto lawyer, Bill Trudell, for Jamie to call.

Just after 1 p.m., the officers and Jamie arrived at Vancouver Police headquarters, where Jamie was allowed to phone home. Finding the number busy, he tried Trudell's office, where he got through. At the end of that call, the police tried calling Jamie's father and stepmother again. This time they got through, and handed the phone to Jamie. There was no answer when the police tried Jamie's mother a few minutes later.

While Jamie was on the phone, Cari was with Bell in another room of the Main Street headquarters.

"Is there anything you want, or anything I can get for you?"

"No."

"Are there any questions you have?"

"I didn't do anything," she said, starting to cry. "I was there, but I didn't do anything. What's going to happen to Jamie over this? He's a young offender. He's seventeen years old."

"There are two options," Ball told her. "He could go to family court, or, because it is a very serious incident, the Crown could apply to have him raised to adult court."

"None of this was supposed to happen. They were supposed to scare him and bring him with them. They were joking around about it, so I didn't take it serious. They were going to make him drive them across the border, and then they would just go."

"How were you going to fit into this?"

"I wasn't. I was going to go home, go to sleep, and go to school the next morning. I wasn't going to see Jamie again."

"But you're still together," the detective said. Cari started crying again.

"Our pictures were in the newspaper. The paper is in my purse, in there," she said, pointing at her bag.

The officer went over and opened her purse. Inside, he found the first two pages of *The Toronto Sun* that had featured Fritch's picture and their own.

MacDonald now came back into the room.

"Have you got a light?" Cari asked, holding a cigarette between her shaking fingers. MacDonald found a match for her and lit the cigarette.

"Do you realize how much trouble you're in?" he asked her. "First-degree murder is life in jail with no parole for twenty-five years."

"I didn't do anything!" she protested.

"You were there."

"Yes, but they were going to make him drive them, and I was going home, and no one was supposed to be killed."

"Where were you when it happened?"

"There was glass where the customers come in, and a counter. He was on the other side of the counter down below it, and I never saw him."

"Well, you saw the body."

"No, I never saw the body," she said.

"Do you want to phone your parents?"

"Yes."

Then, finally, half of Cari's family's worries were ended. Craig and Diane Chisamore got the call they had been begging for. Their daughter was alive and well and on her way home. Now they could focus their worries on an equally serious issue: she had been charged with the highest crime in the land.

Part Two

— Chapter 8 —
And Then
There Were Two

After two years without a murder trial, Halton police and prosecutors had learned that finding the criminals was the easy part of bringing them to justice.

It took eleven months before Halton's Crown Attorney, Paul Stunt, could win a ruling to have Jamie tried alongside Cari and Steve in adult court. It would take seven more months for that decision to be set in stone, though, as Jamie's lawyers, Bill Trudell and Janet Leiper, fought all the way to the Supreme Court of Canada to put him back in youth court. At stake, after all, was the difference between life in jail and a maximum three-year sentence. In the adult system, where a life sentence means a minimum twenty-five years before parole, he would be in jail at least eight times as long if convicted of first-degree murder. Jamie's lawyers said it would be cruel and unusual under the Charter of Rights and Freedoms to take away the protection that the Young Offenders Act offered to people under eighteen by plunging him into the adult system. But the seriousness of the crime, the evidence of planning and Jamie's partnership with an adult who was only five months older weighed against him. After the last appeal had been exhausted, he was finally ordered to stand in front of a jury alongside the two teenagers who had once been his girlfriend and his best buddy.

Of the three, Steve had posed the least resistance to a full-blown murder trial. His early confessions, initial refusal to contact a lawyer and apparent willingness to go to jail had left his lawyer Paul LaFleur and senior trial lawyer Alan Cooper very little room to manoeuvre. Cooper had joined Team Olah, as Steve called it, on LaFleur's recommendation. A lawyer since 1973, Cooper had spent ten years in the provincial Crown Attorney's office in Toronto. In 1984, he left for private practice in Hamilton, where he successfully defended reputed mobster Bruno Monaco during the last stages of a ten-year trial over a home-insulation scam. Steve's case, however, was the most highly publicized in which Cooper had ever participated.

Together, LaFleur and Cooper fought to maintain control over their only hope for an acquittal—an insanity finding—by keeping the prosecution psychiatrists away from their client, even blocking one doctor's surprise Labour Day weekend visit to Steve at the Barton Street jail, three months before the trial. Already, both sides were executing the highly political strategies of insanity cases, where defence lawyers give their experts full access to defendants to prove their clients are insane, and do their best to keep prosecution experts away, rendering their second-hand impressions less credible.

Stunt and Cooper had met in the summer before the trial, when Cooper informed the prosecutor that he planned a psychiatric defence, and gave him a list of the doctors he intended to call as expert witnesses. Although he was not required to do so, Stunt had agreed to notify Cooper when he planned to send his own experts to visit Steve. After arranging through the jail to send Dr. Andrew Malcolm to visit Steve on that Labour Day weekend, Stunt says, he dictated a letter to inform Cooper. Somewhere along the line, though, the taped dictation was detoured and never typed, leaving Cooper no notice about the visit until a call from Steve in jail, asking what to do. Steve was advised not to talk to Dr. Malcolm. Cooper was furious, sensing a deliberate ambush. Although Stunt was apologetic and sent a lengthy letter of explanation to his opponent, the damage had been done, fanning the adversarial fire that was about to break out in court.

In other informal discussions before the trial, Cari's senior lawyer, Jeff Manishen, a Hamilton defence lawyer as prominent as Cooper, asked Stunt to drop the murder charge because of a lack of hard evidence against her. Manishen said Stunt didn't have a case, and asked him to let her go. Stunt agreed to look into the request. Even though he had been nearly as disgusted by Cari's actions as by Steve's and Jamie's, he knew he had to put his personal feelings aside and examine objectively the value of the case against her. While he was making up his mind, though, the charges would stand, and both teams prepared for a trial. Manishen and Martha Zivolak, Cari's other lawyer, argued unsuccessfully that she should get a separate trial.

So far, Stunt had won every major pre-trial victory. Knowing that the high profile and unusual nature of the case demanded a senior trial counsel, he had used his discretion as head of the Crown's office to take the murder trial into his own portfolio. Despite his heavy workload that year, he felt he owed the public at least the reassurance that the region's senior prosecutor was handling it personally. More so than in other cases, he knew the community was watching this one, and demanding that he take every aspect of the prosecution to the fullest extent. Stunt had jumped in early in the case, while Jamie and Cari were still at large, by arguing for the police force's request to identify Jamie in the media. He went to court and won—twice—the forty-eight-hour authority to publish and broadcast Jamie's name and photograph, in a rare judicial dispensation from the Young Offenders Act.

Mounting a three-way murder case was not easy for the Halton Crown Attorney's office. Even before the murder, there had been pressure on Stunt's department. Two senior lawyers, his predecessor James Treleaven and senior assistant Crown John Ayre, had left for more senior positions, and had yet to be replaced. Even though the Halton office was short-staffed, the attorney-general's office in Toronto was pushing for more convictions. The Halton office already had a strong reputation in the community, but the province wanted more for less.

For Stunt, it was the third murder trial of the year. In the spring, there had been the difficult trial of James Otto McInnes, a drifter with a long record of violent and sexual crimes who had murdered a twenty-eight-year-old computer operator while she was sunbathing on Burlington Beach. The vicious psychopath had stabbed her eight times and mutilated her body after she died. The jury took only an hour and ten minutes to convict him. When the jury announced its verdict, he hissed "Fucking rats" at them before he was surrounded by police officers. McInnes, at fifty-three a hardened criminal who had become a friend of Steve's in jail, got life for second-degree murder. At the sentencing, Stunt had called the sallow, rat-faced man a lifelong criminal with an evil, sadistic mind.

There had also been the difficult leftover mob trial from a 1983 contract killing where, only a month before the Fritch trial, Stunt had been able to win two first-degree murder convictions against Peter Monaghan and Graham Court, small-time hoods who killed a Toronto mob boss for $4,700 and a small amount of cocaine.

Before the trial even started, Stunt was feeling more tired and challenged than ever. The aggravation of a bad leg had been forcing him to rest one foot on a chair in court. The combination of the leg and the heavy workload had made it the toughest of his sixteen years as a prosecutor. Still, he badly wanted a full slate of convictions in this case. Although he had not yet firmly made up his mind to leave, this would later prove to be his last murder trial as Crown Attorney, before he left for private practice, where he could have more control over his own schedule.

During this time, Steve and Jamie waited it out at the Barton Street jail. Steve spent his time in the adult wing, where he is remembered by veteran jail guards as a manipulative, unrepentant troublemaker. He had to be placed in twenty-three-hour-a-day isolation after threatening to kill his cellmate. In his isolation, Steve read voraciously, consuming and absorbing four hundred books before his case came to court. Jamie was housed in the youth wing of the jail, where the same guards recall him as a model prisoner, often helping to organize athletic activities and following orders obediently. Jamie sent the guards a letter after the trial, thanking them for his kind treatment there.

Since she was not perceived as a threat to public safety, Cari had been released on bail, an unusual liberty for a person charged with first-degree murder. Once she had been returned to Burlington, her parents signed an $80,000 surety for her, and made a $20,000 cash deposit, calling in some generous offers from friends and relatives. It wasn't easy for them, having recently extended themselves again to buy a larger home for their family on the same street.

Although Cari was free, she had serious troubles of her own. Everyone in the family had made it a priority to keep her within the conditions of her bail, which she followed "impeccably," her father, Craig, said, including an order not to communicate with witnesses in the trial, who included her best friends Andrea Talarico and John Ruttan. One day, Ruttan came to the door with flowers for her, but he had to be satisfied with waving to Cari through a window. Her exile included staying out of regular school, where it was felt her presence would disrupt other students. Instead, she completed her high-school studies at home, and eventually enrolled in a special government program through Sheridan College in Oakville, where she was studying to become a beautician. Her school marks leapt from the mid-sixties into the nineties. She had deferred the rest of her college studies because of the trial, hoping to continue once she had served her sentence. At the same time, she had kept a full-time job as a food server at the Red Lobster restaurant along Burlington's Fairview Street food strip. Cari had started work there about six months after the murder, her name and picture still fresh in the memory of many customers. She worked first in the kitchen, and later as a waitress. Even though everyone at work knew who she was, no one asked her about the murder, and she never brought it up.

"She's a very disciplined individual now. Her maturity has certainly been accelerated by all the events that have taken place," her father said at the time. There was, however, one night when she had placed her freedom and her family's money at stake by failing to report to the Burlington police station, where she was to sign in every Saturday before 6 p.m. The probation officer had told her and her parents, "If it's one minute after six, it's no good."

That afternoon at dinner, she, an asthmatic, had experienced some difficulty breathing, and the sign-in had been forgotten until late that night. Realizing the damage had already been done, the family decided it would be best just to go to bed and report to the police station in the morning, when they would be awake and more reasonable. Early the next day, Craig took her to the downtown station, where she was arrested and initially denied new bail. She pleaded guilty to failing to live up to the conditions, and was later fined three hundred dollars. She was out just in time for Christmas, upsetting many citizens who felt it was outrageous enough to have let her out in the first place, let alone after she had broken the conditions of her bail.

Embarrassed and more frightened, the family now double-checked everything to do with Cari's bail. Realizing how fragile her freedom was, they became obsessive about preserving it. They posted a sign on the inside of the front door: "Sign In," and checked with one another constantly. Through it all, Cari was plagued by recurring nightmares, where the killing played back on the screen of her unconscious mind in several variations. Usually, though, the man being killed was not Joe Fritch, but her own father, who was frequently awakened by her screaming in bed.

By day, the nightmare followed Cari and her family all over Burlington, in the form of curious stares from strangers. This was not a small town, but the incredible attention focused on the case made their faces familiar everywhere.

At a pretrial hearing, Manishen, Cari's senior lawyer, said the saturation coverage of the case would make it impossible to find an objective jury in Halton region. Justice Patrick LeSage agreed to move the trial out of Halton to Brampton, about thirty miles to the northeast in Peel, the next jurisdiction. Although the murder had been widely covered by newspapers, radio and television stations across Canada, the publicity in Brampton was, at least, much less intense than it had been in Burlington and Hamilton, where citizens had demanded to be informed of every small detail of the pretrial machinations. Hardly a week had passed without at least some printed mention of the case, often prominently displayed on the front pages of the sister dailies, *The Hamilton Spectator* and *The Burlington Spectator*, and the thrice-weekly rival *Burlington Post*.

Finally, a date was set for December 2, 1991—two years and two months after the murder—and a room was booked at the busy Peel County Courthouse. From the outside, the Brampton courthouse is a curiosity, standing out like a spaceship in the tundra. The bright white building sends post-modern white legs off its sides, as if it were trying to climb out of the muddy field where it was built in contrast to the boxy high-rises and shopping malls that surround it.

The interior is shaped like a mace. Prisoners, judges and jury members enter courtrooms through the back by private doorways at the large end. Police officers, witnesses, lawyers and members of the public go in through a bank of doors at the small end, passing a number of smaller offices there and walking down a long, window-lit corridor, finally reaching the atrium, from which eight courtrooms fan out. The centre of the atrium is filled with large, institutional plants, ringed by chairs, facing outward. Another larger circle of chairs faces them from the outside edges of the circle. Here, everyone mingles, often in uncomfortable proximity, waiting for the day's business to start. There are no corners for anyone to hide.

Black-robed lawyers whisper among themselves or with their clients, while police officers, many obvious in their infrequently worn suits and short haircuts, talk to each other, usually two levels louder than the lawyers. Nervous families of the accused, usually one for each courtroom, wear the best clothes they have, often showing up day after day in the same outfits.

But on that first Monday of December 1991, by far the largest number of people in that uncomfortable circle had come for the case of *Regina versus Olah, Chisamore and Ruston*. Each accused had two lawyers, who in turn were supported by a changing platoon of clerks and secretaries, running messages, photocopying documents and making phone calls.

Stunt was accompanied by the young but able Susan Lawson, who was working on her first murder case. It is traditional that two Crown lawyers will prosecute a major murder case, and common that one experienced prosecutor will use the case to teach a newer colleague the ropes. Lawson was the only Crown in the office who had not worked on a murder trial, so it was her turn. She and Stunt split the case according to groups of witnesses: the kids from the school and the SuperCentre, the police, the forensic experts, the psychiatric experts, Steve's parents, and everyone who had contact with the accused directly before and after the murder. Stunt, being more experienced, would take the tougher ones, such as the friends from the mall, the school and gas station, whose overlapping and occasionally contradictory memories of the days before the crime formed a patchwork that required an experienced trial lawyer to stitch together effectively.

But Lawson had one of the heaviest responsibilities of the whole trial: delivering the opening address, the road map that the prosecution hoped the jury would follow to reach first-degree murder convictions against the accused.

Each day in court, as over the past two years of minor and major hearings, there were several members of the Chisamore family in the gallery. Almost always, Craig and Diane were there, as was Cari's grandmother. Usually there would be at least one of her sisters, and often there were several of her friends.

Jamie enjoyed the support of his father, Jim, and his step-mother, Karen. Frequently, too, his natural mother, Cathy, and her husband were there, along with a changing assortment of aunts and cousins.

For Steve, attendance was generally limited to his parents, although they had trouble, with their demanding work schedules, getting the necessary time off to be there throughout.

No member of the Fritch family attended court. For Anne Fritch, seeing and hearing the details of her husband's murder, and facing the killers and their families would have been too much, even for the woman who had found the courage to go down to the morgue and identify her husband's body on that first day. Her son Jason once told Sergeant Barker that he would not be able to control himself if he were ever in the same room as the contemporaries who had killed his dad, and so thought it wiser to stay home.

After mixing awkwardly in the hallway on that first day, the families, police, journalists and lawyers filed into Courtroom 2, feigning smiles and putting on polite fictions by holding the doors open for one another. The chamber that had been assigned to this hearing was large and grey, with rows of benches separated down the centre by an aisle. On the left side of the court behind the defense lawyers' tables, the families and friends of the accused and the lawyers' support workers filled most of the space. On the right, behind the prosecutors, sat the police and the Crown's student lawyer. Having no neutral ground in which to sit, the half-dozen journalists and two sketch artists had chosen the less crowded side, where they could sit in the front rows. It was difficult to hear in the echoing, high-ceilinged chamber. Cari sat in front of the bar, between the lawyers and the observers. Steve and Jamie had not yet been brought into the room.

In front of the eight lawyers, just under the judge's bench, were the court clerk and the court reporter, who breathed the transcript into a mask-like microphone. Above it all sat Justice LeSage. His friendly manner and boyish cowlick belied his status in the courtroom, but helped to ease the tension. Just ten days short of his fifty-fourth birthday, he was sitting for what would be only the second murder trial of his fourteen years on the bench. As a Crown prosecutor in Toronto, however, the former fuel-truck driver from Tweed, Ontario, had handled more than two dozen murder cases.

The 150 members of the jury panel, from whom the lawyers would choose 12, were ordered to remain outside. They were waiting to see which of them would spend the weeks before Christmas sitting in two rows of six chairs that had been set up in the jury box on the right side of the courtroom.

An equal space had been built on the left side, but was now filled with boxes of transcripts and tagged, clear plastic bags of clothes, music tapes, two knives and a bright red fire extinguisher.

Paul Stunt, in his black robes even broader and more imposing than usual, opened his binder and smiled momentarily at the photo of a bulldog friends had given him after a weekend newspaper reference to his tenacity. Stern again now, he rose to announce the results of a meeting before the trial.

"Miss Chisamore will not be proceeded with on the charge of first-degree murder," he said, explaining that the young woman would instead enter a guilty plea to the lesser charge of accessory to murder. A whisper ran through the benches, and all eyes focused on Cari, who sat with her head bowed, looking down at her black jacket and plaid kilt. She was conservatively put together for the occasion, as though someone older had dressed her, except for one personal touch: her white lipstick, which made her look hard. The indictment was read out, accusing her of unlawfully and wilfully assisting Steve and Jamie in their escape from the murder—such as by helping them get a hotel room.

"Guilty," she said quietly.

A month before the trial, Cari had agreed for the first time to be interviewed by the police, after Stunt had promised to consider Manishen's request to drop the murder charge. After the interview, Stunt met with Lawson and the two police officers to make a decision. He had been planning to prosecute her on the theory that her presence had acted as an encouragement to the young men to carry out the killing, and that by sitting behind the counter, she had, knowingly or not, acted as a decoy to lure Fritch toward her. Stunt's best hope, however, had been to prove that, as the only person within reach of the panel of switches, she had turned out the lights inside the kiosk to prevent outsiders from seeing what was happening. But without witnesses who could confirm it, and without any fingerprints or other physical evidence, there wasn't much of a case. Did she turn out the lights?

"I don't know. Certainly at the time of the trial, I didn't have the evidence to prove it," Stunt said later. Although he, Lawson and the police officers remained convinced that she had at least been a passive participant in the killing, they knew they couldn't prove it. Stunt and the others had strong suspicions that she had done more than sit and watch—which is not a crime—but Stunt knew they had to separate their emotional outrage from cold, legal reality. It was the toughest choice he had ever had to make as a lawyer, but he decided they would drop the murder charge against her.

"In my seventeen years as a prosecutor, I made a lot of serious decisions. I would expect that this was the most serious decision I ever made. That was probably the most intellectually, legally and ethically pure decision I ever made," he said afterward. "The most that we could prove was that she was there. There was not one shred of physical evidence or reasonable inference that she was part of the murder."

Still, he was determined to get the longest sentence possible for what she did after the murder. Since she had been so active in the escape, after at least witnessing the actual planning and killing, Stunt felt she should get the upper end of the precedent for being an accessory: five years in jail.

"I always had a view that she was a cold fish. I didn't like her. I felt a person who could do that was callous, cold and frightening. If someone could do that without compunction, that's frightening," he said later.

After Cari's guilty plea, court was adjourned and the judge called the lawyers back into his chambers to discuss the fallout from this late development. The jury panel members were still crowding the hallway. They weren't allowed to know the details about Cari's plea, because it could taint them later, during the trial.

After an hour, guards escorted Steve and Jamie into the room through a side door. Shackled hand and foot, the short chains around their ankles limited them to small, quick steps, and the handcuffs allowed Jamie only to squeeze a small wave to his parents. Both prisoners wore grey suits, looking more grown-up than they had at previous appearances. Jamie's hair was parted in the middle, cut at collar level. He had begun to fill out his suit but it was obviously still too large for him. He looked subdued, his face showing no hint of the terror running through him. Steve, on the other hand, looked constricted by his suit, and his hair had grown somewhat longer than the preppie schoolboy cut he had worn at the time of his arrest. His eyes looked heavy, and as he sat in the prisoners' dock beside his friend, he seemed as though he were about to fall asleep. He had been given extra dosages of his anti-psychotic medication to help him stay calm throughout the trial. He had been very excited for it to get started. The guards took off the shackles, but never diverted their attention from their charges.

The judge announced that Jamie's and Steve's jury would now be selected, while Cari's sentencing on the accessory charge would be put off until after the twelve citizens had been picked. Betting in the gallery was that the jury selection would take as long as two days. At that stage, even with the removal of Cari from the proceedings, it was expected that the trial would last more than three weeks, taking it right up to Christmas.

When the jury panel members were finally admitted to the room, they filled every seat on every bench, and stood three deep along the outside walls. The murder charges were read out in front of them and the accused were asked to plead. Steve said nothing. His lawyer Alan Cooper explained his client would stand mute on the accusation, which is interpreted by the court to be the equivalent of a "not guilty" plea. The whole defence strategy involved keeping Steve quiet throughout. If he spoke in his usual articulate style, he would jeopardize his insanity defence, since he might not appear crazy enough. Ruston quietly uttered his own "Not guilty."

The judge asked if anyone among the jury panel was related to anyone connected to the case. None answered. He asked if anyone had firsthand knowledge of the crime. One woman, who told the court that she had friends who knew the victim quite well, was dismissed.

By the lunch break, the court had processed sixty-seven potential jurors, yielding an amazing eight for the trial. So far, three had been excused, Cooper had challenged ten, Trudell had challenged eleven, and Stunt had asked thirty-five to stand aside. After the break it only took nine more candidates before the lawyers had agreed on the rest of the jury. There were three engineers, two independent business people, two clerks, a graphic designer, a head teller, a purchasing manager, a consultant and a retired trucker. Nine were men and three were women.

Judge LeSage told them *they* were actually the judges of this case, and that he was only the referee, there to make sure the facts were presented according to the law. He warned them solemnly not to discuss the case outside court with anyone until after a verdict had been agreed upon.

"That includes anyone and everyone," he said.

The jury was dismissed for two days in order to allow the court to deal with Chisamore's sentencing. This paved the way for her to appear as a Crown witness. Once the jury had been sent home, the judge started listening to arguments on her sentence. Stunt read the prepared statement signed by Chisamore after the interview with police, where she described what had happened at the SuperCentre, and, later, in the kiosk. Although she was to become an important part of the prosecution's proof of planning, Stunt was still giving her a rough ride. He wanted a long sentence for this young woman, and the disgust in his voice and manner were strong as he questioned her and made his case.

She had seen the knives both Steve and Jamie had brought to the station. By 12:10, he said, she knew that they were planning not only a violent robbery but also to kill someone of Joe Fritch's type: small and wealthy-looking. Still, she had ignored every opportunity to leave the station, he said.

In the witness box, she said she remembered Jamie in the booth that night telling Bob Yates, the station's off-duty car wash attendant, which cars he liked, telling him "how nice it would be" to take one of them. She admitted calling Steve at home, knowing it would be in violation of his curfew if he were to join them at the station. She knew they had talked about a "big job," but she maintained she hadn't believed they would really go through with it.

"I didn't think they'd have enough guts to steal a car with someone in it," she said.

She said she didn't watch the beating, but could hear what was going on, even over her own screams.

"I could hear the man breathing. It sounded like he was spitting up stuff. Gurgling," she said. "I remember saying I was feeling like I was going to be sick."

Once Cari was finished in the box, Manishen called a string of character witnesses, hoping to control the damage Stunt had done to his client's chances for a short sentence. First was Brenda Kurth, who had been Cari's manager at Red Lobster. Kurth had treated her like any other worker, despite the fact that everyone on staff knew who she was.

"She was bright, intelligent, easygoing. She got along with everyone. She was a great worker," Kurth said. Cari had finished her job at the restaurant the Friday before the trial, in anticipation of being sent to jail. But, Kurth said, she still had a job waiting for her whenever she got out.

Cari's uncle Darcy, the thirty-nine-year-old brother of her

father, said the whole family believed she had been innocent of murder all along, and told the judge his niece had been a model citizen before and after her arrest for murder.

"She's worked extremely hard, and we believe in her," he said.

Terry Defelice, the Chisamores' neighbour from across the street, said Cari had sometimes baby-sat her two young children.

"Cari has always been a very nice girl," she said. "She's always been very good with kids. She plays with them. I'd [still] let her play with my children. I'd definitely trust her." She credited the Chisamores for having raised their children properly, and for coming through this crisis stronger than they had been before.

"They're a family. They talk. They disagree. They yell. They hug. If anything, the whole thing has brought them closer together," she said. "From the moment I found out, I said, 'No way.'"

With that, court adjourned for the day. Next morning, Cari's father, Craig, dressed in a blue suit and white shirt, took the stand.

Only once, he said, had he and Diane had significant trouble with Cari. She had moved out of their home in 1988, for a total of three weeks, after refusing to adhere to their discipline. She had a lot of friends, and liked to stay out late, but had reformed considerably after coming home.

"I know she would not knowingly do anything that would contribute to the death of another individual. I still trust her. I still believe in her," he said.

The last member of Manishen's bullpen to speak was Cari herself, over the strenuous objections of Stunt, who complained that anything she could possibly say would only be self-serving. Still, the judge agreed to hear her apology, which she had written in pencil on a sheet of three-ring binder paper:

Dear Justice LeSage,
I would like to take this opportunity to express how sorry I am for any participation I had in assisting the escape of James Ruston. Although it was not planned, it was the result of my actions, and for that, I cannot express how sorry I am.

In the past two years, I have done all sorts of things: work, school, and have had my family and friends to support me. I am thankful for these things I have, but not a day has gone by that I have been thankful [and not] turned to the thought of the Fritch family.

I imagine they are thankful they have one another, but their father is gone, and I truly do feel so much compassion for them. I've never had such tied hands wanting to reach and help another. I haven't found the courage.

I may only have been eighteen when this nightmare began, but I've known enough to realize the torment this has put the Fritch family through, although I cannot try and say I know what it feels like because I truly don't. I've never lost a loved one at an age I could comprehend it at.

But I can express my feeling of apology, sincere concern, and frustration that I don't have the power to turn back time, and change all these horrible events.
Sincerely,

Cari-Lee Chisamore.

The look of disgust on Stunt's face had grown uglier with each word she read. Now it was his turn.

He called his only rebuttal witness, Sergeant Barker, to the stand, to describe the search for Cari and Ruston as the most extensive of his thirteen-year police career up to that point, where he and Chapman had been forced to rely largely on other police forces and the media to help them. He remembered his outrage at the killing and dealing with the Fritch family. "It's probably one of the most senseless thrill kills, if you like, that I have seen."

But he remembered very clearly what it was like after six days and nights of looking, when he retrieved Cari and Jamie from across the country. What they displayed, he said, was anything but concern for Joe Fritch and his family.

"What I believe I saw in Miss Chisamore at the time we arrived was concern for herself and what was happening to *her* at the time."

Manishen countered that Cari's life experience up until the time of the killing had left her unprepared to deal with the magnitude of murder. She had never had any experience with the law before she had been charged with Canada's top crime. Since then, he said, she had literally been under house arrest at her parents', and subjected to overwhelming publicity. The most active she had been in the murder was to call Steve down to the gas station, he said, and now she was cooperating with the authorities. Justice LeSage interjected that the recent interview with the police that had provided a chance at having her charge substantially reduced had acted as "a very real carrot."

Manishen argued that his client, even after becoming aware that her boyfriend and his best friend wanted to kill someone, didn't believe they actually could or would do it.

"This crime is so shocking in its brutality...that it is not unreasonable for Miss Chisamore to believe they would not be capable of carrying it out. My submission is that Miss Chisamore never believed they would do what they did."

He said the judge's sentence should not, and could not, ever make her forget what had happened.

"She was a high-school student, and an ordinary, normal teenager," he said. "She will think every day how she would have done differently."

He asked the judge to give her a suspended sentence, which would keep her from having to return to jail.

Stunt, for his part, told the judge that Cari's personal circumstances were irrelevant to what she had done, and that she had willingly stayed at the gas station, even after she had learned a serious crime was about to take place, to the point where she refused a friend's offer of a ride home.

"It became clear that this was not going to be an abduction or a car theft. This was going to be a killing. She did not leave. She did not call the police. She did not call her parents."

She went along on the ride to Toronto, and did not object to watching two movies with the killers, Stunt said. "I dare, your honour, to doubt there was one expression of remorse on the part of Miss Chisamore."

She had breakfast and went shopping with the killers while Fritch's body was still in his car. She knew the police were searching across Canada for her and her boyfriend, but still did nothing.

"There wasn't one shred of human dignity accorded Mr. Fritch. Not one."

He called her letter and her deal with the Crown self-serving. Although Canada does not make witnessing a crime and failing to stop it a crime in itself, it is still repugnant to most people, he said. Cari, who could have influenced Jamie, let it happen.

"She, of all the people in the entire world, was in the best position to try and prevent this senseless killing. And she sat. There was nobody in a better position. Anywhere," he said, his steel-blue eyes glaring. "It is mind-boggling that this could go on. That someone could sit this close, and then travel to Toronto and watch movies and enjoy the credit card of the deceased. The reality is that Miss Chisamore, if she is as capable and bright and likely to succeed as we are told, will do so."

Cari was crying now, quietly, in the prisoner's box, as Stunt asked the judge to send her away for four to five years.

Justice LeSage took the night to prepare his remarks. The next morning, the Chisamore family and their friends gathered in a tiny courtroom on the top floor of the Milton courthouse. Justice LeSage, in his grandfatherly tone, frequently looked up from his page and over his half-glasses at Cari. He said that although Cari had been a passive participant in the crime and had received a small portion of its proceeds, she had still talked her boyfriend into turning himself in at the time of his arrest. He credited her for protesting while Steve and Jamie killed Fritch.

Cari sat quietly, and tears welled up in her eyes as the judge neared the end of his ten-minute statement. He sentenced her to one year in jail. "You have a long life ahead of you. I wish you well."

Stunt was outraged. He later pressed the Crown's provincial office in Toronto to appeal the sentence, but was refused. The young woman who had walked into court that morning with her family left from another door, as a prisoner. With Cari's sentencing complete, the stage was now set for the real trial to begin.

— Chapter 9 —
The Crown's Jewel

The whole cast returned to Brampton the next morning, with the jury, the accused, the lawyers, the families and the journalists. The informal press gallery was populated by newspaper reporters from *The Hamilton Spectator*, *The Burlington Spectator*, *The Burlington Post*, *The Globe and Mail*, *The Toronto Sun*, and *The Toronto Star*, frequently whispering among themselves. Television reporters from Hamilton's CHCH and Toronto's Global and CFTO also monitored the proceedings. Two sketch artists were allowed special seating beside the judge.

Susan Lawson, her blonde hair in a blunt cut, and her peaches-and-cream complexion reddened by the spotlight of attention, took the lectern to lay out the Crown's case.

"This is one of the most callous, senseless and brutal crimes imaginable. This crime was every family's and every community's worst nightmare. This crime was the savage and brutal murder of Mr. Joseph Fritch," she said, looking into the shocked faces of the jury as she described the terrible events of October 18, 1989. The video- and audiotapes of Steve's confessions, she told them, would leave no doubt that it was all true.

"You will have a unique opportunity to see and hear a graphic, chilling confession of Steven Olah as to how this calculated and cold-blooded murder was planned and executed."

Then Alan Cooper let the other shoe drop on Steve's refusal to enter a plea. It was not a surprise, but nonetheless, it changed the course of the trial.

"We admit, on behalf of Steven Olah, that he hit Mr. Fritch on the head with the fire extinguisher and caused his death. It's simply a question of his mental state at the time."

Steve sat, drugged, in the prisoners' box, head bowed, eyes blinking slowly, as the Crown introduced its first witness.

Constable David Banks, a veteran of Halton police's Identification Unit, responsible for collecting and recording evidence, described closing down the station and taking photos there and later at the morgue, more than 250 in all. Selected photos had since been compiled in a dossier, copies of which now went to the jury, one for each two people to share. Before the trial started, the defence lawyers had fought hard to keep the pictures out of the trial, because they were so graphic. They said the photos would unfairly prejudice the jury against their clients. In the end, the judge ruled that the photos were a necessary, although horrifying, part of the case, and allowed them to be distributed to the jury.

The jurors, two to an album, flipped through the pages of four-by-six pictures, past the long shots of the gas station, close-ups of the pried-up floor tiles and bloodstained grouting, to the murder weapon itself—innocuous-looking in an upright position, but suddenly more menacing when turned on its side to show the dents and paint chips on its underside—and worst, the detailed pictures of Joe Fritch's battered head, as his body lay face down on a steel autopsy table. The deep gouges over his ear showed the savageness of Steve's attack. If the jurors had not been disturbed by Lawson's opening address, they were certainly upset now.

Constable Banks's clinical, professional recollections of

taking the photos were lost on the jury members once they had seen the book. They could only think, as average people, of the sickness they held in their hands.

Next, the prosecution called a group of young friends and acquaintances of Steve, Jamie and Cari from school, the SuperCentre, the gas station and car wash, who recalled bits and pieces of conversations that had gone on during the days before the killing: Steve bragging that he was going to jail soon, Jamie asking about ways to kill a man, Steve saying he wanted to kill someone before he died. Separately, they had dismissed each bragging remark about getting out of town or shocking question about killing methods. It had been easy for Andrea Talarico, John Ruttan, Geoff Berendse, Bob Yates, Ed Boutillier, Marino Peric and Nick Santini to shrug it all off. Who could have believed Steve and Jamie were serious? Collectively, however, their recollections formed a damning picture of two young men bent on escape and seriously considering murder.

The testimony of the taxi driver who returned Jamie's wallet to him, the food delivery man, the attendant who opened up the gas station the next day, the hotel clerk and the clerks who sold the shoes to the killers rounded out the credibility and continuity of the case.

The police who first interviewed Steve told how they were surprised by his manner, and later by his graphic confessions, but nothing shocked the jury as much as what they saw and heard on the audio- and videotapes.

They sat transfixed, when, four days into the trial, the Crown played the audiotape of Steve's first confession. Later, they watched in mute horror as the all-too-real drama of Steve's confession flickered on the screen. Even though the tapes had been edited to excise most references to Jamie's participation, there were still parts that couldn't be removed, either because the tapes wouldn't have made sense, or because taking out Jamie's part would also have removed important sections of Steve's own confession. (A confession cannot apply to another accused person unless the first accused person is available to be cross-examined by the other's lawyers. For this reason, Justice LeSage told the jury only to consider the tapes as evidence against Steve. As long as Steve refused to take the stand, the tapes, in law at least, were no good against Jamie.) Still, it would have been impossible to hear Steve's recollections of the crime and not believe that they all applied to Jamie, too. After all, what did Steve have to gain by implicating his friend?

Sergeant George Reynolds, the fraud detective who had originally spoken to Steve, told Cooper under cross-examination that he had felt, before he knew Steve's background or what he had done the night before, that he was talking to a young man who could not cope with life outside jail, and that Steve, whom he saw as a "nice clean-cut looking fellow," had told him, "I need help." Despite his vast experience, he admitted that Steve's comments, especially about the officer thinking about old ladies pushing shopping carts, "totally bewildered him." In other words, Reynolds had been wondering if this kid were insane. Soon afterward, though, his sympathy and confusion had been erased, and he started seeing Steve as cunning, not crazy.

To this point, Steve had never mentioned to Reynolds that he had a history of psychiatric treatment, nor that he was supposed to have been taking anti-psychotic medication. But when he finally came clean about the murder, all prior confusion was erased, Sergeant Reynolds said under final questioning by Stunt, who was obviously annoyed by Cooper's attempts to have the officer back up Steve's insanity defence.

"Mr. Olah struck me as very lucid, very much in control. He certainly struck me as a reasonably bright individual who had a grasp of what he was saying. He appeared to be very anxious to describe what had happened that evening," Reynolds said.

Sergeant John Line, a veteran of murder interviews, confirmed for the jury that Olah had also seemed "cool and calculated," totally in command of his mind during his interview with him. "He never changed. At all times during my presence, he was lucid. He appeared to be very much in control of his thoughts, his speech. That never changed."

What was a jury member supposed to think? Was Steve in control the whole time at the Metro station? Was the reference to old ladies and shopping carts just a red herring, part of Steve's games? Or was he slipping in and out of his delusional world? Cooper took a run at Line, suggesting that Steve's coolness must be an indication of his insanity.

"That's what so strange about it all. One would expect a person to go through a range of emotions when describing these things," the lawyer suggested.

"There are normal people who appear insane and insane people who appear normal," the officer responded. "I'm not an expert on whether a man's insane or not."

"But you have seen it before," Cooper continued. "With all of these gruesome details about family photos, crushing this man's skull, certainly you'd expect him to show some emotion."

"There are people who can do that."

What about Steve emphatically refusing to contact a lawyer, saying, "Christ, no, I want to go to jail for twenty-five years"?

"Did you ever hear anyone say that before?" Cooper asked the officer.

"It's very, very unusual."

"He was offering everything to you on a platter, wasn't he?"

"Yes. He was very cooperative."

And, if this person were strictly a psychopath, Cooper continued, why would he go out of his way to clear Cari of any part in the killing? If he was supposed to be without morals and conscience, why would he be working to protect a friend?

Stunt got one last opportunity to discredit Cooper's attempts to have Line diagnose a killer's mental state.

"I've seen people at both ends," the officer said. "I've seen literally raving maniacs obviously out of touch, and on the other hand I've seen people who in my opinion had all their faculties and could describe something without remorse. I can't judge about mental illness."

Next, Stunt turned to proving Jamie's guilt. Eric Crocker of the Centre of Forensic Sciences in Toronto connected trace fibres from the seats of Fritch's car with the clothes Jamie and Cari were still wearing or carrying when they were arrested. Even more damning, the running shoes Jamie had left behind at the Florsheim shop were clearly stained with Fritch's blood, and later proved to have been carrying fibres which had rubbed off from the victim's pants during the struggle.

Raymond Higaki, a specialist in bloodstains from the CFS, said the reddish brown smears on Ruston's runners and those on Olah's pants and shirt had been formed in patterns that would come from a beating.

Although this evidence had logically linked Jamie to the murder, it still needed buttressing. The blood only matched Fritch's *type*, and could not absolutely be called his. And Olah's confession was, in theory at least, not supposed to apply to Jamie. In order to seal the case, Stunt needed one other corroborating eyewitness to say Jamie had deliberately planned and carried out the killing of Joe Fritch every bit as much as Steve had.

That was Cari-Lee Chisamore, who was summoned from jail and put in the stand to testify against her old boyfriend and his best friend.

The Cari-Lee Chisamore who was led into the courtroom was much changed from the one who had left the sentencing hearing in Milton just a few days earlier. She was now in the drab clothes she wore at the Vanier Centre for Women in Brampton. Her face was scrubbed clean of all make-up, and her hair was pulled back in a girlish ponytail. Cari's face was drawn as she swore on the Bible to tell the truth. After three and a half hours of testimony, during which she had gone over virtually every line of her fourteen-page statement to Halton police, she had made it clear that Jamie had discussed killing someone well before Fritch had arrived.

She was calm and rational as Stunt led her through questions about the days and hours before the killing. She had been able to provide incriminating answers to questions about Steve and Jamie without any problem, even though they were sitting watching her from the prisoners' dock, where she might have been sitting, too. Instead, they were watching her seal their fates. But now, as Stunt worked up to the terrible moments of the killing itself, she was overcome and started to cry.

"Did you try to leave?"

"No."

"Did you pick up the fire extinguisher?"

"No."

"Did you take part in the killing?"

"No."

"Did you ever move from your seat?"

"No."

"How fast were things moving, in your understanding?"

"Very fast."

"Did you take any steps to try and stop it?"

"No. I did not."

"How did it sound?"

"It sounded terrible."

"Was there a struggle?"

"I don't believe so, no. I just saw one hit."

"What part of his body was hit?"

"His head."

"How hard?"

"Very hard."

She said she listened to Steve hit Fritch ten to twenty times before she heard him fall to the floor, where the beating continued.

"I was trying to tell them to stop."

"Did that seem to have any effect on them?"

"No."

"What was being said?"

"To keep hitting him again, because he wasn't dead yet."

"Who said that?"

"Jamie."

Without knowing it, she had just said the one word that would prove Jamie's guilt more than any other. Until now, his only hope had been to prove that Steve killed Fritch on his own, by going beyond their plan for a robbery and abduction. But now Jamie's former girlfriend had just told the jury, by quoting his own words, that both of them had meant for it to be a killing all along.

That night, she said, she knew that Steve and Jamie would not stop until they had stolen a car. She knew they could and would go through with it. She had seen Jamie cross off the last item—kill a man—from a list of things to do and pitch it in the garbage. She had seen them move the weapon into place and saw them act far more aggressively and hyperactively than ever. She knew they were going to knock out their victim with a large, heavy weapon. Still, she said, she did not believe they would actually kill someone.

"I couldn't believe it. It's not something your friends do," she said.

Alan Cooper now took over questioning Cari, in the hope of discrediting her damning statement and answers to Stunt's questions.

He reminded the court that there was still $100,000 in bail guarantees outstanding on her, and that the matter of her parents getting it back was not to be resolved until after the trial—a tacit suggestion that the money may have been the motivation for her sudden cooperation.

"You'd like your parents to get that money back, wouldn't you?"

"Of course."

Although she had just ruined Jamie's last chance of beating the first-degree murder charge, she seemed quick to agree with Cooper's theory that Steve was insane, both when he killed Fritch and at other times.

"You thought Steven Olah was crazy."

"Yes, I did."

"You thought he had a severe, severe mental disorder?"

"Yes."

"You thought he was crazy in a big way?"

"Yes," she said. "I always related Steve with drugs, and whenever he was on drugs, he was crazy. Without drugs, it could vary. He could be a very understanding person or not."

"Like a Jekyll and Hyde?"

"Kind of. Yes."

After twenty minutes with Cari, Cooper handed her over to Bill Trudell, who tried to find a way to salvage Jamie's case.

"Because you thought Steve Olah was crazy, you didn't like Jamie hanging around him, did you?"

"No."

She had seemed so sure of the planning, and of Jamie's orders to keep hitting Fritch until he was dead, that there wasn't much he could ask her, beyond how she had felt since the killing.

"I know that for everyone in this courtroom, this is really a nightmare," he began. "You must have gone through horrible feelings."

By now, she was crying again, and pulling tissues from the box the court clerk had placed on the witness stand for her.

"It's been a nightmare since it started, hasn't it?"

"Yes it has," she said, sniffling.

She agreed when he suggested to the court that she had suffered nightmares of the beating happening over and over again.

Finally, in the mix of memories and watching her recall the terrible consequences of the murder he had committed, Jamie himself began to cry in the prisoners' box, the first time during his murder trial that he had shown any identifiable emotion.

Trudell walked over to the witness stand and pulled a tissue from Cari's box and took it over to her old boyfriend to wipe his tears.

Court recessed for the lunch break.

After lunch, when both Cari and Jamie had calmed down, Trudell had her agree that her memory of events after the murder was clouded partially by her attempt to block it all out of her mind. She admitted she hadn't actually read the list of things to do that Jamie had thrown out. She agreed she had been panicky and hysterical inside the kiosk while Steve and Jamie were murdering a man. Despite Trudell's brilliant questioning and timing, she confirmed that she definitely heard Jamie say, "Hit him again, he's not dead yet."

Now, the case seemed so certain that apart from having him confirm the videotape statement and give details about how it had been made, there was not much that Paul Stunt needed to ask the next witness, Sergeant Jim Chapman. Everything seemed very straightforward, according to his testimony.

But tension ran high in the courtroom as Alan Cooper asked Chapman about Steve's mental state throughout their time together. Cooper tried to get the officer to agree that Steve's behaviour and statements were far out of the ordinary, especially for an eighteen-year-old who had just been arrested for murder. But every time Cooper tried to pull out an answer, Chapman dug in deeper. Cooper recalled part of the conversation between Steve and Chapman in the cruiser on the way back from the Toronto police station: "What's life now, twenty years?" Steve had asked.

"To be honest, I don't know. First-degree is twenty-five years, but that varies with parole," Chapman had replied.

Cooper now turned to the officer in the stand, and asked: "Do you get the impression the man *wanted* to go to jail?"

But he didn't get the answer he expected or wanted.

"Not particularly, no."

Next, Cooper recalled Steve having told the officer of his plan to bury Fritch's body "in a shallow grave by the Lake of the Woods."

"Isn't that too poetic?" the lawyer asked.

"I think he used it because that's what he was going to do with Mr. Fritch."

Chapman wasn't giving an inch.

Cooper mentioned Steve's telling Chapman in the cruiser that he was supposed to be on tranquillizers, and that he wished he had been committed to psychiatric hospital when he had asked to be, so the murder would never have happened.

"Weren't you concerned about that?" the lawyer tried again.

"Not in the back seat of the car. No."

Chapman was clearly stonewalling him.

What about Steve's flat responses during the one-hour interview, where he had described, in full detail, every aspect of the grisly killing?

"He showed normal emotions throughout the videotape," the officer said.

"I suggest that there's not a bit of emotion," the lawyer argued.

"I disagree with you."

Cooper remained as genteel as ever, but was clearly growing frustrated with Chapman's curt responses and unwillingness to go along with his suggestions.

"Sergeant Chapman, I know you're very keen on your case, but wouldn't you agree that these kids were just planning an abduction?"

"I do not agree."

"You just do not want to budge from your position, do you?"

"I do not agree," was all the response Chapman was willing to give.

After a few more abortive attempts to raise a response

from the officer, Cooper finally sat down, clearly exasperated by the exchange.

After watching Cooper's frustration, Trudell had no questions, and Stunt rose in front of the jury.

"That's the case for the Crown, your honour. We're a week ahead of schedule."

— Chapter 10 —
The Voice Said "Kill! Kill! Kill!"

Now began the uphill battle of the defence. It was clear, based on the physical evidence and admissions of the two young men, that they had killed Fritch. That was the easy part to see.

The job ahead for these boys' lawyers was to prove that it wasn't their fault. Cooper and LaFleur enjoyed the most material from which to draw. They had already got it across to the jury that Steve was to have been on anti-psychotic medication for a serious incident prior to the killing. They had already presented his diary, with its references to another force in Steve's mind that seemed beyond his control. Cari Chisamore had confirmed she had always thought Steve was crazy, and that he had been acting even more so on the night of the killing.

Of course, Cooper and LaFleur were operating within quite a narrow framework for proving their client was not responsible for his actions. They had to show not only that Steve was crazy, but also that he was crazy at precisely the moment he killed Fritch, and that his craziness was so overpowering that it had overcome his obviously strong and intelligent personality. They were hampered by conversations with friends that showed he had thought about killing someone.

There was less material available for building Jamie's defence. Here was a young man who had obviously used his job to find a victim to rob. There was no evidence to suggest he had been forced by uncontrollable demons to kill. All his lawyers had to work with was the thin premise that he had not meant for this to turn out as a murder, only a robbery and possibly a kidnapping.

Since his own girlfriend of the time had just finished saying she heard him yell at Steve to hit Fritch again because he wasn't dead yet, and Steve's taped confessions had already implicated him, there was only Jamie's own word about what the plan had been that night, and of course, out of self-interest, he would deny planning the killing in the hope of getting some reduced conviction—anything less than first-degree murder and a life sentence.

Before the defence was to have its turn with the jury, Trudell and Leiper asked Justice LeSage to throw out the possibility of finding Jamie guilty of first-degree murder. There had been, they said, no direct evidence of planning and deliberation on his part. Under law, Steve's statements were not admissible against Jamie, and even Cari's adoption of them did not render them direct evidence of Jamie planning a murder. As far as Jamie's comments about putting somebody in the trunk of one of the nice cars at the gas station were concerned, they did not necessarily apply to murder. Leiper also said that Cari had only *assumed* that Jamie had had a list of things to do, that she had never actually seen such a list and none was ever found.

Nonetheless, the judge rejected the request and ordered the trial to continue according to the original indictment, since there had certainly been at least enough evidence of planning and deliberation to keep the trial going.

The next morning, the jury sat down to hear the first of the opening statements for the defence. Alan Cooper, tall, square-jawed and lanky, and wearing dark-rimmed glasses, rose with the dignified air of a church deacon, to tell the jury about Steve Olah. He stood in studied casualness by the jury box.

"The first day of the defence happens to be Friday the 13th, but I hope you aren't superstitious, because we are not," he said with a slight smile.

If he had meant the icebreaker to get the jury to lighten up, it didn't seem to have worked. This was one of the toughest juries he had ever stared down: they stared right back. He jumped directly to the heart of the matter. He wanted the jury to believe Steve had taken his parents at knifepoint to the hospital to get help for a mental problem that was already out of control, and still he was released. He promised to bring in some of Canada's foremost psychiatrists to prove Steve was out of his mind when he killed Fritch.

"They have examined him. They have determined that he's suffering from a recognized mental disorder: paranoid schizophrenia. That's a psychosis: a break with reality," Cooper said. "He was insane at the time Joseph Fritch was killed."

This was the first time that Steve's insanity defence had been so plainly spelled out for the jurors, although it had been clear by Cooper's questions during the Crown's case that that's where he had been planning to take his defence. He promised to bring Frank and Beth Olah to the stand, in order to make the jury understand what Steve had been like as a boy.

"You'll find them to be decent people who suffered greatly through this, like a lot of other people suffered."

Cooper finished his address by telling the jury that something had failed along the way, making Steve as much a victim as a killer.

"He wasn't accurately diagnosed on August third and fourth, and if he had been, we might not all be here today."

That was the nub of the Steve's defence: that he was a psychotic as well as a psychopath. To the layperson, both are disorders capable of rendering a person mentally unstable; both can make a person what is considered crazy. But to the courts and mental health professionals, they are from different leagues. A personality disorder—in this case psychopathy—is a serious mental problem, but it does not interfere with the mind's ability to think logically. A psychopath has no morals or conscience, but still understands the difference between right and wrong, and is able to control his actions to conform to the law. On the other hand, a psychosis, such as paranoid schizophrenia in Steve's case, can overpower the mind's ability to think logically. A person acting under paranoid delusions is capable of acts that are beyond his control, and therefore may be judged not responsible for actions that are otherwise considered criminal. A patient who suffers from both problems is difficult to understand and potentially extremely dangerous. Cooper could easily show Steve was a psychopath, but proving he was also a schizophrenic would be much more difficult.

Cooper started his case by going back to the hospital on the night of the knife incident. He summoned Marianne Czerechowicz, a records keeper at Joseph Brant Memorial Hospital in Burlington, where Steve had originally forced his parents to drive him.

Clearly uncomfortable with the idea of reading from confidential medical notes in open court, the health-records technician nonetheless was obliged to go through the records left by emergency room physician Dr. Kevin Batten, and nurses Barbara Dallariva and Joanna Greco.

The doctor's notes said Steve had arrived with a knife to

his father's belly and his arm around his mother's neck, demanding a straitjacket and becoming abusive to staff when he didn't get it right away. "*Initial diagnosis: hostile patient.*"

The records detailed Steve frantically smashing at the window of the emergency-room waiting area, while his father screamed for him to give up the knife. The hospital staff recorded their attempts to bargain with him and trade the knife for the straitjacket he wanted.

Steve had responded only with more threats, saying if they didn't cooperate, "he would smash the bottle over his mother's head."

The nurses' notes end with Steve being taken away by Halton police to St. Joseph's Hospital in Hamilton, and an uncharacteristic editorial comment: "Thank God!!!"

When Cooper next called Czerechowicz's counterpart from St. Joseph's, he expected and met the same resistance to reading out from confidential medical records: after all, it was a matter of professional conduct, whether in a court of law or not. But when Valerie Fitzell finally opened the file she had brought from the Hamilton hospital, Cooper and LaFleur made an exciting discovery, something they hadn't known was in Steve's records. It was the Mental Health Act Form 1 in his name, showing that a physician had believed Steve so mentally unstable and potentially dangerous that night that he had been held for psychiatric observation. Obviously, that physician had been overruled, but the existence of the Form 1 opened the door a good crack further on the possibility that he had in fact been misdiagnosed.

The form had been completed by emergency-room physician Dr. Kevin Dwyer, who had noted that Steve fulfilled every criteria for restraint: he was a threat to himself and to everyone around him, behaving in a "bizarre" fashion, and claiming to be hallucinating. There was evidence, in the doctor's opinion, of problems between Steve and his parents, with school, and recent criminal charges over the smoke shop break-in. He ordered that Steve be held in a medically safe and secure environment at the hospital at least until he could be detoxified and assessed "over a period of time."

Every single box that was open to the doctor to fill in his justification for issuing the order had been checked off.

"I am of the opinion that the said person is suffering from a mental disorder."

The notes from St. Joseph's described Steve as restless, abusive, alert, angry, aggressive and, apparently, intoxicated. They described his surprising escape from leather restraints, and his placement in the secure, barren room. A brief, cryptic note suggested a conversation between overnight emergency room staff and police who came to secure him in leg irons and handcuffs, about the "politics" of police and the Mental Health Act. By 4 a.m., Steve was still described as "loud, obnoxious and vulgar."

The subsequent report from psychiatrist Dr. John Deadman, written several hours later, when Steve had calmed down considerably, noted his criminal history and his long-time abuse of drugs and alcohol: "Two weeks ago, apparently told sister he had heard voices after using drugs," said one note.

There was no indication, according to Dr. Deadman's notes, of Steve ever having a desire to kill himself or others, and he seemed to be free of family problems and abnormal thought processes.

The report rescinded the Form 1 by concluding that Steve should be "dealt with through the legal system," since he was suffering from "substance abuse and conduct disorder."

Cooper called Dr. Emil Zamora to the stand, a forensic psychiatrist from Stoney Creek, adjacent to Hamilton. The doctor's qualifications included affiliations with McMaster University Medical School, the Hamilton Psychiatric Hospital, Chedoke-McMaster Hospitals and St. Joseph's Hospital, all in Hamilton. He estimated he had testified between seventy-five and one hundred times on the insanity issue, for both the defence and the prosecution.

The doctor testified that because of a tremendous shortage of psychiatric beds, there would have been pressure to examine Steve as quickly as possible once he had dried out.

Dr. Zamora said he had seen Steve's diary only after diagnosing him as a paranoid schizophrenic, but said it only substantiated that diagnosis.

"It gives further evidence of someone within himself, someone different than himself, that he refers to as 'it,'" Dr. Zamora said. The diary showed a clear progression as "it" took over Steve's mind, he said.

The symptoms of schizophrenia, he said, include a blunting of feelings and the development of a numbness toward others, as Steve had described in the final passages, where he said he didn't feel close to anyone, including his family and best friends, not even his soul mate, Jamie.

In addition, he said, Steve is clearly an antisocial personality, otherwise known as a psychopath or sociopath. Of the classic acute symptoms of paranoid schizophrenia, Dr. Zamora said, one of the chief is delusions, either heard or seen or both, where the patient focuses on and overvalues a certain idea. There is often a kernel of truth that has been layered over many times with delusions, he said.

The difference between Steve's psychosis—paranoid schizophrenia—and his personality disorder—psychopathy—he said, is that personality disorders do not generally make people kill. He said the Halton police video of Steve's confession was most striking to him because of the flatness with which Steve delivered his confession, including all the details of the killing, clean-up and escape.

"He certainly was not upset about it," the doctor said. "He showed no remorse about it."

That could be the sign of an antisocial personality, a psychotic or both, he said. Steve's answers on the same personality inventory that had earlier shown Jamie's emotional disorder revealed a "very bizarre scatter" of responses that meant one of two things: he was faking his answers in a bid for attention, or his thoughts were so truly fragmented and distorted that he was beyond conventional classifications.

A CAT scan and an electroencephalogram showed no signs of abnormal brain activity or brain damage, but the doctor said he would have far preferred to do a magnetic resonance imaging test, a more comprehensive procedure that could have shown if the insulation of the brain's transmitters had been lost, causing abnormal thought processes.

Dr. Zamora said Beth Olah's difficulties during her pregnancy with Steve could have caused him permanent brain damage. Further contributors to his current mental state could have been his heavy drug use over at least the past five years and a habit of banging his head on walls as a teenager and holding his breath until he fainted. Dr. Zamora had first seen Steve four weeks after the murder, and had visited him six times, the last visit as recently as two weeks before the court date.

In addition to interviewing Frank and Beth, he said, he had spoken with Steve's family doctor, J.G. Wakefield; his child psychiatrist, Paul Denew; and the staff psychiatrist at the Barton Street jail, Dr. Guyon Mersereau. Dr. Mersereau had prescribed heavy doses of two powerful antipsychotic drugs for Steve: chlorpromazine and Stelazine.

When Dr. Zamora had asked that Steve be taken off his medication for a short period to do a "clean" assessment of him, Dr. Zamora said Dr. Mersereau had urged caution, telling him Steve was "extremely dangerous, one of the most dangerous patients he had encountered."

Steve had described his younger sister as a "self-centred little bitch," but Dr. Zamora said all other evidence pointed to the contrary, especially her volunteer work with mentally challenged youngsters. But Steve's description had not surprised Dr. Zamora, who said there was a general lack of affection within the family.

"There wasn't a lot of warmth," the doctor said. "There wasn't a lot of intimacy."

Steve, he said, seemed to be most angry with his father, for having failed to live up to his potential. Steve felt his dad should have achieved a higher status in the world, and had embarrassed him. At the same time, Steve resented the pressure from his family to do well in school.

"He was an obsessive child in an obsessive family," he said, reinforcing Steve's perception.

His interviews with Steve showed that from as early as Grades Four and Five, he felt others were conspiring to keep him from power, since he was smarter than everyone else. And indeed he was smarter than most, testing in the top percentile in an intelligence test administered after he had set fire to the closet.

At the Barton Street jail, Steve referred to "him," instead of "it," but the hallucinations seemed to have consistency, Dr. Zamora said. Throughout his period without medication, Steve's hallucinations became stronger when he was fearful, weak or angry, like a "devil's voice," he said. Sometimes the voice would be seductively kind, and at other times it would be menacing. It was often accompanied by screams, banging, rhythmic drumming and the sound of nails dragged across a chalkboard. Sometimes the voice made him feel unusually powerful, including one time when he felt that he had the power to drive a car from the back seat, the doctor said.

"Much of his fantasy life involves violence, killing and murder," Dr. Zamora said, and most of Steve's fantasy victims are men.

One of Steve's most prevalent fantasies was ruling the world, like Adolf Hitler, only in a kinder fashion. He honestly believed this was his destiny, and that everyone around him, especially teachers and doctors, was conspiring to keep him from his rightful position. In a world run by Steve Olah, prostitution, gambling and drugs would be legalized as a quick and efficient way to erase the national debt.

Among all the interviews, Dr. Zamora said, these were the only times when Steve would brighten from his stonefaced stare. "He definitely has had murder, mayhem and violence in his mind for years," the doctor said.

Steve had made other bizarre statements in the interviews before the trial. Once, he told the doctor he wanted to go to California and live in a redwood tree. He said he would go blind from time to time, and experience strong musky smells and tastes. He felt the jailhouse public-address system was calling to him by using the number 521 to refer to him. He said he recognized he was mentally unstable and would have to spend very long periods in jail or mental hospital to keep him from hurting other people. The psychiatrist believed him and said that in his professional opinion, the voice had taken over Steve's mind and changed him from a robber into a killer.

"With the first hit, the voice said, 'Kill! Kill! Kill!'"

Dr. Zamora said. "At this point, he was simply losing control and wanted to stop the noises coming out of the body.

"He, in fact, lost control. He was controlled by the voice and in fact, had to silence this piece of meat."

Dr. Zamora carefully spelled out for the jury the details of the Criminal Code's version of the McNaughten rule, from an 1843 English case. Daniel McNaughten claimed he had been commanded by God to kill Prime Minister Robert Peel and mistakenly killed Peel's secretary. The English court ruled that a defendant is not legally responsible for his actions if he is suffering from a "disease of the mind" that makes him incapable of knowing what he is doing or knowing that it is wrong. Canada's version, Section 16 of the Criminal Code, says the defendant must be incapable of "appreciating" the nature and quality of his actions, or knowing that they are wrong.

"In my opinion, I do not feel that he knew what he was doing. He was quieting a piece of meat."

Less than a month before the trial started, Steve had claimed the same voices had returned, so his medication was increased.

But then it was Stunt's turn to question Dr. Zamora. Eager for a conviction, he knew that his biggest obstacles to putting Steve in jail for life would be the defence psychiatrists.

Stunt started off angrily, inviting the doctor to stop using the term "piece of meat."

"I'm sure that there will be people who will be offended by that, including Mrs. Fritch," he said.

Dr. Zamora had to agree with Stunt that Steve was a self-centred psychopath, bright enough to realize that whatever answers he had given to the doctor would one day end up in front of a jury: "He definitely is capable of manipulating the results."

He could easily have faked the answers on the personality inventory test to make himself appear crazy. Yes, the doctor admitted, a thirty- or sixty-day assessment at a mental-health centre could more easily have separated manipulation from true hallucination than his series of short-term visits.

"A plan is devised, a weapon is selected, a class of person is selected, and it was executed, perfectly. That's in control, isn't it?" Stunt asked sarcastically.

"That's planned," the doctor admitted.

Stunt went on. Steve and Jamie were able to plan the cleaning of the station, while Olah was thinking clearly enough to move the car out of sight behind the station. They were able to buy expensive clothes, and Steve was able to play cat and mouse with the police, wasn't he?

"All of these are clear examples of his psychopathy," Dr. Zamora answered. Steve was able to use his brilliant mind to escape detection and protect himself, which is one of a psychopath's main goals.

"Knowing, remembering it and recalling it, right down to the sausages and eggs he had for breakfast?"

"He didn't care," the doctor said.

"He is quite clearly a dangerous psychopath," Stunt said.

"He is quite dangerous," the doctor agreed. "But he is more than a psychopath."

Laughing as he dumped the body in the trunk is a telling match-up of the frightening capabilities of a psychopath and schizophrenic, the doctor said. Steve was able not to care about the body he was dumping in the trunk, and the schizophrenia caused an inappropriate reaction, so he laughed.

Stunt had one more set of questions for the doctor before he sat down. On this one, they would finally find some agreement.

"We have here an accused who is capable of inhuman brutality. Would you agree?"

"I would totally agree. Yes."

"He is, therefore, I would suggest, a very, very dangerous individual."

"On that, sir, I would not disagree with you at all."

Next, Cooper returned to the lectern to question Dr. Basil Orchard, recognized as one of the country's top courtroom psychiatrists, the author of several books and scientific articles, a staffer at the Clarke Institute of Psychiatry in Toronto for nineteen years, and, at the time, acting chief of psychiatry at Credit Valley Hospital in Mississauga. Among more than three hundred murder cases that had brought him to court as an expert was serial murderer Clifford Olson's.

Dr. Orchard said it would have been better after Steve's attack on his parents to have sent him for a full psychiatric assessment than to jail. At the time he was interviewed at St. Joseph's, he would still have been partially drunk from the Southern Comfort, he said.

But, given the lack of secure facilities at most hospitals to deal properly with potentially dangerous mental patients, most doctors exercise their choice to send those patients to jail instead. Only with great reluctance will a doctor send an extremely dangerous patient to the Queen Street Mental Health Centre in Toronto or to Penetanguishene. The process starts with a Mental Health Act Form 1, like the one Dr. Dwyer had completed, but which Dr. Deadman had cancelled. Only about one in forty patients committed for mental treatment is placed in a facility against his will, Dr. Zamora said.

"Most of us don't write those very easily," he said. "That's a pretty extreme measure to take."

Steve's diary shows very clearly, he said, the degeneration of his mind, starting with his reference to "it," telling "it" to shut up, sensing his own frustration and resentment giving "it" power, and finally fighting against the force that was trying to control him.

"It would tell me he is already experiencing, at that point, the kind of distress, the thinking and feeling associated with schizophrenia. It's a major mental illness with loss of contact with reality. A person can't tell what's real and what isn't."

Most often the type of schizophrenia experienced by Steve begins to present itself in people in their late teens and early twenties, he said. Cooper asked him if he had any doubt that Steve was a paranoid schizophrenic: "No. None whatsoever."

Part of the make-up of someone suffering paranoid delusions such as Steve's, he said, is a flatness of emotion where one would expect to see strong reactions, and strong reactions where one would expect none.

A step-by-step plan to rob someone, threaten him, and finally to knock him out could easily and suddenly change very drastically in the mind of a schizophrenic, he said. Plotting a robbery would create significant stress in the mind of the criminal, and the strain could take him over the edge and beyond the control of his own mind, even though he might appear to be in control.

"When someone feels they're fighting for control of their mind and actions, there's going to be periods when they are very flat," the doctor said. The emotions disappear from the surface because the person's energy is all focused inward, on the battle within himself. Any other outside influence on the mind can make all of these symptoms worse, he said, identifying alcohol and drugs as particularly dangerous.

Cooper asked if the hashish Steve and Jamie had smoked could have pushed him into delusional thinking.

"An amount that would hardly affect a normal person can make a person like this very ill," he answered. "A toke off a joint, that is no harm to anybody, can make them desperately ill. Small quantities will do much more to them than large quantities will do to a normal person."

Furthermore, he said, the most common reason for any of his schizophrenic patients suffering relapses is their decision to stop taking their medication, as Steve had done in the days before the murder. Over the course of his visits with Steve, he said, he noted that the progressively stronger doses of anti-psychotic medications he was receiving were having a very positive effect. During those visits, first in April 1990, and then just before the trial, he said Steve showed no remorse or horror at what he had done, but that at the same time, he seemed to have strong reactions to unusual provocations.

Dr. Orchard's conclusions about Steve, however, were slightly different than Dr. Zamora's. He said he felt Steve could be suffering from "pseudo-psychopathic schizophrenia," meaning he is primarily a schizophrenic whose illness gives him some of the symptoms of psychopathy. He was saying that along with delusional thinking, Steve loses emotions and caring about others. Under treatment, such patients can enjoy a return of spontaneous, appropriate emotions, he said.

Regardless of how his psychopathy and schizophrenia are linked, the doctor said, Steve is a very dangerous person. And like others with his illness, he tends to reverse reality, feeling everyone else is sick, and he is well. During the police interview in Toronto, Steve's comment about the officer thinking about old ladies and shopping carts shows how much he was caught up in his own importance, the doctor said. The comment, contrary to Stunt's assertion that it was contrived to feign insanity, was quite the opposite, Dr. Zamora said.

"It's an illogical thought, not connected to any previous conversation," he said. "That's very common, that people feel thoughts have been inserted into their minds. He was getting a lot of attention, being centred out, and he would tend, under those circumstances, to be very expansive."

Steve's bizarre results on the personality test, he said, appeared to be genuine. "There's no doubt in my mind that he's got schizophrenia of the paranoid type."

From his study of the murder, he concluded there had been a psychotic "flavour" to the whole crime. The vague need Steve had expressed to get away from Burlington and the people he felt were controlling him there was not surprising, the doctor said, and could easily have been the symptom of his ongoing paranoia, and the motor that drove the Big Job.

"I think that flavoured the whole thing from the first, took away the feelings that one would have about whether this was an appropriate thing to do," he said.

When a schizophrenic feels he is losing control, he can become very impulsive and try several different ways to regain control. He said families and communities are often scared of all schizophrenics, even though the vast majority are not dangerous.

The illness itself is characterized by bursts, as opposed to a constant state, as is commonly believed. Steve, Dr. Orchard said, was likely in the early stages of a psychotic episode before the killing, but it bubbled over and took control once he began beating Fritch.

"In my opinion, he was unable to appreciate, because of the schizophrenia, the consequences and nature of that act."

Although they had come along different routes, both Dr. Zamora and Dr. Orchard agreed that Steve was legally insane.

When Stunt took over the questioning for the prosecution, he tried to have the doctor agree that Steve's behaviour on the night at the hospital was merely the result of his drunkenness.

While Dr. Orchard agreed that Steve was drunk that night, he said the explanation for Steve's behaviour was much more complicated than that. He said he would have sent Steve from the hospital to a more secure setting as quickly as possible, admitting that he, too, would have looked on Steve as a simple drunk at the time, because the on-again, off-again nature of schizophrenic delusion makes it difficult to detect at first.

"The trouble with schizophrenia is it all of a sudden appears full," he said. "If the patient can conceal everything, it's easy to miss."

"The trouble with *psychopaths* is they know exactly what they're doing, and they re-offend," Stunt shot back, his voice sharp with sarcasm.

"Yes." The doctor had to agree.

He also had to agree that Steve's history of behaviour problems, his school difficulties, his substance abuse, criminal activity, lying and manipulation were all classic symptoms of psychopathy. Psychopaths are also generally bright, clever and insightful. Since Steve was no exception, Dr. Orchard had to keep agreeing when Stunt suggested he could easily have faked his personality test answers to make himself appear crazy.

"He has exhibited these traits. He certainly wants attention when he's disturbed. He has done very extreme things to get attention," Dr. Orchard stated.

Still, he said, although a patient such as Steve might be able to fake the results of a written test, it's another matter when it comes to faking in front of a trained specialist such as himself.

"It's very hard to do. It's hard to continue the illogic and loose associations for any length of time, for more than a few sentences, without losing it."

But Stunt wasn't buying it. He pointed to Steve's and Jamie's plan to assault and abduct someone, and later decision to kill him to make their getaway easier. The doctor admitted that it had all taken some thought, including the decision by Steve that he would do the hitting, since he was bigger and stronger than Jamie. Steve, Stunt said, planned enough to sneak out of his home to avoid getting caught. He knew enough to pick out a specific type of victim and to assign roles in the crime, and he remembered enough about it later to describe it—twice—in chillingly accurate detail.

Dr. Orchard admitted that at the time of his arrest, Steve didn't say anything about hearing voices as he had killed Fritch.

"In fact, the only voices he heard were Jamie saying, 'Hit him again, he's not dead yet,' and Cari-Lee Chisamore saying, "Stop!" Stunt said. "He did it just like he was told, not by a voice in his head, but by the voice of the guy beside him."

"Yes," the doctor admitted, surprisingly.

Stunt asked if Steve were so uncaring about others and so incapable of logical thinking, how could he deliberately have misled the police in Toronto about the location of the car, in a bid to give Jamie time to get away?

But Dr. Orchard said the bizarre thing about that whole aspect of the confession was that after lying to protect his friend, Steve had turned right around and revealed everything Jamie had done in the crime.

Dr. Orchard said that even telling the story was a symptom of Steve's sickness. Despite the sharp detail Steve had used during the confessions, they were strange. His use of police and court jargon showed he knew all the terminology of the system. That meant, too, that he knew the criminal's unwritten rules of being arrested, the first being that you never rat on your partner.

"That's a very risky thing to do. On the other hand, he did it in exquisite detail," Dr. Orchard said. "There is logic even inside delusion."

Another of the bizarre leaps between rage and tranquillity Steve had made, Dr. Orchard said, was calmly advising Cari that she would need help, just minutes after the killing.

"He knew that he was taking another man's life," Stunt said.

"Yes."

"Quite clearly."

"Yes."

"He followed a plan."

"Yes."

But the doctor insisted Steve did not appreciate the nature and consequences of what he was doing. He had been right on the balance point between criminal insanity and sanity, but edged over into the insane, he said.

Stunt's frustration with the psychiatrist's rhetoric began growing and he grew more aggressive.

"Thrill kill. Psychopaths often engage in thrill kills, don't they?"

"They may."

"You've seen it, haven't you?"

"Yes."

"That's what this was: a thrill kill. Two guys out looking for something to do," Stunt said, spitting out the words. "He blames the system. Blames his parents. Blames his sister."

"Yes."

"Everyone but Steven Olah."

"Yes."

"Here is a man in perfect contact with reality at the time he kills Joseph Fritch," Stunt said. "He described it in perfect detail."

"With remarkable detail and remarkable flatness," Dr. Orchard countered, and Stunt finally sat down.

Cooper's job, when he stood up for his final questions to Dr. Orchard, was to win back as much credibility as possible for the evidence of one of his star witnesses. The doctor told Cooper that if Steve had been simply a psychopath, he would not have made the remark about old ladies and shopping carts at the Toronto police station, and he would not have written in advance about voices in his head trying to take him over.

"A psychopath isn't ever in conflict with himself," he said plainly.

After the lunch break, it was Beth Olah's turn to take the stand in her son's defence. She told the court about Jennifer, then nineteen, a Grade Twelve student planning to go to college or university.

"She's absolutely delightful," she said, her motherly face an odd mixture of pleading and intensity, as if she were trying to make sure that her obvious sincerity was understood by everyone.

Turning to Steve, she remembered her rough pregnancy, the bleeding, the threatened spontaneous abortion, the medication, the final weeks when she was toxic, and lastly the rapid labour and more bleeding. But Steve had appeared to be normal, and although he was troublesome as a young child, she didn't consider it anything outside the acceptable range for a growing young boy.

"He was mischievous, kind of like Dennis the Menace. He was a good child."

In fact, the first time she ever had any serious concerns about Steve's behaviour was when he was eight years old, and set his bedroom closet on fire from behind the closed door.

"I was panic-stricken. I thought there was something really wrong," she said.

The whole family went for psychiatric counselling after that, and while everyone else proved to be fine, Steve got worse.

"It was always felt that he was being blamed for other people's misdemeanours, pranks and things like that," she said.

By the time Steve was seventeen, his parents' concern had grown strong again.

"We felt we needed help. We wanted to do something to help him. We didn't know what to do. We felt we couldn't handle his problems any more. We had tried and we weren't successful."

She retold the story of the night Steve used a kitchen knife to demand a bottle and a ride to the hospital.

"He looked really wild. His eyes were bulging, flaring, his hair was wild," she said. "I really feared for my life. I was terrified."

Once they had delivered Steve to the hospital, she said she and her husband felt relieved that Steve would finally get the help he needed. She supported the Form 1 detention of her son for psychiatric evaluation. "Definitely," she said. "I wanted help for him. Medical help. Psychiatric help."

When it became that apparent that even his outburst had not been enough to secure such help for his illness, she said, she and Frank agreed to make yet another effort, by trying to get Steve released from jail. That way, she said, they knew they would be able to get individual psychiatric help for their boy.

"We honestly and truly believed that the only way to get it was through medical avenues," she said. "I strongly believed that that was more appropriate than jail."

And so, they got him out, and tried, unsuccessfully, to line up more help for him. She bought Steve the diary, but she never read it until after her son had been arrested for murder.

"The things he wrote in it were strange," she said. She noticed how his handwriting had slipped as the diary went on, finally becoming hard even for her to read.

"Did you know what was going on in Steve's mind at the time?" Cooper asked.

"No."

That would have been difficult. Steve's schoolwork—two weeks behind when he entered Central High School after leaving the Barton Street jail—was caught up in just a few days. But it wasn't long before things had started going bad again, she said. On October 16, the school called to say Steven had been skipping classes. And that night he missed his 8 p.m. curfew. Given that the last time he had been out this late he had threatened to kill her and her husband, Beth called the police in the hope they would pick him up for violating his curfew. But somewhere between Cartier Crescent and the Elgin Street police station downtown, the message got mixed up, and no police were dispatched to track down the psychopathic boy.

At 11 p.m., though, Steve called home on his own, asking if his father could come and pick him up at a submarine sandwich shop not far from the gas station where he would kill Fritch the next night.

"He looked very, very dishevelled," Beth recalled. "Not at

all like Steve, who was generally well groomed. He liked to look nice."

She told the jury about Frank leaving for his business trip the next day, and the dinner Steve made for her. Things seemed to have calmed down again. But the next morning she realized they were worse than ever when she discovered that he had left home, placing a pile of clothes and a soccer ball under his covers to make it look as though he were sleeping in his bed. Her first call was to the probation office. She went to the bathroom and counted his pills. She was surprised to find he hadn't been taking his prescription.

Now it was Susan Lawson's turn to cross-examine the witness. Her style was very different from Stunt's. She was much less confrontational. Although there was more sympathy in her voice, she still cut right to the point. Beth agreed with Lawson: Steve had grown up knowing how to get his way when he wanted it.

"He was able to influence people, to get them to do the things he wanted them to do," Beth remembered. Steve's manipulation grew worse as he got older, and he began to drift into drugs, drinking and crime. The first time she had found Steve's dope-smoking tools in his room, she kicked him out of the house.

"I wanted no part of it," she said. It was quite clear that she had had her share of this uncontrollable son, although it was equally clear she still loved him in spite of everything he had done. That was why she got so angry when Lawson asked her about October 16, the night before Steve murdered Fritch. Beth had seen him in this wild state once before, when she herself was the victim and he was holding a bottle over her head. She recognized the danger when she saw it again, had tried to stop her son from doing something violent again.

"That's why I phoned the police. I wanted him to be charged," she declared. "I was concerned. I didn't know what might happen."

Cooper now called Frank Olah. Compared to his wife, Frank was much quieter, his hooded eyes darkened by the circles that come from worrying when your son is on trial for murder. Frank was more apt to recall the brighter parts of Steve's childhood and adolescence. Yes, he was a hellion, but "also excellent in sports."

"He was a charmer, even as a kid, but I wouldn't call him a manipulator, in such strong words," he said.

Frank looked sad as he remembered the struggle of sending Steve to the high-priced private school in Hamilton in an effort to make sure he would realize the potential of his intellect. And later, not wanting to create unfairness in the family, they sent Jenny there too, so she wouldn't feel like a "second-class citizen."

But after four years of debts and spending vacations at home in order to pay the tuition bills, the burden had become too much, he said, and they reached the painful decision to bring their children back to the public system.

— *Chapter 11* —
Jamie's Tears

Cooper now handed the trial over to Trudell and Leiper, who called their first and only witness: Jamie Ruston.

Jamie, still in the grey vested suit he had worn since the first day of his trial, moved from the prisoners' dock to the witness stand, quietly sat down and folded his hands.

Trudell, in his half glasses, got up from the lawyers' table and started walking toward the witness box, and spoke in fatherly tones.

"You lived with your father and stepmother, sitting here?" he asked, taking off the glasses and using them to point to Jim and Karen Stinchcombe, who faintly tried to smile back at their son.

Before he could answer yes, Jamie's face screwed up and turned bright red. He cried in deep sobs, and never fully regained his composure throughout Trudell's questioning.

Still, he managed to sketch a picture of his life just before the killing. He said he had been failing in school, because he rarely went. He was working only part-time at the gas station, and so far, his career plans consisted of working during Grade Twelve, saving his money, and going out west to work in construction with his uncle. But mostly, he agreed, he had been living just to get high on hash.

"I'd have it literally for breakfast," he said. Often, he'd smoke up again at lunch, and after school. Frequently, he'd just skip school altogether.

"Why?" Trudell asked.

"I don't know. It got me high, I guess. It made me relax, forget about problems."

Trudell asked him to describe what he felt when he got high.

"It relaxes you. You kind of see things differently. Sort of like a camera lens that's different. Sounds are different."

Jamie admitted he'd even been stealing money from the station to finance his drug habit.

"You were playing fairly fast and loose with money from the till. Is that right?" Trudell asked.

"Yes."

His plans to save up and go out west were not working out. He had spent more than he earned on drugs, and had been forced to quit his job at the gas bar. The build-up of problems and pressures that he perceived had made him want all the more badly to get away.

"I was having difficulties. I had been in trouble with the police on two occasions. I was having trouble in school. I was having trouble at home," he said, speaking more clearly now. "I decided to go to Vancouver."

He said he had spent the middle days of October thinking of ways to get out west as soon as possible. With no money, he thought the easiest way would be to steal a car, but he denied telling friends at the SuperCentre he was going to do it. He denied consulting with John Ruttan on the best way to kill a person, painting the conversation instead as a discussion of war movies.

"Did it have anything to do with your intent to go to B.C., or your plan to steal a car, or anything to do with that kiosk?" Trudell asked, trying to wipe away the Crown's case for premeditation.

"No," Jamie answered flatly.

"What was your plan?" Trudell asked.

"The same idea as the day before," Jamie said. "Stealing a car."

Trudell slowly edged his witness up to the killing itself, pushing gently but firmly against Stunt's evidence of planning.

"Did you ever say to John Ruttan or anyone else that you'd hurt someone or kill someone if you had to, to get away?"

"No."

"Did you ever intend to kill Mr. Fritch or anyone else?"

"No."

"Did you ever intend that someone else kill Mr. Fritch or anyone else?"

"No."

"What was your plan before you went to work that day?"

"Rob somebody of their car and their cash and credit cards."

Why then, Trudell asked Jamie, did he come to work with a knife in his jacket pocket?

"To rob somebody," Jamie said.

"Had you ever robbed anybody before?"

"No."

"Did you think about what you were going to do, how it was going to happen?"

"No."

Why, then, did he call Steve Olah?

"I asked him if he could get any drugs and hash, and I told him to come down, because I had a plan to rob somebody," Jamie said. "I guess I was hoping he would come down and he and I would figure something out. It developed. There really was no plan until that night." Jamie had openly contradicted

Steve's confession to police, where he said he and Jamie had in fact planned out the crime over several weeks.

"Did you ever say to Mr. Olah that you should kill someone?" Trudell asked.

"No."

"Was there any effect of narcotics on you after you had them that night?"

"Yes."

"Did you see Mr. Fritch drive in?"

"Yes," Jamie said, his breath quickening as Trudell got closer to the questions he knew were coming.

"What happened?"

"He drove up and started pumping gas. Steve went around the back of the kiosk and waited between the back of the kiosk and the automotive centre. I had a garbage bag and I took it to the customer side and I knelt down on the ground, pretending to pick up garbage.

"I suddenly thought: I don't want anybody else to see Steve hit this guy. I stood up and said [to Cari], 'That's the set of lights I want you to turn out when you see me put this bag over his head.' She said, 'Okay.'

"Mr. Fritch came into the kiosk and I stood up and put the bag on his head," Jamie paused, hyperventilating, trying to get his breath as he cried again uncontrollably. "And Cari turned out the lights and Steve came in the customer door and picked up the fire extinguisher ..." Jamie was sobbing loudly now, gasping for breath. "And he hit him. And he didn't do anything. And I said, 'Hit him again,' about three times."

"What was happening?"

"Nothing."

"Why did you say that?"

"Because he wouldn't go down. He didn't do anything."

"When Steven Olah hit him with the fire extinguisher, Jamie, what was supposed to happen?"

"He was supposed to fall down."

"Did you ever say, 'Hit him again, *he's not dead yet?*'"

"No. I said, 'Hit him again.' I never said, '*He's not dead yet.*'"

Trudell continued asking Jamie about the plan, but it was becoming more difficult for Jamie to answer. He tried one last question.

"Was he supposed to die?"

"No!" Jamie screamed out, his sobs bouncing off the high ceiling and landing on the silent observers on both sides of the room. Justice LeSage ended the day early. As the jury rose to leave the room, Jamie reached down and yanked his tie to loosen the knot around his neck.

The next morning when court resumed, the red tie was back in place and Jamie looked calmer. Trudell skipped past the murder to the escape. He asked his client how he felt when he and Cari saw their pictures on the front page of *The Toronto Sun*.

"Scared. Confused. I don't know. It's hard to believe," Jamie said.

After helping Jamie into the day's testimony with some easier questions, Trudell knew he still had to return to the murder scene. He had Jamie describe the clean-up and putting the body in the trunk.

"Were you laughing?"

"Nobody was laughing."

Jamie admitted he went through Fritch's wallet in the car on the way to Toronto.

"There was credit cards and, uh, there was a picture of his wife and his kids and that was all," he said.

He remembered getting the room at the Carlton Inn, watching movies, falling asleep and getting up the next morning to go shopping.

"And all this time Mr. Fritch's body is in the trunk of the car?" Trudell asked. It was better than letting Stunt ask. *He* wouldn't be as nice.

"Yes," Jamie answered. "It was weird. I thought about it. I don't know." He was very quiet.

Then Trudell came to the heart of the planning issue. He reminded Jamie of Steve's last diary entry, where he had said he was going to do a Big Job. Jamie, who had earlier said he had never seen the diary until the trial, also denied knowing about any plan to do a Big Job.

Furthermore, he rejected Steve's claim that the two of them had gone for many walks during the weeks before the killing, figuring how they would carry out this big job.

"Did you ever have these discussions with Steven Olah?"

"No."

"Did Mr. Olah ever tell you that he heard voices?"

"No."

"What do you think about Steven Olah now?" Trudell asked. Jamie didn't even look over at his friend.

"I don't know. Maybe the doctors are right."

Now Trudell gingerly picked up the murder weapon. The red fire extinguisher looked even larger in the hands of the small lawyer. It was still in its plastic evidence bag.

"Was it decided this fire extinguisher be used to hit Mr. Fritch?"

"Yes."

Jamie admitted he had moved the extinguisher from behind the counter to the customer area on the other side of the kiosk.

"Why did you move it?" Trudell asked.

"So that it could be used to knock out the customer," Jamie answered.

"Was that discussed?"

"Yes."

"When?"

"A couple of minutes before Mr. Fritch drove in."

"Was there any talk before that couple of minutes?"

"No," Jamie answered.

"The plan was to cover his face with the garbage bag and knock him out with the fire extinguisher."

Jamie started crying again when Trudell asked how they got the body from the kiosk to the car.

"After he was…ah…" Jamie broke down again, but tried to keep answering. "He was laying down and Steve said, 'Pull around to the kiosk and open the trunk.'"

Trudell moved farther back in time now, to the precise point where Jamie had had to be stopped the day before.

"When Mr. Olah was hitting Mr. Fritch, where were you? Where were you standing?"

"I was holding onto the bag."

"And then what happened?"

"Steve said, 'Knee him in the balls.' I tried to, but I couldn't do it. Steve kind of moved in between us and did it himself. I stepped a couple of feet back."

Jamie had now completely departed from Steve's version of events. Not only did he deny planning a killing and urging Steve to keep going until the victim was dead, but he also tried to remove himself from any participation in the act beyond holding the plastic bag during the first series of blows.

"What did you think would happen if someone were hit with this?" Trudell asked, indicating the fire extinguisher again.

"I thought they would fall down, unconscious," Jamie said.

Next, he denied having the list of things to do, which Cari had described him throwing away after he crossed off the last item: kill a man.

"I didn't have a list," he said.

Then, he denied ever having a conversation with Steve about it being easier to kill their victim than to go to the trouble and risk of letting him live.

"Did that conversation ever take place?"

"No."

Finally, at the end of the morning, Trudell came to the last of his questions.

"Do you know why Mr. Fritch is dead?"

"No. I don't"

"Is there anything else you'd like to say?"

Jamie's mind was already past Trudell's question. He cried and wiped his face one last time before the real test: Paul Stunt.

The air was heavy in the room as Stunt stood straight up, despite the leg that had been throbbing throughout the trial. This was what everyone had been waiting for. Both sides were silent and transfixed.

Stunt first took Jamie through his criminal record: the convictions for the chip-truck heist and the break-in at the smoke shop. Jamie once again admitted that he had a nearly daily hashish habit, and that he also drank heavily.

The night before the killing, he was drunk and stoned when he and Steve broke into the auto dealership office. Despite his intoxication, he had still managed to get in.

"You and Steve had sat around and decided to do that?"

"Yes."

"Didn't you once say to somebody that you didn't want to work?"

"Probably, yes."

"Life was just going to be a big party, right?"

"No."

"But you thought about it."

"Sure. But it wasn't realistic."

"Where did you get the money to buy drugs?"

"From working, I guess."

"You dipped into the till pretty frequently, didn't you?"

"Yes."

"For drugs?"

"Sometimes."

Stunt turned to the night of the crime, which he described as Jamie's last opportunity to use his job to carry out his escape plan.

"You used your position at a late-night gas bar to effect a purpose?"

"Yes."

"Solely for your own gain, you and Steven Olah."

"Yes."

"Your pal, your buddy, your partner in crime."

"Yes."

He asked Jamie to recall Geoff Berendse's testimony, where Berendse described Jamie wanting to do one more big crime.

"Did you agree with that?"

"No."

"He's mistaken?"

"Yes."

Bob Yates, the car-wash attendant who said Jamie had shopped for cars among his customers, was also wrong, Jamie said.

"You certainly think a lot of people are mistaken about what they heard or saw?"

"Yes."

"But *you're* right."

"I was there. I know."

The list of denials grew longer as Jamie refuted John Ruttan's testimony about Jamie saying he was going to steal a car and hurt or kill someone if he had to.

"I would never have said I would kill someone for that purpose."

Stunt went down the list. Talarico. Santini. Boutillier. Cari. Steve. All mistaken, according to Jamie.

Jamie admitted taking a knife from home before the killing. He admitted he planned to have it later in the day, when he would meet up with Steve. He admitted he had someone call Steve to set up a meeting later at the gas station to finalize their plans for getting a car.

But he balked when Stunt suggested the knife was actually to be used as a weapon.

"At the very least, you took it to hold in somebody's face and make them drive you somewhere."

"No. I didn't know what I was going to do with it."

Jamie admitted he was aware of the order preventing Steve and him from speaking to one another, and of Steve's 8 p.m. curfew. Still, he told him over the phone that he was carrying a knife.

"So that he could think about what to do," Jamie said. "How we'd rob somebody."

He told Stunt first that Steve came down to the station with a piece of hash between a half a gram and one gram in size, and then changed it to more than a gram. Stunt pointed out that the same piece had now more than doubled in size compared to the day before, when Jamie had claimed it was less than half a gram.

"I never said that. I don't remember saying that. Did I say that?"

Justice LeSage looked in his own notes and told Jamie that he had.

Now that Jamie was off balance, Stunt worked up to full boil.

"When you killed Joseph Fritch, the two of you, you were pretty clear about what you were doing."

"I didn't know."

"You knew *he* was going to take a thirty-pound fire extinguisher and drive it into the man's head, didn't you?" Stunt was yelling now, and pointing at Steve.

"Yes."

"What was he going to do? Struggle for his life, maybe, while *he's* smashing that thing into his head? You knew that didn't you?"

"He was only supposed to hit him one time."

"Oh. Until you said, 'Hit him again.' That, and the kneeing in the groin, was the last little indignity you applied to this man? Is that what it was?"

Jamie started crying for the first time during Stunt's questioning, but the prosecutor was not willing to wait for him to stop.

"Well?" he demanded. "This guy didn't have a chance, did he, Mr. Ruston?"

"Nobody was supposed to die," Jamie protested, sobbing loudly.

"You didn't need a knife. You didn't need a plastic bag. You didn't need a fire extinguisher. You waited until you got somebody small. Didn't you?"

No answer.

"You only thought of all the things you needed for yourself. Isn't that what you did?"

Jamie cried again, and finally Stunt backed away, momentarily at least.

"Mr. Ruston, let's do it one step at a time," he said in the voice of a frustrated schoolteacher almost at the end of his patience. "You decided to pick somebody small, right?"

"Yes."

"Somebody the two of you could easily overpower."

"Yes."

"Somebody who had the things the two of you wanted."

"Yes."

Jamie continued to agree with Stunt, including the suggestion that it was an ambush.

"With the two of you guys there, and poor little Mr. Fritch, you didn't really need a fire extinguisher, did you?"

"We wanted to knock him out."

Stunt tried to get at Jamie from another direction now, questioning him on his plan to go out west.

"You could have said to your parents, 'I want to go now.'"

"I had no means of getting out there," Jamie pleaded. "I was spending all my money on drugs."

"You really had no intention of changing your lifestyle. None at all," Stunt scowled.

"Yes I did," Jamie protested. "It was to go to Vancouver and work with my uncle."

Stunt asked Jamie why he didn't get his parents to help him pay for his trip to Vancouver.

"Money is kind of tight around the house," he answered.

"You had a job."

"I was spending all my money on drugs."

"Nobody was holding a gun to your head. Or a knife. Or a fire extinguisher."

"No. They weren't."

Next, Ruston denied another statement from an earlier witness: he said he didn't tell Yates he was worried about a big scene happening. Stunt tried to punch open the hole in his credibility even further.

"A lot of people seem to be mistaken about things that were said, but you, who have the most to gain, seem to be perfectly clear," he said, rhetorically.

Ruston said that the reason he threw a bag over Fritch's head was to keep him from identifying his attackers, and maintained that the fire extinguisher was only to be used to knock Fritch out.

"There were all kinds of things in that kiosk, I suggest to you, that you could have used to knock somebody out, including your hands," Stunt said. Jamie and Steve also had the advantage of size, numbers, and most of all, surprise, Stunt said, as he walked over and picked up the fire extinguisher.

He carried it over to the witness box.

"THIS is what you decided on, isn't it?" he bellowed, dropping the heavy weapon hard on a wooden counter. The silence after the boom seemed to last minutes.

"You picked it up, and Olah said..."

But then Ruston burst into tears again.

"Had enough?" Stunt asked, before bringing the weapon right over to Jamie.

"Take it in your hand, and just show us," he taunted. "Show us what you did, just before Mr. Fritch was beaten to death. Come on, Mr. Ruston, take it."

Jamie only stared and cried, and Stunt went after him again.

"If you can decide to beat a man..."

"He wasn't supposed to get beaten!" Jamie blurted through the tears.

"Bonking him on the head is not a beating?" Stunt asked, incredulously. "A defenceless man in a plastic bag, taken by surprise by two people, doing something as simple as trying to buy gas. Isn't that a beating?"

"He was only supposed to hit him once."

"Until you said, 'Hit him again.' Three different times. How many times did he hit him?"

"I don't know."

"Lots, wasn't it?"

"Yes."

"The only words that you spoke were 'Hit him again.' Not once did you say stop, did you?"

"No, I didn't."

"If you didn't want him dead, why did you want him to hit him again?"

There was no reply.

"You were holding him while he struggled. The man fought, didn't he?"

"Yes."

"The man struggled for his life, and you said, 'Hit him again.'"

Stunt was building up steam again, hoping to crack Jamie completely.

"You didn't knee him to render him unconscious. You kneed him in the groin, Mr. Ruston, so that he could be on the ground while Mr. Olah finished him off."

"Mr. Olah told me, 'Knee him in the groin,' so I did."

Jamie had just admitted delivering the blow that forced Fritch to the ground, precisely the same thing he had denied before. Any credibility he had managed to hold on to was slipping fast.

"He struggled, didn't he?"

"Yes."

"And he fought?"

"Yes."

"But he couldn't even get his arms up from inside this

plastic garbage bag, could he? *That's* what it was for. Wasn't that what the bag was for?"

"No."

"He wasn't able to get his arms up, was he?"

"Yes, he was."

"The bag sort of stopped the blood from spattering about, didn't it?"

"I don't know."

"Just like on the tape, you dumped this man's body in the trunk, just like a bag of garbage, didn't you?"

Jamie didn't answer. Stunt had him in a tight corner.

"Then you cleaned up the kiosk, nice and clean, to clean up the evidence."

"Yes."

"I guess, in a fit of remorse, you decided to smoke a couple of more tokes."

"We smoked some more, yes."

"While you were going through the remnants of this man's life. You checked into the Carlton Inn. God, I guess *choked* by remorse, you watched *Roadhouse* and *Ghostbusters II*."

"Yes."

"While that man's lifeless body was probably still oozing with blood."

This was Stunt at his peak: sarcastic, bullying, merciless when he knew somebody was guilty and lying.

"Before you went on your little shopping spree, you went back to that car, didn't you?"

"Yes."

"To put your things away so you wouldn't have to carry them."

"Yes."

"What you wanted to think about was five-hundred-dollar leather coats, Ralph Lauren shirts, Florsheim shoes.

Is that right?"

"I didn't want to think about him."

"So that was the next best thing, right?"

"Yes."

"There was no problem leaving when Steven Olah was caught, was there?"

"No."

"There was no problem taking every step you could take to get as far away as you could to save your own skin, was there?"

"No."

"You were able to do it all, weren't you?"

"Yes."

Stunt went through the whole escape: the laundromat, the stop for supplies, never stopping to call home.

"All you were thinking about was yourself. Isn't that the case?"

"No."

"Were you thinking about Mr. Fritch or his wife, or his four children?" Stunt snorted. "Were you?"

Jamie cried again.

"I was trying not to."

"Mr. Ruston, your lawyer asked you if you knew why Mr. Fritch was killed. The only reason Mr. Fritch is dead, would you agree, is because he happened to be driving a nice car, he wasn't very big, and he looked like he could be carrying credit cards and maybe money?"

"No."

"The only reason he's dead is because you and Steven Olah killed him," Stunt said, his voice growing louder and angrier with every suggestion.

"No."

"He was beaten senseless with a fire extinguisher while

you held him to stop him from struggling."

"It wasn't supposed to happen!"

With that, Stunt slumped back into his chair, shaking his head in disgust and disbelief, while Ruston wiped away the last of his tears.

From the other end of the lawyers' table, Bill Trudell rose quietly.

"That's Jamie Ruston's explanation and that's the defence."

Chapter 12

The Jury Decides

Now the Crown got one last opportunity to refute evidence raised during the defence.

Stunt called Dr. Andrew Malcolm, the author of *A Craving for the High*, about the psychology of drug use. A specialist in brainwashing, cults, and marijuana and its derivatives, Dr. Malcolm had already testified at more than three hundred trials, and in front of Canadian and American Senate committees examining drug use. He was no stranger to this setting.

Dr. Malcolm explained that he had been forced to base his opinions of Steve's sanity strictly on reports and taped confessions, since he had been denied access to interview him. Stunt led him through a clinical definition of psychopathy. Once, a person was called morally insane. Later, one was called a sociopath, then a psychopath, and in the new correct coinage, an antisocial personality. Whatever the label, the disorder has always represented a deficit of morals and conscience.

Dr. Malcolm referred to the psychiatrists' recipe book: the *Diagnostic and Statistical Manual of Mental Disorders*, compiled by the American Psychiatric Association. This book is used universally as a guide to the mind, helping doctors put labels on sets of symptoms. According to *DSM*'s description of antisocial personality disorder, Steve fit the bill, Dr. Malcolm said.

He was equally certain that Steve was *not* suffering from paranoid schizophrenia, a much worse problem, potentially severe enough to alleviate his responsibility for the killing.

"I couldn't really see that myself," he said. "It is really important for me to do a clinical interview with someone suspected of having schizophrenia."

In fact, the only characteristic of schizophrenia which Dr. Malcolm could find in Steve was the flatness he showed during his confessions. And even that could be explained as simple psychopathy.

"I couldn't find any delusional thinking at all," he said.

In response to Dr. Orchard's diagnosis of pseudo-psychopathic schizophrenia, Dr. Malcolm said he had never even heard the term. It's not listed in *DSM*, he reminded the court.

But Dr. Malcolm did acknowledge that psychopathy, as is clear in Steve, is considered by psychiatrists to be a major mental illness, although it's in a different category than thought disorders such as manic-depressive disorder, schizophrenia, or organic problems, such as brain injury.

Dr. Malcolm said unequivocally that Steve met neither clause of Section 16's tests: that a person was insane if he could not appreciate the nature of what he was doing or know that it was wrong.

"I couldn't see any delusions at all," Dr. Malcolm said. "My impression was that he could measure and foresee the consequences of his actions."

That took care of the *either*. Now the *or*.

"It was my impression that he knew it was wrong, both legally and morally."

That was that. In this psychiatrist's view, Steve was definitely mentally ill, but not in the way that would keep him out of jail.

"He had an antisocial personality disorder. He had a mental illness in my opinion, but it's not what lawyers call insane in courtrooms," he said.

And with that, Stunt sat down again, satisfied.

But Cooper still had a shot at Dr. Malcolm.

Dr. Malcolm could not dispute the credentials of the other psychiatrists who had reached the opposite conclusion: that Steve was criminally insane when he killed Fritch. Dr. Malcolm admitted also that he had no current affiliation with any hospital or university, unlike Dr. Orchard, who was then overseeing hundreds of schizophrenic patients at Credit Valley Hospital in Mississauga. Still, he said, his total experience with schizophrenics was likely the same.

Malcolm complained he had not been allowed to interview Steve. Cooper said that was because Stunt had not forwarded the paperwork; the remark brought the Crown Attorney to his feet.

"Maybe if Mr. Cooper would like to go into the witness box," he said testily, "I've got another story."

Justice LeSage sent the jury out. They weren't to hear arguments like this. Once they were gone, Stunt told the judge his expert had twice been refused permission to see Steve, and that his sending a letter to Cooper's office was not a requirement, but only a professional courtesy.

He said the Crown's application for a thirty-day assessment of Steve's mental status had been refused, and the judge ruled that despite who sent what letters, the jury was to be made aware of that. But, Cooper complained, the Labour Day visit to the jail had been planned as a deliberate surprise to catch the defence off guard.

"I'm suggesting you've done that many times at the request of the Crown," Cooper said to Dr. Malcolm, who did not reply.

Justice LeSage called the jury back, and the questioning resumed.

Cooper asked the doctor if defence experts would have better assessments of Steve's psychiatric make-up.

"You let *them* in to see him," Malcolm replied. "Yes."

Cooper asked Malcolm to take out his copy of *DSM* and look up the definition of schizophrenic. With the book open, he agreed with the lawyer's suggestions that schizophrenics experience delusions, hallucinations, inappropriate behaviour, and appear flat. Cooper compared these symptoms to Steve's.

"He was completely detached about horrible things. He didn't even seem moved by it," Cooper suggested.

"Yes," Malcolm said.

Cooper pointed out the differences that would elevate Steve's illness from psychopathy to schizophrenia. A psychopath, he said, is an egotistical schemer who does anything to avoid detection. Steve, on the other hand, had told his friends that he wanted to go to jail, and at Joseph Brant Memorial Hospital had demanded attention in a dramatic fashion.

"Well, he was drunk," Dr. Malcolm said. "He was highly intoxicated on alcohol. Such people can say anything." Besides, he said, it's not unthinkable for psychopaths to call for help "when they find it's a little too tough steering their boat upstream."

Dr. Malcolm disputed defence expert Dr. Orchard's assertion that a small amount of hashish could have unlocked the schizophrenic fury that made Steve kill Fritch.

"I've been a student of drugs for a long time, Mr. Cooper," he said. "If he says a small quantity could have a severe effect, I would have to disagree."

Cooper tried another tack: wasn't Steve's bizarre statement

to the Toronto police evidence of delusional thinking? Why, Cooper asked, in the middle of a criminal investigation would he suddenly mention little old ladies pushing shopping carts?

"Anyone can say an off-the-wall statement, especially when a person has been playing games with police in the last few minutes," Dr. Malcolm said. "If you get delusional thinking at one time, you get it at a thousand other points in time, also."

What then, about Steve's diary, and his repeated references to "it"? Didn't the journal offer the other examples he was talking about?

Even the bizarre diary entries, Dr. Malcolm said, were not outside the range of normality. Anyone can feel there are external forces guiding aspects of his life. A full-blown thought disorder, he said, is far more global.

In absolute contradiction to Drs. Orchard and Zamora, he said there was no way that Steve was a paranoid schizophrenic, calling the possibility "so remote as to be not even worth considering."

Stunt had one more expert witness to call during his rebuttal. The fourth and final psychiatrist to take the stand was Angus McDonald, from the Clarke Institute of Psychiatry in Toronto, where he assessed people facing criminal charges. He was responsible for 85 per cent of the assessments for the institute for the criminally insane at Penetanguishene.

In his career, he had been called to the witness stand as an expert about two thousand times, more than any of the others. When he had testified in insanity cases such as this, he had testified one hundred times that the accused was insane, and only ten times that he wasn't. This would be the eleventh.

Like Dr. Malcolm, he had not had any access to Steve, and was basing his opinion solely on Steve's medical records and taped confessions to police. Of all the pieces of information he had used to put together his diagnosis, he said, the videotape was by far the most important.

"What is there that would suggest the presence of a major mental illness?" Stunt asked.

"The short answer is nothing," Dr. McDonald answered. "The impression I get from listening to that videotape is one of extreme psychopathy."

Like Dr. Malcolm, Dr. McDonald agreed that Steve had more than fulfilled the *DSM* requirements to be labelled a psychopath.

He said if Steve had also been suffering from schizophrenia, his sentences would likely have been jumbled, and his thinking delusional. There was no evidence of that on the tape, where Steve had spoken clearly and logically, he said. Where in the videotape the defence psychiatrists had seen the flatness that comes over schizophrenics who are not registering what's going on, Dr. McDonald saw instead "gross insensitivity." Instead of failing to understand what he had done and what would happen as a result, Dr. McDonald said Steve appeared to know exactly what was going on, but just didn't care.

"In the videotape, there was nothing to suggest he had schizophrenia then," he said.

Concerning the wild scores Steve had registered on the personality profile, Dr. McDonald said it was not rare for written results to contrast with personal interviews. The test results taken on their own, he said, would show that Steve was "quite psychotic." But, he said, the interviews he saw and heard showed the opposite.

All that remained before the jury would be sent to sort it

all out were the final addresses of the lawyers and instructions from the judge. This was where the lawyers on all three sides would cap off two years of work on this difficult case, trying to sell twelve laymen on the idea that they were right, by using the evidence from the last nine days as their proof.

Since Steve was named first in the indictment, Cooper would go first. He turned the lectern toward the jury box and for the last time faced the panel which would decide if Steve was a calculating, heartless killer, or a pitiable madman who had no way of controlling his actions.

"Mr. LaFleur and I have a great responsibility to Steven Olah and his family to do our best for him," he began. "But you have a greater duty."

Steve, still heavily sedated, stared blankly ahead, while Frank and Beth watched from the front row of the gallery.

"Steven Olah was raised in a good home by good parents. They did all they could to nurture him to grow up to be a good person," he said. "You might ask how this can happen. Steven Olah suffers from a mental illness over which he has no control. This is a boy who never hurt his sister, who loved his family dogs. Something changed later on."

He reminded the jurors that Steve had taken his parents hostage and forced them to drive him to hospital and demanded to be restrained because he himself sensed he was losing control over his mind.

"He begs to the people there, 'Pay attention to me! Put me in a straitjacket!'" Cooper said. "Does that sound like a drunk to you? Is that your experience seeing drunk people? Do they ask for straitjackets? That's not a drunk. That's someone who's mentally ill, crying out for help."

He reminded the jurors that Steve's mother, a nurse, was capable of recognizing the signs of mental illness, and tried to get help for her son more than two months before he killed. "His mother begged for psychiatric treatment, and this is a woman in the medical field," he said. "This man desperately needed treatment, and he still does, and only you, members of the jury, by your verdict can see that he gets it." He reminded them that a doctor had once filled out a form saying that in his mental state he was too dangerous to be free, but that the order had been revoked.

"Mr. Fritch might have been alive if someone had done something about it," Cooper said. He pointed out that his side didn't contest the majority of the Crown's case, except for the allegation that Steve was not a paranoid schizophrenic. His intent, he said, was not to diminish the impact of Fritch's death and the outrage that followed.

"We understand. How can you not understand?" he asked, pointing to the murder weapon. "When it's crashed to the desk, how can you not understand how horrible it must have been to Mr. Fritch?"

"I only hope [his survivors] know the degree of sympathy the Olah family and Jenny feel for them, and if Steve could feel it, I'm sure he would."

Cooper said Steve had started out with a conscious plan to knock out a victim with the fire extinguisher, but was driven to greater violence by the voices in his head that ordered him to kill.

"It was just to knock him out, but something went desperately, desperately wrong," he said.

Cooper called Olah "lucky" because he had recorded his own descent into madness in his journal before the killing.

"Just use your common sense," Cooper urged. "You don't need a psychiatrist to determine whether these writings were normal or abnormal.

"We're so lucky in this case that they exist, because they lend tremendous credibility to the fact that Steven Olah was a paranoid schizophrenic before the offence," he said. "This isn't something that was manufactured. This is something that shows Steven Olah's state of mind before the event."

If Steve were strictly a psychopath, Cooper said, he would have been too clever to do—and later admit—what he had done. Cooper called his actions "so half-baked, so goofy and so scrambled" that they didn't measure up to Steve's known intellect. "You don't screw up like Steven Olah screwed up in this crime," he said.

Whether or not they decided he was insane, he said, the jury could be assured that Steve would be out of society for a very long time. The difference, he said, was that as a convicted murderer, he would be locked away in jail with no guarantee of treatment. If he were locked in a mental institution, he would be treated for his problems. Either way, he would likely be free one day, and it was up to them to decide how he would come back.

"Without treatment, this man is extremely dangerous," he said. "Wouldn't you rather have a man return to society who has had psychiatric treatment?"

If the jury were to decide that Steve Olah was not insane, he challenged them to find anyone who was insane.

"You may want to hate him for what he did to Joseph Fritch, but how can you hate someone who's sick, who doesn't know what he's done?" Cooper asked.

He reminded the twelve that even Steve's parents preferred the uncertain long-term stay in an institution to a fixed term in jail, as long as he could get better.

"What a waste of a human being, this person who was once his parents' little boy," he said. "He should have a good life ahead of him: an education, a job, a family. Now it's all gone."

Cooper chose to adapt a poem from Steve's diary to close his address. He took the words from Steve's *Hello, My Name Is Love*, substituting the word fate for love.

Hello, my name is fate
For you I can sail on the wind
And soar like a dove
For you I can break all convention
Leave tradition in the past
Or hurt you
If I kiss you tonight, sweetly,
I will kill you tomorrow, surely.
Hot, humid, passionate fate, but not.
Cold and cruel and hurtful, but not.
I feed on feelings and excrete pain.
I have no feelings and feel no pain.
My morals are non-existent, and I don't discriminate.
Hello, my name is fate.

"I couldn't have written it better," Cooper said. "I ask you to do the right thing in this case. Thank you."

Cooper sat down, feeling he had done the best he could, but knowing it wasn't going to be good enough to keep Steve out of jail.

"What was tough was the jury. This was such a grim one, and you're acting for a guy who is accused of the very brutal murder of an innocent man," he said later. "You just knew they weren't buying it. They weren't smiling at all. They were serious as hell, and you could tell it wasn't going anywhere."

Before starting, Bill Trudell looked into the gallery at his own son, who had come especially to hear his closing address. Trudell said he didn't need long to address the jury:

Jamie Ruston had said it all from the witness box the day before, when, weeping uncontrollably, he had told them there was never a plan to kill Joe Fritch.

"What is so frightening about this case—and it is frightening to all of us—is that it is random. It could have been me," Trudell said. "But our job here is to look at the evidence and then decide.

"We don't act on the basis of rage. We don't act on the basis of getting even. We trust you to take these horrible facts and decide in law whether Jamie Ruston is guilty."

He asked the jury to remember that Jamie was only seventeen and "still developing" when he threw the bag over Fritch's head.

"It is horrible to try and imagine the nightmare the Fritch family must feel. It's just incomprehensible. But this community has lost two of its young people, now adults."

He wasn't asking them to excuse Jamie's behaviour, but pleaded emotionally and eloquently for them to use their power to keep other young people out of trouble. Trudell was thinking not only of Jamie, but also of his own son.

"When we walk from this courtroom when this is all over, we have to remember one thing: that is to go and grab our young people and hug them, and say, 'What is going on?' None of us knows what pain they're masking, what fear they're masking."

Jamie was under no obligation to testify in his defence, Trudell said. Instead, he chose to do it to tell the truth.

"I just ask you to look back and think about the answers he gave," he said. "It screamed, his testimony, of honesty."

He reminded the jurors that Jamie admitted taking a knife to the gas station that night, and that he admitted that he and Steve were trying to abduct Fritch, but said a murder was not what Jamie had in mind.

Jamie recognized he would go to jail, but Trudell asked the jury to believe Jamie when he said he did not mean for Fritch to die. Even though six other people had given conflicting testimony, he told the jury Jamie was the one telling the truth.

"He said it wasn't supposed to happen. No one was supposed to die. He screamed out his evidence and that's what happened here," he said. "Ladies and gentlemen, this young man was as honest as he could be with you."

Trudell finished with a quotation from John Donne:

Tears
Fruits of much grief
They are emblems of more.

The fatal fire extinguisher sat in front of the jury box as Paul Stunt began his final address. It was one week before Christmas, and he was to be the last lawyer the jury would hear before getting instructions from Justice LeSage and finally deciding if Steve and Jamie were guilty.

Stunt began his address with Jamie, scoffing at his evidence that the fire extinguisher sitting in front of them wasn't meant as a murder weapon.

"His story is riddled with implausible, hopelessly contrived falsehoods and lies," he said. "What can possibly be the result of taking that item and smashing it into his head while another person is holding him? What could be more fatal than that?"

Stunt spared no graphic detail in creating the picture of the crime for the jury, hoping to disgust and enrage them into bringing back two murder convictions. He gave a haunting description of Fritch's last moments, gasping for breath in darkness and confusion as blood flowed through his broken skull and into his airway.

"Joseph Fritch drew his last breaths. They were not easy breaths. They were choked and drowned by the blood that was rushing into his lungs."

He called Steve and Jamie two "self-centred, cowardly individuals motivated by their own greed."

"They shed no tears for Joseph Fritch. I suggest they never have, never did, and never will."

He reminded the jury that Jamie had talked to a friend about killing a man by hitting him on the head. "Is that coincidence that that's exactly how Mr. Fritch met his death?"

He said Jamie was lying when he told them that he had only meant for Fritch to be knocked unconscious.

"If, as Mr. Ruston said, there was no plan to kill that man, where is the shock? Where is the outrage at what Steven Olah had done?"

Instead, Stunt said, Jamie methodically cleaned the kiosk, picked through the dead man's wallet, checked into a hotel, watched movies, and slept serenely.

Jamie cried only because he was upset over not being able to answer Stunt's questions, not because he was sorry, the prosecutor said.

"The tears, if there were any, were certainly not for Joseph Fritch and his famly. They were for James Ruston because he now knows he is in serious, serious difficulty."

Stunt dismissed Steve's insanity defence by saying it would have been impossible for him to have planned the murder so carefully if he had been in an uncontrollable psychotic rage.

"If Olah only killed because he heard these mysterious voices, how could he think so clearly about who would do the hitting?"

And why, he wondered, if Steve were truly insane, would the defence have prevented Crown psychiatrists from examining him?

"The answer is quite simple: It's because he is a fake and a fraud."

Like Cooper and Trudell, Stunt chose a quotation to end his address. He said his, also from John Donne, was more appropriate than Trudell's, because we are all diminished by the death of Joe Fritch:

Never send to know for whom the bell tolls;
It tolls for thee.

"We ask for no compromise. We seek no middle ground. Both of these men are guilty of first-degree murder and nothing else."

The rest of the day and the first part of the next morning, Justice LeSage gave a lesson in murder and insanity.

"There's no question that Mr. Olah inflicted the wounds that caused the death of Mr. Fritch," he said. "There's equally no question that Mr. Ruston put the bag over his head and held him and said certain things."

The judge gave them three options in deciding on Jamie's guilt: first-degree murder, second-degree murder and manslaughter. A conviction for first-degree murder meant they thought Jamie planned the murder ahead of time and carried it out deliberately. Second-degree meant that he decided only at the moment that it would be a killing. Manslaughter meant they believed Jamie intended nothing more than an assault and robbery.

Justice LeSage went over with them the legal definition of insanity—that during the attack, Steve would have to have been incapable of appreciating what he was doing, its consequences or that it was wrong. The jury could also convict him of a lesser charge if they decided Steve's mental state had robbed him of the ability to plan the attack.

Above all, Justice LeSage reminded them, they were to remember that both Steve and Jamie must be presumed innocent until proven guilty beyond any reasonable doubt.

"If you have such a doubt, you must give the benefit of the doubt to the accused," he said.

Finally, the jury rose and filed out to its secret room to decide. But the action was not over. On his way out of the room, one of the jurors, a self-assured young man with a slick haircut and a dark tan, wearing plenty of gold and a fashionable sweater, looked out into the courtroom and winked deliberately at Paul Stunt.

Once the door had closed and the jury was out of earshot, Trudell jumped up to his feet.

"Juror Number Two winked at Mr. Stunt," he said.

This was not the first thing that Juror Number Two had done to alarm Trudell and the other defence lawyers. He had smiled knowingly at Stunt several times, and had often nodded in agreement during the prosecution's questioning and closing address.

"This conduct is inexcusable, and I wanted to bring it to your attention this morning," Trudell said.

But Stunt said that juror and some of the others had been unusually talkative and easygoing, much more relaxed than a usual murder jury, but not inappropriately so.

This was a highly unusual development in any case, let alone the especially charged atmosphere of a murder trial, and it seemed to take a moment for Justice LeSage to get his wind.

"Although it is a very inappropriate thing to do, I do not

feel it is grounds to relieve that person from the jury," he ruled. "Because the jury is relaxed does not mean that they don't take their role seriously."

Cooper complained that Justice LeSage had not given the jury enough room to consider a second-degree murder or manslaughter conviction for Steve. But Stunt said there was no legitimate way, given the confessions, for the jury to work its way down to a manslaughter conviction for Steve. The jury was allowed to continue deliberating; these protests were for the purpose of the record, to be recalled later, during the appeals process.

After ninety minutes, the jury asked for a copy of the Criminal Code of Canada so they could refer to the definitions of insanity and degrees of murder.

And so the wait began. The uncertainty over how long the deliberations would take added to the tension in the corridors, which resembled the opening day, when no one knew what to expect. Darkness fell, and the courthouse eventually emptied of everyone except the families, lawyers, police and reporters. Now there were more reporters than ever: this was the last day, the quick and easy big story for the out-of-town media, who could swoop in and grab the juiciest emotional highlights, the last minutes of more than two terrible years for everyone involved.

Jamie's family clustered together, quiet and anxious, fearful for their son. Steve's parents were more talkative, sharing memories of Steve as though they were in a staff lounge at break time. They were obviously concerned, but seemed to know that worrying could not help Steve now.

Finally, after eight hours of deliberation, everyone was called back into the courtroom. The bailiff anounced that the jury had reached a verdict, and the doors were sealed. Trudell gave his rival Stunt a friendly pat on the shoulder, and Steve shook hands with LaFleur, while Trudell moved over to put his hand on Jamie's back. Justice LeSage warned that anyone who created a disturbance would be ejected from the courtroom immediately.

Now the jurors filed slowly back to the seats they had occupied for more than two weeks. Many were red-eyed, and several clutched tissues.

Steve was ordered to stand as the foreman read the verdict: "Guilty as charged."

No emotion registered on his face.

Jamie stood next.

"Guilty as charged."

Together in the first row, all the parents wept quietly. Jamie sat down, only a slight look of disbelief crossing his prematurely hardened face.

Justice LeSage turned to the jury.

"It is not an easy task that you have just performed. It is apparent, just looking at you, that it's been difficult," he said. "You have been the administration of justice."

Trudell asked for Jamie's sentencing to be put off until the federal Senate had passed a bill that would limit jail terms for youths who had been raised to adult court to a ten-year maximum.

"I am totally opposed," Stunt said, rising angrily from his seat.

Justice LeSage said he would not consider the legislation, since it had not yet been ratified.

Cooper asked that Steve be sent to a mental hospital instead of to jail, even though it had never been done in the history of Canadian justice.

Instead of immediately handing down automatic life sentences, as usually happens in first-degree murder convictions, Justice LeSage agreed to hold separate sentencing hearings. He wanted to consider Trudell's request for a shorter sentence, and to think about what to do with Steve and his mental condition.

After setting the sentencing dates, Justice LeSage congratulated all the lawyers for their skill, and turned to the murderers.

"Mr. Olah, Mr. Ruston, you were adequately and superbly represented in this case. The Crown was equally adequately and superbly represented."

They were led away out of the courtroom and prepared to be taken away in the prisoner van. Their ties were taken from their necks, the belts from their pants and the laces from their shoes.

"Bullshit verdict," Jamie spat out as soon as he was out the door.

But Olah asked the obviously pleased Chapman and Barker to pass along a message for him: "Tell Mr. Stunt he did a good job."

In the hallway on the other side of the courtroom, reporters crowded around the families of the convicted murderers. Jamie's father and stepmother waited for Trudell to catch up. Clearly too devastated to say much more, they said they respected the judge and felt Jamie had had a fair trial.

But Frank Olah was as angry as he was saddened, and he wanted to say something.

"As sure as hell, he's going to kill again if he doesn't get this treatment," he said, trying to cling to another hope for the system to redeem itself. He wanted the judge to send Steve to a mental hospital instead of a jail—not so much for himself, or his son, as for the community Steve would eventually re-enter. A life sentence's twenty-five-year parole eligibility, dating from the time Steve was charged with murder, meant Steve could be out by the time he was forty-three years old. Even after a life sentence, then, he could still be freed a younger man than the one he had killed. After that long in a hostile prison atmosphere without proper treatment, Frank worried Steve would be even more dangerous than he had been on October 18, 1989.

Packing up their office, which had been crammed with documents, Stunt and Lawson were obviously relieved by the verdict, but Stunt had not lost one ounce of the intensity he had shown throughout the trial.

"For the people of Burlington and communities like it, it certainly is a sign that this kind of behaviour, when inflicted on an ordinary citizen, will be dealt with in a most emphatic fashion," he said. "Convictions don't offer any solace to Mrs. Fritch, other than having these proceedings terminated. It's now behind her and her family."

Exhausted, he described the case as one of the toughest he had ever faced.

"The facts were so outrageous. The consequences were so outrageous. I think it's tough, emotionally. I think a lot of people don't want to face up to the fact that this goes on and it can happen anywhere."

After leading Jamie and Steve past the photographers and cameramen to the prisoner van, Sergeants Chapman and Barker were preparing for a celebration.

"After two years, justice has finally been done," Barker said.

Inside the prisoner van leading them back to the Barton Street jail in Hamilton, Steve looked at Jamie, and they both fell to the floor, laughing hysterically for half the trip there.

Part Three

— Chapter 13 —
Jamie's Fate

After more than two years of waiting for a conclusion, everyone the tragedy had touched was tired: the families, the lawyers, the police, the journalists and the community in general. Like few other cases, this one was not going to go away. The facts were so unspeakable, the criminals so young, the community so unprepared for something this brutal to spring up from within itself.

"I don't know if anyone could come out of this case, whether it be lawyers, judges, jurors or reporters, without some pretty strong personal reaction to it," Stunt said later. "It was right at the top of the scale." Convictions having been won, though, there were still two young murderers to be sentenced.

Steve was first. There was no reason to put off his sentencing. Compared to the complex constitutional arguments being prepared for Jamie's sentencing, his case was simple: he was indisputably an adult when he murdered Joe Fritch, and the jury had delivered a straightforward verdict. Without a finding that he was insane, there was nothing Justice LeSage could do but send him away for life.

On January 8, 1992, the judge agreed to put off Jamie's sentencing, but he dealt then and there with Steve's. Justice LeSage said that despite the failure of the insanity defence, there was no question the trial had proven Steve was seriously mentally ill. In an attempt to resolve this conundrum, which clearly frustrated him, he took his mandate as far as precedent would allow, recommending that once he was sent to the federal penitentiary system, he should be thoroughly mentally assessed and treated accordingly. But that was where his jurisdiction ended. Once Steve was under the power of the federal penal authorities, the trial judge's words, at their strongest, could form only a recommendation, which he later described as nothing more than a "pious hope."

No one could force them to treat Steve, and because he had not been found legally insane, Steve himself was fully within his rights to refuse any treatment that was offered, however impaired his judgment might be by his illness.

For Jamie's part, the sentencing was complicated by Bill C-12, legislation then being considered by the federal government, which would allow adults convicted of murders they had committed as youths to be eligible for parole after as little as five years, instead of twenty-five. By the time of Jamie's hearing in February 1992, the House of Commons had passed the bill, but it had yet to be ratified by the Senate. His lawyers argued that the pending legislation should apply to Jamie anyway.

Although he was still being represented by the team of Bill Trudell and Janet Leiper, the sentencing was chiefly Leiper's responsibility. For her arguments, the hearings were held back at the Milton courthouse in the original jurisdiction of Halton, since the jury's work was finished and sentencing was Justice LeSage's responsibility. Leiper would continue the argument that sentencing Jamie to life as an adult constituted cruel and unusual punishment under the federal Charter of Rights and Freedoms.

The first meeting on the sentencing was held on

Valentine's Day, when Leiper argued that under the Charter, it would be unfair to elevate Jamie from a maximum three-year sentence to a minimum of twenty-five years. Allowing that he had committed the Criminal Code's highest offence, she argued it was the timing of the crime and not its nature that should be the deciding factor.

"Young people are capable of doing horrible things, just as adults are," she said, but our modern law says they must be treated specially because of their lower level of maturity and understanding. "In a maturing society, we're moving to a point that resolves this gross disproportionality between three and twenty-five," she said, referring to proposed amendments to the Young Offenders Act which would elevate the potential sentence for youths convicted of murder. Justice LeSage warned he would not permit the sentencing to become a repeat of the lengthy transfer hearing, where similar arguments had failed to keep Jamie out of adult court. Leiper acquiesced, but said she still wanted to present a short line-up of witnesses to testify about the effects of a life sentence on a young person such as Jamie. Stunt was incensed. He reminded the court that just thirty years earlier, a murderer like Jamie would not have enjoyed even the possibility of getting out of jail, ever. Now, he said, there was even the "faint-hope clause," which allows a murderer to have a special judicial hearing after fifteen years, which may result in even earlier parole than the twenty-five-year minimum.

"It is an enormous benefit that accrues to people who in 1960 would have been hanged by the neck until they were dead," Stunt said.

Stunt argued that the test of a sentence's appropriateness should not be its effect on the accused, but on the community. If a murderer doesn't get life for taking a life, he wondered, what kind of faith and security could society have in its justice system?

"The public concern would be outraged if in this particular case this accused were treated differently than his counterpart, who is five months older," he said. "It was an execution. It was arbitrary. It was nothing more than a thrill kill perpetrated by two devious and outrageously dangerous people."

Still, the judge agreed to wait two more weeks before hearing Jamie's lawyers' arguments. Jamie wasn't going anywhere, and the whole cast assembled again for the next session, when the hearing finally got going in earnest.

From the back of the courtroom, the first witness rolled his wheelchair to take the stand. Tom French, a convicted and paroled murderer who under previous rules had been sentenced to life in 1975 and served ten years before parole, represented Lifeline, a provincial group helping inmates serving life sentences. His responsibility for the past two and a half years had been to help inmates with the transition from maximum-security prisons back to society, as they flowed through progressively more lenient institutions and finally made their way into halfway houses before being reintegrated fully into independent society. Of his three hundred clients, most were murderers. Part of his job, he said, was to help them see themselves as "professional prisoners" instead of offenders.

A burly man in a ponytail who had since his release from jail lost his leg in an accident, French hardly looked like a typical social worker, and his formal education had extended only as far as high school. Once, he had stood six feet two and weighed 450 pounds. He had been imposing enough that in jail no one had challenged him. He spoke with authority and sensitivity about the effects of a life sentence on an inmate. He described what goes through a prisoner's mind as he begins the most difficult early years of incarceration, a phenomenon prisoners call "tunnelling," where one tries to cope with the enormity of his sentence.

"When you first go in, you don't grasp it," he said. Prisoners serve the first one to three years with a certain hopefulness and denial, since they still have appeals to be heard. But once the appeals are exhausted, he said, depression frequently sets in. Once the inmate realizes his appeals have failed, a new process starts: the effort to get out sooner than twenty-five years. Their only focus, their only means of coping with the enormity of their sentences, he said, is knowing that one day they may be released.

"It's like looking down a tunnel, and hopefully you see something at the end. It's certainly not a blinding light, but there's a flicker down there. It's a long road. It's depressing," he said. "I can't visualize twenty-five. I could see a flicker at ten. But if you slap another fifteen on that—I don't know."

Most inmates, he said, look toward their fifteen-year faint hope hearings. As an inmate's only prospect, it becomes the next plateau. Until then, the inmate's only relief from the depression is to make the imaginary light brighter by speeding the passage of time in jail. That means blending in, and avoiding trouble with guards and prisoners alike. Socialization within maximum security institutions such as Kingston and Millhaven penitentiaries is a survival skill, he said. Minorities in the prison, such as natives and Sicilians, have an easier time making friends within their own ethnic groups. For the rest, it's tough to crack the cliques and understand the different rules of life inside. There is a whole other language that only fellow prisoners understand. Without learning it, you're in trouble.

"It's not a *sentence* inside that will get you in trouble. It's one *word*. One word inside will get you killed," French said flatly.

Along with the stress of adjusting to life inside comes the inevitable depression of growing gradually more isolated from one's family and friends.

"Families turn their backs on people after a short time. That's a big, big punishment," he said. "Anyone who was your friend on the outside—trust me, you're dead when you're gone."

Trying to shed the prison socialization becomes more difficult with each passing year, he said: "If they do twenty-five, it will take another ten to get them ready for the street."

French recalled one inmate who, after twenty-two years, had finally been allowed an unescorted pass from jail. He took a cab back to the jail early, unable to cope with life on the outside. Even French said that in jail he was big enough to avoid other prisoners touching him, but once he was outside, he wasn't able to adjust to the idea of literally rubbing elbows with people in crowds.

"I still don't go to stores. I don't go to malls," he said. "People ask me if I've adjusted to society. No."

The memory of jail alone is enough to keep him from ever committing another crime, he said.

By the time he got up to question French, Paul Stunt had remembered that the man in the stand had once been the subject of a famous trial where, like Steve, he had lost his bid to be found insane. He reminded the judge and French himself of his record: break and enter, keeping a gambling house, common assault, extortion and, finally, murder.

"It's like a smorgasbord of crime, isn't it?" the prosecutor asked. There was really no other way for French to answer but, "Yes sir."

Stunt reminded French he had appealed his own case all the way to the Supreme Court of Canada, but had steadfastly refused to admit that he had deliberately killed someone.

That, Stunt said, was typical of a prisoner serving a life sentence: "They never face the reality that they deliberately killed somebody."

"I don't see the point in that," French replied curtly, although he added a footnote: "I take responsibility for why I was put in jail."

Stunt said prisoners know the National Parole Board wants to hear them express remorse. He was working to make sure that the court's sympathy did not shift from Fritch's family to the killer.

Before excusing French from further questions, Stunt reminded the court that prisoners commonly take advantage of institutional programs that allow for counselling, religious worship and education, all as a means to win points at their parole-board hearings.

Dr. Clive Chamberlain, a psychiatrist specializing in adolescents who had testified at Jamie's transfer hearing, took his place next in the stand.

"I felt Jamie was an emotionally disturbed young man," he said. Jamie, he said, had been unable, since he was a young child and watched his brother drown, to express his emotions properly, especially frustration and anger. Instead, he had internalized these feelings. The pressure caused by the feelings grew until he committed murder. On the outside, though, he had appeared to be affable and easygoing. Any time a difficult situation arose, he pretended it didn't affect him, leading Dr. Chamberlain to label him a "conflict avoider."

"He went into a tailspin and slipped into drug abuse and criminal behaviour to avoid the pain he couldn't face," he said. In a way, he said, Jamie was just as sick as Steve was. There aren't tidy, diagnostic words in the psychiatric lexicon to describe what troubled Jamie, he said. In fact, Jamie had been so affected by the events in his life and his failure to deal with them that he had become, at the same time, suicidal and antisocial.

Still, he was not a clear-cut, textbook psychopath like Steve.

"A psychopath has no emotional blocks at all," Dr. Chamberlain said. "Jamie is suppressing a lot of feelings."

For confirmed psychopaths, there is very little hope for recovery or treatment. But for someone in Jamie's position, having developed the outward but not the inward symptoms of antisocial behaviour, there is a great deal of hope for treatment. For this reason, he said, sending Jamie to jail would tend to fortify his emotional wall, and perhaps leave him untreatable by the end of twenty-five years inside.

"I can't think of an environment better organized and calculated to make this kind of problem worse," he said. "The longer a person expects to be in an environment like that, the gloomier are the prospects for any change."

Dr. Chamberlain tried to move away from the legal system's fixation with remorse, saying it was impossible to determine how sorry a person is for what he has done.

"I think perhaps we make too much of remorse. It's difficult to really know what another person is feeling."

He said Jamie had the capacity to feel sorry for what he did, but in his fragile, immature emotional state, did not have the tools for it.

After dealing with many other patients who had committed murders as adolescents, he said he had recognized a common pattern: they don't do it again. "It is generally recognized in most societies that there is a period where impulsivity and foolish, poor judgment are present, but not necessarily going to be part of the adult picture," he said.

Murderers between ten and twenty-one years old, he said,

are not generally mindful of what punishment they may face.

"The whole thing is a bit of a chaos and a jumble. They're idiosyncratic, cataclysmic events. They're not logical."

Dr. Chamberlain said protecting society should not be a major consideration in sentencing such youthful criminals as it is for adults. The probability of murderers such as Jamie killing again is "exceedingly low," he said. Instead, he argued, the potential for harming their personalities by imposing long sentences is far more worrisome. "I'd rather take my chances with an intensive treatment program over a shorter period."

Again, when it was his turn to ask the questions, Stunt returned to the reality of what Jamie and Steve had done. He reminded the court that Jamie had initially refused to discuss the murder with the psychiatrist, and later recanted, admitting that everything Steve had said in his statements, including planning, was true, with only minor discrepancies. Stunt reminded the court that Jamie had agreed when Steve had suggested the robbery could not be successful unless it included killing their victim, and that Jamie had shown his agreement by holding the plastic garbage bag and yelling, "Hit him again! He's not dead yet!"

"How does the diagnosis that this man suffers from an emotional disorder explain his participation in this outrage?" the prosecutor demanded to know.

"It doesn't explain it," Dr. Chamberlain said. But he did remind Stunt that Jamie's disturbance had been exacerbated by confusion and rage over his brother's death and back-and-forth movement between his separated parents.

Stunt countered that regardless of his emotional incapacitation, Jamie had been able to make independent, selfish decisions to commit crimes, skip school and take drugs.

"This is a person who is driven to avoid pain," the psychiatrist interjected. "This is a person who knows exactly what he's doing, but he may not appreciate it in a full sense."

Stunt and Chamberlain continued to joust over Jamie's responsibility, with Stunt saying Jamie was fully aware of what he was doing but didn't care, and Chamberlain countering that Jamie was not capable of appreciating what he was doing because of his emotional impairment.

Stunt said it was clear Jamie was a psychopath, just like Steve: "If you open up the manual, there he is."

He said the only evidence of Jamie's remorse for killing Joe Fritch was a momentary twinge of guilt when he found the family pictures in his wallet on the way to Toronto. Apart from that, he was concerned only with getting away. Stunt reminded Chamberlain and the court that another psychiatrist had found Jamie to be a classic psychopath.

"A lot of other people might find themselves in Mr. Ruston's circumstances," Stunt said. "But it is a very small number of people who would go and do what Mr. Ruston and Mr. Olah did."

Chamberlain maintained there was a very low risk of Jamie ever committing another murder.

Leiper's last witness was Graham Stewart, executive director of the John Howard Society of Ontario, a volunteer group of advocates for prisoners' rights. Like French earlier that day, Stewart said he was concerned with the prisonization of people serving long sentences, particularly if they were young. For them, he said, the focus shifts from punishment and reform to preoccupation with doing their time with the least difficulty possible and making it go by as quickly as they can.

In order to do so, he said, prisoners adopt the rules and codes of jail, and deliberately learn how to lose track of time. In order to succeed, they keep their mouths shut and their backs to the wall.

They purposely become "zombies," he said, by cutting themselves off from others, focusing on banal daily concerns such as getting extra socks and proper meals, forgetting about larger ideas such as the outside world and how they will re-enter it eventually.

"Younger people are much more susceptible to being influenced by that prison culture," he said. "I'm not aware of anyone who can think in terms of twenty-five years. Trying to focus on release in twenty-five years is impossible."

A young person such as Jamie is not able to visualize a sentence that is even longer than the total of his life so far, he said.

The most dedicated families eventually lose the ability to communicate with relatives who are serving life sentences, he said; faithful visitors even find themselves with less and less to talk about. The prisoner doesn't know or care about what's happening outside the jail, and the visitors can't relate to what the prisoner's life is like, he said, so they drift apart.

Stewart argued that Jamie should get a shorter sentence, one that would be possible for his young mind to visualize, to keep the troubled young man from losing all hope. Once a prisoner is given the ability to see the end of his sentence, his potential for overcoming jail and becoming productive expands tremendously, he said.

After a brief cross-examination by Stunt, Stewart was released and Janet Leiper prepared to make a summary of her arguments.

"The issue is whether or not there is going to be any flexibility provided," she said. She noted that French had provided a good example of the benefits to a prisoner of being able to see a light at the end of a long sentence. She pointed out that the Canadian government was well on its way to passing a law that would recognize the difference between young and adult murderers, and adjusting their sentences accordingly.

"We have to prepare the person for a return. We have to look for some sort of redemption in these things," she said. "Surely, it's got to be acceptable to the population."

She said it would be unfair to say Jamie deserved the same sentence as Steve on the basis that they were only five months apart in age. The law, she said, has drawn a line at age eighteen, and Jamie was short of the line; the appropriate minimum before parole for Jamie would therefore be ten years at the longest.

But Stunt was unsympathetic.

"This is it. He has committed the worst offence in the Criminal Code," he said. "He has committed it in the worst way: with planning and deliberation. Nothing you've heard today would suggest that a life sentence is grossly disproportionate."

With those brief remarks, he sat down confidently and the judge announced he would be ready with a decision in two weeks, when the group assembled for one last time.

As tradition dictates, Jamie was asked if he had anything to say to the court before he was sentenced.

"No sir, I do not," he answered quietly.

In typical fashion, it didn't take long for Justice LeSage to deliver his remarks to the hearing, in one of the Milton courthouse's small basement courtrooms. Like Steve, Jamie would serve life in jail, he said. He had found considerable merit in Leiper's arguments for a shorter sentence, but in the end was forced to reject them.

"Twenty-five years to anyone, let alone a very young person, whose life experience is less than twenty-five years, is virtually impossible to visualize," he said. But, turning to Jamie, he reminded the hearing that one must not discount the potential of the human spirit to overcome adversity.

"I find it difficult to conceive of a crime that calls for greater punishment. You will still have a life ahead of you after parole. Joseph Fritch will not."

With that, Jamie was taken away, as his parents cried in the front benches, yet again. In the hallway, there was frustration and outrage among family members, who brushed past reporters and photographers without comment.

Bill Trudell promised that the effort to save Jamie would not end there. There was still the appeal process.

"We've tried to keep the spark alive and we will continue to do that. He's a kid worth saving," he said with conviction impressive enough to transcend his black lawyer's robes and recall the teenage years he had spent in the seminary.

Chapter 14

"Why the Hell Don't They Act on It?"

We need more than a "pious hope" that Steve Olah and others like him will be treated. There is a tragic flaw in a justice system that precludes a judge from reassuring society that a killer who is universally acknowledged to be mentally ill will be treated.

The jury of twelve ordinary men and women, certainly no experts in psychiatry before they had entered the Brampton courtroom, had left it with more knowledge of human behaviour and mental disorders than most ordinary citizens. After all, they had been treated to lessons in psychiatry from some of the country's foremost experts in criminal mental illness. But even these experts had failed to reach any consensus.

Part of the problem is the way criminal courts try to determine truth. Representatives of the prosecution and the defence, trained in the art of rhetoric and debate, use adversarial argument to prove their conclusions, leaving jurors to judge who is correct. In specialized cases such as these, experts are called in to explain the complexities of the arguments. These experts take judges and juries down incredibly complicated and often baffling paths of scientific knowledge. Their purpose is to explain the complicated—to make it easier for juries to do their jobs. But they have instead become levers for lawyers on both sides of the courtroom to help make their cases for them.

Although he would not speak specifically about this case, Justice LeSage, a ten-year member of the Law Reform Commission of Canada's judicial advisory committee, said in an interview that the courts rely too much on experts.

"The whole role of experts in law has taken on an importance and significance that I think should be really carefully assessed," he said. "I think we are putting far too much weight and emphasis on the testimony of experts in areas that are nothing more than common sense."

It is easier for juries to compare witnesses in simpler cases, where, for example, they must weigh the evidence of a jail-bird against the testimony of a model citizen. When a doctor goes up against a doctor, though, and both have mile-long résumés, how is one to determine who is correct? Unable to draw distinctions between the validity of experts' testimony, juries are left to decide on the basis of rhetoric and delivery instead of information.

Unlike lawyers, doctors are trained to work in a cooperative, collegial atmosphere and reach conclusions based on consensus, not confrontation. In other words, lawyers make cases *for* or *against*. Doctors just have cases. Period.

For the purposes of the courts, however, they are unnaturally plucked from their cooperative environment and stretched across the adversarial frame, where they are divided and conquered, forced to defend their beliefs against those of their colleagues.

Not only is this unnatural for the witnesses and confusing to the jurors, but it also forces psychiatric experts to warp their views to the Criminal Code's narrow definition of insanity. In the medical world, they measure madness along a continuum, where fine gradations and overlapping symptoms lead to complex diagnoses. But in court, they are required to use only the legal definition, based on an ancient British model. It doesn't work.

"The medical model doesn't fit very well with the criminal model. The criminal system finds pigeonholes to fit things in," Stunt says. "If you don't fit one of the two holes of the McNaughten test, you're not insane."

Psychiatrists are taught in school to avoid the conclusive labels that the justice system demands. But school doesn't help them in court.

"Lawyers are lawyers for a reason. They know how to get out of you what they want," says Dr. Guyon Mersereau, chief psychiatrist at the Hamilton-Wentworth Detention Centre and a lecturer in psychiatry at McMaster University. "This is part of the barrister's art—to put a wedge between people and get what you want. We're just putty in their hands. It always leaves me uncomfortable. You're always coming away saying, 'Did I say that? How could I say that?' I have a constant tension in doing both jobs."

They have become so frustrated, in fact, that several top forensic psychiatrists have begun meeting with all the experts in a case beforehand and thrashing out the issues on their own. Even so, the lawyers often manage to divide them once they get them on their own turf.

"It's the problem you have with the insanity defence: dealing with something lawyers and legislators have come up with to address their concerns," Dr. Mersereau said. "A jury can't come up with a diagnosis. The process is not designed for that, and our medical procedures are."

Justice LeSage favours codifying a procedure for psychiatrists from both sides of a case to meet among themselves *before* trials to establish their views.

Not only would it make their eventual testimony less

confusing to juries, but it would also recognize that insanity trials are not strictly legal matters to be resolved entirely by adversarial arguments. Allowing doctors to form opinions based on their own methods would begin to harmonize the legal and medical systems at the place where they meet.

In the 1960s, Justice LeSage—then a Crown prosecutor—and defence lawyer Arthur Maloney successfully arranged such meetings on an informal basis.

"I like that, but I don't think most Crowns and defence lawyers would go along with that," he said. "If it became an accepted practice, that would be a positive development."

Dr. Nizar Ladha, head of the Canadian Psychiatric Association's forensic section, agrees.

"I think the adversarial setting is very difficult to be in," he said. "In an ideal world, I think four people should meet: two psychiatrists, the Crown and the defence. Outside an adversarial situation, there is much more agreement among witnesses."

Given the impossibility of providing definitive, empirical answers in psychiatric cases, the best that experts can offer are their opinions. Even if they were relieved from having to battle one another in court, there would still be no pure, objective truth for them to find. Such is the embryonic nature of psychiatry. Among all the sciences, it is the child which the courts ask to be the man.

Without doubt, the jury system is our best test for determining guilt and innocence in criminal cases. It is fair, balanced and participatory. But in cases of criminal insanity, society is not asking twelve common people to determine whether someone committed an offence. Instead, it is asking them to decipher a medical diagnosis of the highest complexity. Without giving them the benefit of decades of training and experience, we risk letting them decide on the basis of who puts on the best show, or on their personal reaction to a crime.

Steve's many statements, both to the psychiatrists and to the police, offered little help in figuring out whether he was truly insane. Despite the advancements of science, it is still impossible to determine the absolute degree of anyone's truthfulness. For all anyone knew, Steve could have been a very sick man or a terribly great actor. He is more likely an indecipherable combination of both. He certainly had the intellectual ability to concoct a bogus psychosis, and in fact, his antisocial personality, which seeks only to protect himself, would have driven him to do so.

For both sides of this case, the outcome turned on the diary. It is difficult to believe that the journal, written well in advance of the murder, could have been deliberately prepared to trick others into believing he had been losing control over his mind bit by bit during the weeks before the killing.

"That diary was a gold mine that I think the jury should have acted upon, but I think that juries are very skeptical," Cooper said. While Cooper pointed to it as the best card in proving Steve's insanity, Stunt claims it was his own trump in showing exactly the opposite. He considers the diary to have been one of the most important pieces of evidence in proving that Steve was *not* crazy. Despite its references to "it" and the voice inside his head, it showed Steve's increasing disposition toward murder and mayhem, which, Stunt says, is proof of planning.

Steve was the one person who could have cleared up the uncertainty over the diary. But his lawyers chose not to introduce him as a witness. They were concerned that whatever he said, he would have appeared too *sane*. Their fear was that a jury of lay people, with no qualifications in psychiatry, would have judged his detachment as proof that he was simply callous, not crazy.

"We thought if he testified, he would appear too *normal* to the jury," said his lawyer Paul LaFleur.

Psychiatrists, on the other hand, are trained to react professionally, not emotionally, to patients' statements. They know that a person can appear perfectly lucid on the outside and still be a mess on the inside.

Asking if Steve was insane was an impossible riddle that was unfairly and inappropriately posed to twelve ordinary people. Undoubtedly, they considered the consequences of their decision. Finding Steve guilty would at least have guaranteed the longest sentence this country can give an offender, at the same time as it would have provided a tidy explanation for his behaviour: that he is plain evil. The alternative, a finding that he was insane and therefore not responsible, would have left more questions than answers, not least of which was when he would be released. These jurors were the same people who were forced to view the photographs of the impossibly battered head of a kind-hearted father, and compare them to the almost prideful confession of his killer. No ordinary human could suppress his outrage of what those pictures showed, or fail to be shocked by the callousness with which Steve had described the murder. But at the same time, no human is capable of saying precisely or conclusively what deficit in his brain caused him to behave like that. To put such a question to twelve ordinary citizens is the greatest challenge any jury could have, and more of a challenge than one should have to face.

Although we cannot legally know what they talked about in their deliberations (it is illegal to ask them or for them to discuss it), Stunt and Cooper now agree that it's likely they considered the consequences of a not-guilty verdict, even though they were supposed to have decided purely on the basis of law.

"I think a lot of members of the jury thought he probably was insane, but they probably wouldn't decide that he was because he would get out sooner," Cooper said. "If jurors are thinking this guy's going to get loose because of some psychiatrist, then it doesn't matter what the law is."

Stunt agreed that conflicting information from psychiatrists would serve to push a jury toward conviction, if only to keep the offender off the street for as long as possible. Jurors are more likely to make *themselves* the gatekeepers, rather than hand the responsibility to professionals who can't seem to make up their minds. "If he's found insane, these guys, who can't even agree on whether he's sane or insane, will be the ones who decide when he'll get out," Stunt says.

In other words, if psychiatrists can't as a group decide if he is sick, how are they supposed to know when he is *well*?

For his part, Steve knows many are cynical about his claim to have been insane at the time he killed Joe Fritch. He recognizes that many think that he is a lifetime con man trying to pull his biggest job ever by manipulating psychiatrists, lawyers and the public.

"I think it's got some merit," Steve says contemplatively of the argument. "I think I've got the brains to pull it off. But I don't see the validity in their assertions. If I'm so brilliant and I can fool them so well, it would have worked."

He also knows there is virtually no public sympathy for him.

"I think they think I'm a monster. I'm not a monster. I'm just an ordinary guy who happened to have a few things wrong with him. I don't feel like a killer. I don't feel like a monster."

Although Steve's father felt some relief when the judge had recommended psychiatric assessment and treatment, he worried the words would once again ring hollow, just as they had when a doctor promised he would be held for observation after the summer night when he had turned on his own parents. Frank and Beth Olah knew firsthand what it was like to look into the murderous eyes of their son.

"We're not looking for an easy way out," Frank said. "If he doesn't get treatment, he'll do it again. There will be another life lost along the way. He's sick and he needs treatment."

Furthermore, they say, if their son was simply a lustful murderer and not a madman, why didn't he kill *them* when he had the opportunity and a weapon in his hands?

Now that both Steve and Jamie have been proven guilty of murder, the rest of us are left to grapple with the issues that transcend those terrible moments in the gas bar. How did these kids get themselves into a place where they wanted to kill a person? Why didn't someone stop them long before they ever got there? Despite the confusing and contradictory opinions of experts in the legal and psychiatric fields, it is clear that both young men were on a destructive path well before October 18, 1989. Starting with Joe Fritch and his family, continuing with the Olah, Ruston and Chisamore families, and the community at large, we are all still paying for the execution of an innocent man by two boys who felt the only way they could find happiness was to slaughter someone, spend his money and drive his car as far away as they could. It's not as though they were oppressed in a political or financial sense. They were living in *Burlington*, after all, a place that if anywhere in Canada, was protective of its safety and its children, where there were plenty of alternatives, and more opportunities for help than in most of the rest of the country. Still, it happened.

The search for answers must start with Steve, and stem back to his childhood. Here was a boy who proved he was very different from his classmates, who relished stealing from them and hurting them, not as an end in itself, but rather as a way to draw attention to himself. Here was a boy who, although smarter than all his peers, was still unwilling or unable to fit in. This was a child who, by all later descriptions, fit the classic profile of a developing psychopath, not only by his proclivity for violent and selfish acts, but also by his inordinate intelligence and ability to manipulate people. Even today, it is difficult to say where Steve's manipulation stops and where his real personality begins. Not even his parents can say.

"I can't really tell what's true and what's not true any more," Frank Olah says.

Steve's parents, loving, able people, literally put themselves into debt trying to get some help from a school system that wasn't capable of correcting something so sinister. Not even *they* were aware of the degree to which he was manipulating them. They had no idea of the double life he had been leading at home.

They knew he drank, they suspected he was using drugs, but they were shocked to learn they had become practically daily habits. They knew he had committed petty crimes, but they had no idea he was constructing grand plans under their own roof, even after they had taken the ultimate risk of bringing him back home after he had threatened to kill them. Beth knew something was stirring in him in the hours before he escaped through his bedroom window to go to the gas station, but she had no idea that murder was Steve's plan the night he had cooked a special dinner for her.

He was a child with a mother who, as a nurse and nursing instructor, was professionally associated with the community that should have been doing something to help him, a woman who, among everyone, knew what buttons to press to make things happen, but was still unable to prevent her son from slipping out his bedroom window to kill someone.

Perhaps our finger automatically points to the psychiatrist who let Steve out of the hospital that night when he took his parents hostage. After another doctor saw him during five hours of absolute, incoherent rage and destruction and decided to keep him in psychiatric custody for observation, how could this psychiatrist, after a brief consultation the next morning, say that he was a better candidate for jail and punishment than for a mental institution and treatment? But the answer is not as simple as it may first appear.

For Dr. John Deadman, a veteran of more than thirty years in psychiatry, a man with impeccable credentials and a former head of the Ontario Psychiatric Association, there is no reason to rationalize his decision: he had no choice.

The province's Mental Health Act, once a rigid document that allowed a general practitioner to consign his patients to psychiatric care on the simple suspicion that they were mentally ill, has since gone far in the opposite direction. Before a sweeping series of changes designed to recognize the rights of patients to liberty and control over their treatment, Dr. Deadman said, he would have kept Steve under psychiatric supervision.

"Thirty years ago, I would have," he said shortly after the trial. "I wouldn't have taken a chance on this guy."

Now, though, he says he must constantly take chances with patients like Steve Olah. Any one of them is potentially capable of doing what Steve did, but it is impossible to predict with any accuracy what small minority of them may do so. Once, the law allowed doctors to hold patients for their own welfare. Then it limited them to holding anyone they deemed to be a general risk to their own and others' safety. Today, it must meet an even stricter standard of proof. Doctors must believe the patient to be an *imminent* danger. Imminent is a word professionals take literally: that the patient will, within hours of release, do something destructive to himself or someone else. In a climate charged with fear of litigation and complicated appeals of assessment orders involving patient advocates, psychiatrists feel they are constrained from doing the job they were trained to do: identify the people who are dangerous and help them.

Few would question that it is necessary to grant the maximum opportunity for all people to function in our free society. But this is where the rights of the individual and the rights of society come into conflict.

The road to reforming the Mental Health Act started with Barry Swadron, a Toronto lawyer who rewrote much of the legislation in 1967 to bring it more in line with the social thinking of the day. At that time, patients had only to be considered dangerous to be held for treatment. As a result of the reforms, hospital review boards were established as a check against the arbitrary authority of individual doctors. Later, patients won the right to refuse treatment, and the danger provision was tightened further. Later still, the province established a system where lay people act as patient advocates to oversee psychiatric treatments and intervene on patients' behalf. Throughout, psychiatrists have felt under fire: that their authority was being eroded, and that the public was showing less trust in their ability to do their jobs, while at the same time as it was making the impossible demand that they predict patients' behaviour. As professionals, they generally regard themselves as instruments to carry out the standards set by the community. If we tell them that we want them to intervene less often to care for patients, they feel duty-bound to oblige.

"There has been the perception on the other side that we are part of an oppressive regime," said Dr. Mersereau. "Our hands are tied under the Mental Health Act."

The problem is that most people have unrealistic expectations of psychiatrists' ability to diagnose and treat mental illness. Unlike other fields of medicine, psychiatry is still an embryonic science. Despite massive advances, one must remember that this is still a field where only fifty years ago, syphilitic patients were put into sweat boxes to cure their insanity. This is a science where crude electroshock therapy and frontal lobotomies were considered acceptable treatments as recently as a generation ago.

Psychiatry cannot explain what causes psychopathy or schizophrenia, and when top experts argue with one another in court, it is clear that the science still has trouble identifying when these major mental disorders are actually present.

Still these doctors are forced to be the gatekeepers who decide who stays in and who gets out. Among one hundred Steve Olahs who come to St. Joseph's or any community hospital, it is not unreasonable to say that perhaps one will go on to cause serious damage to himself or to someone else. Now, though, society has sent the message, through its elected legislators, that it is better to preserve the freedom of the ninety-nine at the risk of the one, than to keep all one hundred and thereby preserve the safety of citizens that the one may hurt. Psychiatrists are only too happy to admit that they don't have the absolute ability to distinguish the one from the ninety-nine. Human behaviour is unpredictable. There is no blood test they can do to say someone is going to kill, but we expect them to reach definitive conclusions, because they are *doctors*.

"That is the latest formulation of what society wants us to do, but we're hard pressed to make those determinations," Dr. Mersereau said. "We're not very good at predicting behaviour. We're not in that business. The people who do that are astrologers and teacup readers, but that is society's expectation."

If they could meet the expectation, they certainly would. Their families are as much at risk from madmen as our own. But when our community standards grant freedom to a raging, violent and powerful young man who had even demanded to be kept inside, it is the community which must bear responsibility when they result in death. Within a twenty-nine-month period, in Hamilton and Burlington alone, six deaths were attributable to five people, including Steve and Jamie, who had clearly demonstrated they needed psychiatric help.

Paul Rhora, a thirty-five-year-old Hamilton man, killed another prisoner at the Hamilton-Wentworth Detention Centre in April 1991. After smashing up his apartment, convinced that someone was trying to kill him, he called police, whom he greeted with a knife in his hand and a pellet pistol in his pocket. He was taken to the jail, where he stomped a cellmate to death, nearly killed a second, and tried to kill himself. He had been treated nine years earlier for manic depression, and had suffered a severe blow to the head shortly before the jail incident. At the Barton Street jail, he did not see a psychiatrist until after he had killed a prisoner. Later, Rhora was found not guilty by reason of insanity.

Jonathan Yeo, a thirty-two-year-old Hamilton steelworker who committed suicide after killing two women in August 1991, had tried for nine years to get psychiatric care for the condition that caused him to be aggressive and violent toward women. He had been released from the Clarke

Institute of Psychiatry eight days before his cross-Canada killing spree, because he was not perceived to be an imminent danger. His brother-in-law called it a case of "patients' rights gone amok."

John Michas, another thirty-five-year-old Hamilton man, had a long history of hospitalization for his schizophrenic condition. He was taken to St. Joseph's Hospital emergency psychiatric unit in September 1991, after smashing his TV set at home. Once there, he assaulted an elderly man with an intravenous stand, was arrested and taken to the Barton Street jail. The next morning, he was found in his isolation cell, bleeding from self-induced injuries to the head. He was treated at hospital and returned to the jail. Before he could attend his first appointment with a psychiatrist at the jail, he had set himself on fire and died.

As issues of law and order rise on the public agenda, the question to be answered is whether the pendulum that started swinging toward patients' rights in the 1960s has now swung too far away from the rights of the rest of the population to be protected from the tiny but very dangerous minority of them who may kill us.

Today, even Swadron admits that the pendulum that he started swinging may now have gone too far, pushed along by civil libertarians and well-meaning patient rights advocates.

"I think communities are being outraged, particularly recently," he said. "I think we have to maintain an even keel. People who need hospitalization should get it. We shouldn't go so far as to say a person has to be almost murderous to get in."

Even if they found themselves with the mandate to hold the Steve Olahs, psychiatrists would have nowhere to keep them. Since the liberalization of mental health laws in the province of Ontario, the system for holding and treating potentially dangerous people has been largely dismantled. At the Hamilton Psychiatric Hospital, for example, there are only six beds reserved for potentially dangerous criminal patients. The hospital serves a population base of more than one million people, stretching from the Niagara Peninsula, through Burlington, and the counties that border Lake Erie to the south.

"Clinically, there's a large number of people who are suffering from some form of mental disorder," said Dr. Marcel Lemieux, head of forensic services at Hamilton Psychiatric Hospital, who supervises those six beds. "Because of the narrowing of the Mental Health Act, a certain number of patients are not admissible legally."

Instead, those patients are often dumped in the next best secure setting: the jail. Here, the focus is on detention, punishment and rehabilitation, not mental treatment. Although jails are staffed by psychiatrists, their workload is so heavy that it is impossible for them to treat individual patients with anything approaching the attention they need. At the Barton Street jail, Dr. Mersereau said, he is troubled by the number of patients who come to him when ideally they would be observed and treated better in more appropriate facilities.

"We have one hell of a problem," he said.

Even Paul Stunt, who argued that Steve should be jailed for life, agrees that the Mental Health Act should have closed the door that allowed Steve the freedom to kill someone.

"The Mental Health Act is really a lousy companion to the criminal law. Opportunity for assessment is very limited," he said. "That's just a bad marriage: provincial mental health legislation and the Criminal Code. It's ill-fated. It's just not going to work. As soon as the danger is passed, they're going to let him loose."

Cooper, Stunt's opponent in the case, feels, not surprisingly, even more strongly.

"As a private citizen, I say you can only see this so many times. When there are obvious warning signs, as in Steve's case, that he needs to be treated for a serious mental illness, why the hell don't they act on it? With a little insight, they could have acted in a different way and saved two lives: Joseph Fritch's and Steve's."

The problem is complicated by the random scattering of the dangerous few among the harmless majority of patients who, just as inappropriately, end up in jails instead of hospitals. Those in the majority are the ones who roam the streets muttering to themselves, poorly dressed against the weather, often smashing store windows or drawing attention to themselves in a way that lands them in jail cells. After a short period, they wind up on the street again, and the cycle repeats itself, seemingly without end. The distraction of dealing with them in this inappropriate manner further compounds the difficulties of trying to spot the dangerous ones who shouldn't be in jail cells or on the street.

Even while Steve was in the Barton Street jail awaiting trial, he nearly killed a cellmate. He and the man, accused of a much less severe crime, had become friends, playing cards often late into the night. But after the man had gone to bed one evening, Steve, who had been taken off his antipsychotic drugs for testing purposes, said he felt the force creeping up in him again. At 2 a.m., when he couldn't sleep, he had taken a sharpened pencil in hand, intending to use it as a weapon. On the verge of stabbing the sleeping man in the throat, Steve called over a guard and told him he was about to kill his cellmate and demanded to be placed in an isolation cell. If not for this momentary lapse into reality, it is likely that the decision to jail Steve Olah instead of hospitalizing him could have resulted in a second murder.

And today in Kingston Penitentiary, Steve refuses to take his medication or accept psychiatric help from the staff there. This is his right, having not been found insane in a legal sense. He may refuse all treatment. After a conflict with his psychiatrist in jail, he has declined counselling, and because of the side-effects of his anti-psychotic medication, he has refused to continue taking it. This is common in schizophrenics: because the medication works, they feel better, and gain a false sense of being cured and no longer needing it. Most of these medications bring some form of unpleasant side-effect, which speeds their desire to be free from it. For Steve, the drugs create the sensation of a feather in the middle of his brain tickling to get out. He complains that every anti-psychotic medication he has taken has left him continually drowsy. In jail, he says, he needs to be alert to work at such jobs as barber and cook. If he were taking the drugs, he says, he would not be able to get up in the morning, and would lose the job that provides him the pocket money for the only comforts he says there are in jail: coffee and cigarettes.

Furthermore, he says, no matter what the drug and the dosage, none has succeeded in stopping the music that plays constantly in his head. For these reasons, and his general lack of trust in psychiatry, he sees no point in taking any drugs. He would rather live with his illness and whatever consequences it brings than put up with the discomfort and inconvenience of being drugged.

This is a man who once demanded treatment. When he didn't get it, his family took some comfort in his being sent to jail. They believed that treatment there would be automatic and mandatory. They were wrong. Given his illness and unstable but brilliant mind, he is likely to continue resisting offers to help him. Even after serving the longest sentence our judges can order, he will be in at least the same position as he was—if not a worse one—than when he murdered a man in cold blood.

In view of its inability to treat the psychopathy that robs him of his ability to care about the moral consequences of crime and the apparent schizophrenia that drives him to acts of violence, how can society risk having him out in public again?

It is too late to stop the death of the innocent man who was so callously killed by two teenagers. Although it would require initiative and determination on the part of healthcare professionals, enforcement officials and politicians, it is not impossible to change the way we evaluate and confine mentally ill dangerous people, both before and after they commit serious crimes.

It is not too late to stop the circumstances of October 18, 1989 from being duplicated in the future. For the specific case of Steve Olah, regardless of whether one loathes him or sympathizes with his problem, he must be treated. If not for him, we owe it to ourselves. Even he knew it once.

"I hope the next person who hurts somebody or kills somebody gets the help he needs. That's my concern," he said. "It's too late for me."

As each day passes since he stopped taking the drugs that have been prescribed for him, his willingness to be treated wanes. As recently as the week he was sentenced, he told me he was still hoping for treatment.

"The thing is, I'll get out some day. It may not be tomorrow, it may not be next week or next month, but it will be some day. Without treatment, I don't know what I might do," he said. "If I could still get away with it, I'd rather be on the street. But I still don't think I could survive. I still don't think I'm ready for the street, so in a way, I'm glad I'm here. I don't like it, though."

Since he has stopped taking medication, his paranoia appears to be welling up and taking control again. He admits it himself, and in a letter said that he trusts no one, and travels nowhere without a long, sharpened pencil in his front pocket. In the controlled environment of a maximum security federal prison, a pencil is a serious weapon. One word from the wrong person at the wrong time, and he could easily kill again, he told me in a visit at Kingston. In an environment where the murder rate is already more than twenty times that of the regular population, the possibility that Steve will use his weapon or have it turned back against himself is very real. In a secure treatment facility such as Penetanguishene, where he would receive full-time psychiatric help, this possibility would not exist to nearly the same degree.

If he manages to hold himself back, he may complete his sentence and be released on parole in the minimum twenty-five years. Frank Olah says he is sure his son will be paroled at the earliest possible date.

"Steven will feign remorse. He will be a model prisoner, and he will get out and do it again."

Acknowledgments

In preparing this book, I have had the good fortune of meeting others who share my thirst for explanation and resolution of the problems which it examines. I wish to thank them for their generous help in making it possible. Although their help has been invaluable, I accept full responsibility for the content and accuracy of this work.

Because of pending lawsuits and appeals, several parties were unable to provide material for this manuscript, but were nonetheless gracious with their time and support during the investigation and trial.

Anne Fritch granted me perhaps the most touching interview of my career. Her admirable insight helped me to understand the impact of this tragedy. William Trudell and Janet Leiper, the lawyers who represented Jamie Ruston, provided important explanation and background during the most difficult moments of the court case. James and Karen Stinchcombe, Jamie's father and stepmother, and Cari-Lee Chisamore's parents, Craig and Diane, despite unbearable stress, were courteous, polite, helpful and understanding during innumerable court hearings. Cari-Lee Chisamore's lawyers, Jeffrey Manishen and Martha Zivolak, despite our sometimes conflicting roles in the courtroom, were generous with their time and explanation in the corridors.

I wish to thank the Halton Regional Police Service. Chief

W.I. James Harding and Deputy Chief A. John Barratt granted permission to the investigating officers to share their personal and professional insights into this case. To those officers, Sergeant Joe Barker and Sergeant James Chapman, I owe a debt of gratitude for sharing many hours of personal time to assure I had the fullest picture possible of this case.

Crown Attorney Paul Stunt, now in private practice, offered important background and candid insights into the case, both during court proceedings and afterward.

I am grateful to Justice Patrick LeSage for allowing himself to be interviewed and offering frank and candid views on the relationship between mental health and the law.

I appreciate the extra work of Halton court reporters Margaret LeClair and Emma Perno, who located obscure transcripts and copied them quickly.

Many professionals in the criminal and mental health fields offered valuable insights and explanations of complicated issues. Chief among them were Dr. Guyon Mersereau, psychiatrist for the Hamilton-Wentworth Detention Centre, Dr. Nizar Ladha of the Canadian Psychiatric Association, Dr. John Deadman of St. Joseph's Hospital in Hamilton, Dr. Marcel Lemieux of the Hamilton Psychiatric Hospital, lawyer Barry Swadron, and Duncan Gillespie of the Hamilton branch of the John Howard Society.

I am grateful for the access granted by the staff at the Hamilton-Wentworth Detention Centre, the Metropolitan Toronto East Detention Centre and Kingston Penitentiary. I am thankful for the work of Pascale Therriault of Statistics Canada.

Throughout the trial and afterward, Steve Olah's lawyer Alan Cooper was generous with his time and insights, particularly with respect to the relationship between mental health and criminal issues.

To his colleague Paul LaFleur, I owe a special thanks for four years of advice, hours of personal time, access to background materials, and explanations of complex legal terms and processes.

I cannot adequately express my gratitude to the Olah family, without whose help this project could not have been completed. Frank, Beth and Jennifer Olah were exceedingly generous and hospitable to me. I admire their dignity and deeply appreciate their trust in me. Steve Olah readily provided many hours of interviews and opened his personal life to me. I appreciate his candor, effort and patience.

My professional colleagues at the sister newspapers, *The Hamilton Spectator* and *The Burlington Spectator*, and at Southam News in Ottawa, offered valuable encouragement and advice, often during trying times. Without their inspiration, support, flexibility and generosity with resource materials, I doubt this work could have been completed. Although they number in the dozens, I would like to single out some of the most helpful: *Spectator* editors Ron Albertson, Godfrey Booth, Bill Dunfield, Howard Elliott, Doug Foley, Gary Hall, Robert Howard, Ken Kilpatrick, Dan Kislenko, Brent Lawson, Denis LeBlanc, Brian Porter, and Southam News editors Roger Gillespie and Les Whittington. Among my fellow reporters, I am especially thankful to: Ray Di Gregorio, Andrew Dreschel, Carmela Fragomeni, Eric Kohanik, Paul Legall, John Levesque, Dave Rashford, Craig Sumi and Belinda Sutton. Photographer John Rennison generously helped to compile and reproduce most of the photographs for this book. *Burlington Spectator* librarian Kathi Aitken went far beyond the call of duty in helping to catalogue and compile the news clippings and photography files related to this case.

Among my newspaper friends, I would especially like to

thank four special mentors who made careful readings of the work in progress and offered invaluable advice for improving it. Paul Benedetti's support, encouragement and good humour were important to me. Wayne MacPhail of Southam's InfoLab offered solid journalistic advice and generous time in helping with technical computer matters. Rob Austin read the manuscript, granted important permissions from the newspaper and offered detailed suggestions along the way. John Gibson, my first editor in Burlington, honoured me by assigning me to this case from the first day and keeping me on it until the killers were sent to jail. I aspire to his standards of authority and sensitivity in reporting. His encouragement and advice in this project have been particular inspirations.

Many personal friends offered support, guidance, understanding and encouragement during the four years spent preparing this book. They include: Katherine Ammendolia, Miriam Blumstock, Jeff Bradley, Tremaine Burrows, Jane Campbell, Don and Madeline Carlson, Norman and Ann DeBono, Desmond Ellis, Madeline Ellis, Mike and Sandra Garvey, Shaun and Julia Herron, Gord Kolle, Patricia and John Kolovos, Mark and Linda McNeil, Annie and George Maly, Paddy Moore and Martha Hodgson, Quincy Morgan, Gary and Madiha Nolan, Leif, Wendy and Duncan Peng, Ken and Melanie Peters, Jim Riches and Barb Swayze, James Robb, Carolyn Rosart, Michael and Judi Shekter, and Mark Walma.

In particular, my dear friend Megan Ellis brought confidence and inspiration to me during many of the most difficult moments of the project.

My family—particularly sister, Lesley, and brother, Daniel, aunts, uncles, cousins and my grandmother Norma Hemsworth—have shown incredible faith and understanding.

Special thanks to my uncle Gregory Hemsworth who offered generous, sound legal advice in arranging for this book to be published.

My sincere gratitude and admiration go to Penguin Books Canada publisher Cynthia Good, her assistant Cathy Leahy, and copy editor Mary Adachi, all of whom made the process much easier than it could have been. Finally, I would like to thank my agent, Denise Bukowski, for knowing exactly when to praise and when to criticize.

Wade Hemsworth
Hamilton, Ontario